NOTHING IS EVER FOREVER

TED TAYLER

Vinci Books

vinci-books.com

Published by Vinci Books Ltd in 2026

1

Copyright © Ted Tayler 2015

The author has asserted their moral right to be identified as the author of this work in accordance with the Copyright, Designs and Patents Act 1988. This work is a work of fiction. Names, characters, places and incidents are the product of the author's imagination or are used fictitiously. Any resemblance to actual persons, living or dead, places and incidents is entirely coincidental.

All rights reserved. No part of this publication may be copied, reproduced, distributed, stored in any retrieval system, or transmitted in any form or by any means, including photocopying, recording, or other electronic or mechanical methods, nor used as a source for any form of machine learning including AI datasets, without the prior written permission of the publisher.

The publisher and the author have made every effort to obtain permissions for any third party material used in this book and to comply with copyright law. Any queries in this respect should be brought to the attention of the publisher and any omissions will be corrected in future editions.

A CIP catalogue record for this book is available from the British Library.

Paperback ISBN: 9781036700515

The EU GPSR authorised representative is Logos Europe, 9 rue Nicolas Poussion, 17000 La Rochelle, France
contact@logoseurope.eu

By Ted Tayler

The Phoenix

The Olympus Project
Gold, Silver and Bombs
Nothing Is Ever Forever
In the Lap of the Gods
The Price of Treachery
A New Dawn
Something Wicked Draws Near
Evil Always Finds A Way
Revenge Comes in Many Colours
Three Weeks in September
A Frequent Peal of Bells
Larcombe Manor

The Freeman Files

Fatal Decision
Last Orders
Pressure Point
Deadly Formula
Final Deal
Barking Mad
Creature Discomforts

Silent Terror
Night Train
All Things Bright
Buried Secrets
A Genuine Mistake
Strange Beginnings
Dead Reckoning
A Normal November
Into the Sunlight
Tame the Storm
One True Friend
Whispered Truths
A Morning Murder
Quick to Anger
Red Herring Season
Gathering Clouds
Still Standing

Chapter One

Monday, September 3rd, 2012

The Olympics were fading from the headlines. Every day, something else crept into the headlights of the media's all-seeing eye. Memories for those involved faded a good deal slower. The athletes would keep their successes and failures for years to come. Spectators at the packed stadiums could always say, "I was there."

Those caught up in the bombings in the capital and those who saw the would-be bomber executed at Weymouth bore the scars and the memories forever. But, at Larcombe Manor, time and tide waited for no man as its agents continued to carry out direct action against those who sought to bring the nation into disrepute.

Phoenix had been in the thick of the action in London. Kelly Dexter and Hayden Vincent were in Weymouth. Others had been positioned around the country, ready to strike where required. But, throughout August, Rusty had been stuck at Larcombe, waiting to join in the fun.

On the first Monday of the new month, that time arrived. Erebus invited Rusty to join him in the orangery alone. Rusty was slightly surprised; Phoenix generally attended these special meetings with Erebus. Now and then, the old gentleman condescended to letting the tough ex-SAS sergeant join them. A face-to-face meeting was a privilege not to miss.

Rusty arrived at the orangery at the appointed time. He wore a clean t-shirt for the occasion. Erebus nodded at Rusty and noted the slogan across his chest; SAS–Super Army Soldier. He passed no comment.

"Thousands of foreign domestic workers live as enslaved people in Britain, suffering sexual, physical, and psychological abuse by their employers; over fifteen thousand migrant workers come to Britain every year to earn money to send back to their families. Many endure conditions that amount to slavery. They can suffer physical and psychological abuse. Thousands are not allowed out alone. They never have a day off, work all the hours God sends, and receive a pittance. Foreign diplomats are among the worst offenders. Unlike those brought in on a domestic worker visa, their workers cannot change their employer and face being homeless or deported if they run away. To prosecute diplomats for treating their workers as enslaved people is extremely difficult. One young girl was trafficked from Nigeria to London when she was twelve. The girl's employer worked as a cultural attaché at the Embassy. The young girl was a domestic servant. Behind closed doors, she was raped and beaten. Aged fourteen, her employer threw her into the street. What had been her crime? She asked for a day's holiday. The attaché left her with nothing; terrified and alone, she could do nothing but sit on the street, waiting for her abuser to change his mind. He relented in the morning, and she returned to household duties and be at his beck and call whenever he wanted her. In June this year, she took her own life by drinking bleach. Her employer was adamant that there had been no signs that the girl was unhappy. She had been a good worker, always willing, and they missed her smiling face around the house. Extreme mistreatment such as that is commonplace. Migrant domestic workers are in a uniquely vulnerable position. Thousands of miles from home, they rely on that single employer for their accommodation, work, and immigration status. Mostly, they are isolated and don't mix with anyone. When this young girl died in June, a woman who cooked for the attaché contacted her family in Bandung to tell them what she knew. She was frightened of going to the police because her employer told her she faced deportation if she didn't have her visa and documents. The cultural attaché retained those, and he intimidated her too much to ask him to return them. We intercepted her story in text messages she sent to Indonesia. The cook said this child worked from dawn to midnight. The young girl feared what might happen to her at any time. The cook told them what had happened to the young girl and suspected her employer had raped her. That had been the reason for her taking her own life. The older woman feared she faced assault too if she kept working there."

"Beggar's belief, doesn't it?" said Rusty. "I find it difficult to get my head around the massive numbers involved."

"There are more servants in the UK now than in Victorian times, Rusty. This is contributed to by the growth of childcare and the lower cost of domestic staff," said Erebus.

"I'm hoping that folder in front of you holds the identity of the bastard involved. Excuse my language, Sir."

"Everything's there, Rusty," said Erebus. "I want this job

carried out without delay. I believe the bastard concerned has outlived his usefulness as a cultural attaché to these shores. Please arrange for his repatriation at once."

"Consider it done, boss," said Rusty, and he picked up the file from the table and left the orangery to return to his quarters to prepare.

Rusty often sat in with Phoenix to watch the master planner at work. He had picked up a few tricks of the trade in the past two years. But, with the hours of training that Rusty gave Phoenix when he first arrived at Larcombe, it seemed only fair it became a 'two-way street.'

Solomon Okonkwo was forty-six. He had been with the High Commission for three and a half years. The high-rise apartment he occupied was impressive and situated in Marylebone. Rusty always imagined that these blokes gravitated towards Mayfair or Knightsbridge. Their government picked up the tab. Rusty flicked through the information that Giles and his team had put together.

He was interested in learning that five million bought you more space in Marylebone than in the more upmarket areas of central London.

"Who knew," asked Rusty, to nobody in particular, "how the other half lives, eh?"

Rusty read further. Marylebone had transformed itself into a great destination with a lovely village feel and, some would argue, the best high street in London. Marylebone's international diversity with Russian, American, and African inhabitants was part of its charm.

Rusty checked the easiest route to Northumberland Avenue to get to the Embassy. He had photographs of his target and could pick him up from there and follow him home. While Solomon was at work, he wanted to look at the apartment block itself. Gaining access would not be an issue. Phoenix knew at least half a dozen methods, tried and tested, and half a dozen that never failed. One of those was sure to serve his purpose.

Rusty believed Solomon Okonkwo deserved to pay the price for his actions, but he went through the data on the young girl just the same. Olabisi Promise Chukwu had been only twelve years old when she arrived in the UK on a flight from Lagos. An elderly relative, said to be an uncle from her village, accompanied her.

Olabisi arrived at Solomon's new apartment only days after he had collected the keys from the letting agents. The diplomat stayed at a five-star hotel for the first two months after taking up his new position at the High Commission. Solomon was a single man with specific needs. Olabisi carried out the domestic duties and soon discovered the other more personal services required of her.

As well as Olabisi, Solomon employed an Indonesian woman, Nurul Ruby Pohan, a thirty-nine-year-old mother of four, who had worked in London for seven years. Mrs Pohan came to the flat seven days a week to cook.

Rusty looked at the photographs of the two desperate women. Then, he studied the long list of crimes that diplomats were responsible for in the past year. They included robberies, sex attacks, fraud, grievous bodily harm, drink-driving, and shoplifting. One suspect had made a bomb threat.

"You couldn't make it up," muttered Rusty.

International treaty rules give immunity from prosecution to diplomats and relatives living with them. Rusty was appalled that serious offenders escaped justice. The privilege granted exemption from arrest or detention.

"Well, in my book, Solomon's immunity doesn't exempt him from having a nasty accident."

Everyone at the Olympus Project agreed. Serious offenders escaping justice was not an option.

Rusty went through his outline plans once more. He felt happy. Transport could be arranged for the morning to have a day in the big city. He looked at his watch. Yes, he had time to drop in to see the lads in the armoury — time to choose the proper kit and then walk to the pool. A hundred lengths should give him time to go through every step of his plan just once more. One can never be too careful. 'Fail to prepare; prepare to fail' was Phoenix's mantra. If it was good enough for him, it was good enough for Rusty.

The following morning, Rusty was up bright and early. The transport would arrive at the stable block at seven-fifteen. The seven forty-three train from the old Spa station would arrive at Platform Five at Paddington just before a quarter past ten.

Rusty collected his kit bag and started the journey. As the train sped through the Wiltshire countryside, he thought through the timetable for the first part of his mission. Straight ahead to the Tube, then the Bakerloo Line to Northumberland Avenue. That should get him outside the Nigerian High Commission before eleven.

The concourse wasn't that crowded on this Tuesday morning. Rusty strode through the slow-moving crowd of commuters, tourists, and students. Why were there always students around, no matter what time you travelled? Late for wherever they ought to be, he imagined. Either that or they selected a course where lectures were scattered throughout the week, ensuring lots of free time.

Twenty minutes later, Rusty studied the front doors of the building. There was no disputing the place had character. His mobile phone vibrated in his pocket. He had received a message from Giles. Giles had hacked into the CCTV in the vicinity and checked that Solomon Okonkwo had arrived for work. Giles confirmed that Solomon was definitely inside the building. The coast was clear for Rusty to pay a visit to Marylebone.

Rusty had another short ride underground via Green Park, and he craned his neck to see the floor on which his target lived. Rusty knew that his choice had been perfect as the crick in his neck increased. What he needed to do now was gain access. It was time to use one of Phoenix's ruses. He removed a clipboard and Hi-Viz waistcoat from his kit bag.

He strolled up to the nearest pedestrian crossing, donning his disguise as he went. As he waited for the lights to change, he kept an eye out for any movement at the front entrance to the apartment block.

There! A postwoman with a trolley. It was early September, and she was wearing shorts, but then they wore shorts, whatever the weather these days. In her case, it was a mistake. The postwoman was old enough to be his mother, with legs that should stay hidden by law. The lights changed; as the mighty noise of traffic paused, Rusty crossed the road.

He hoped that a bit of charm would win the day. He held back for a second as she searched through her bunch of keys. Finally, the woman found the one that allowed her entry into the foyer and the post boxes on the wall.

Rusty sprinted forward.

"Here you go, sweetheart, let me get that for you," he said, holding the door back to get her trolley through.

"Oh, thank you, my love," the old postie cooed. "I'm getting too old for this game."

"Too old?" said Rusty. "Don't be daft. The council has

sent me around to check flats on the top floor; they keep hearing pigeons in the roof spaces. I might have to get rid of vermin later."

"Bloody nuisance, pigeons," the postie agreed, dishing out the post. The pile disappeared fast.

"Nearly done?" asked Rusty. "They can wait for me a few seconds longer; I'll help you get out without scratching those pins."

She was putty in his hands. She slotted the last gas bill into No 84 and wheeled her trolley back to the door. Rusty let her out.

"Have a nice day!" he called after her.

"And you too, love, you too," cried the postwoman.

Rusty had already reached the lifts. Floor after floor slipped by in silence, and then he was there. Finally, when the doors opened, the only thing Rusty heard was his breathing. It was quiet as the grave, which was perfect.

Getting inside Solomon's flat presented no problems. The ability to pick a lock was one of the many skills that Rusty had acquired over the years. Once inside, he moved around quickly and quietly, just in case people were at home in the adjoining apartments. More than likely, the occupants would be at work. These weren't flats a single mum with a nipper could afford on benefits. So Jeremy Kyle seeping through the walls was out of the question, which was always a blessing.

Rusty crept towards the windows. He peered out behind the curtains to ensure that nobody watched him from the flat across the street or idly glanced up from street level. There was no one. He tried to open the sash window, but it was stuck or secured by something.

"Back to the kit bag," he muttered. "Just as well that I collected a few bits and pieces from stores."

Fifteen minutes later, the window opened. It slid up and down smoothly, perhaps better than it had done for fifty years.

"Job's a good one," said Rusty. "Time for lunch, I reckon."

Taking as much care returning to the foyer as he had on the way up, Rusty exited the apartment block. He shared the lift with a Jewish couple and met a lady with sunglasses and a large handbag sashaying into the foyer. Nobody challenged the man with the hi-viz waistcoat and clipboard. Why would they? People who could afford these apartments didn't talk to 'the help', did they?

Rusty removed his waistcoat and stored it along with the clipboard in his bag.

He planned to find a decent pub for a pint and a bite of proper nosh. Two hours later, fed and watered, he strolled through Regent's Park. Rusty made a mental note to thank Phoenix for telling him to take twice the cash you thought you'd need on a mission. Rusty thought that was overkill, but a pint and proper nosh set you back a pretty penny around here.

Nurul Ruby Pchan was due to get to her employer's flat at six o'clock. She was going to prepare a meal, cook it, and serve it at seven-thirty as usual. Everything would be in the dishwasher before eight. Nurul would be out the door as fast as her little legs allowed before Solomon got any ideas.

Rusty made his way back to Northumberland Avenue. He wanted to arrive in plenty of time. These cultural attaches didn't work late. So Solomon might leave early.

Rusty wandered the street opposite at just half-past three. There was a crowd of people going in and out of the building. Rusty concentrated hard on making sure he didn't miss him.

At around half-past four, the door opened. Solomon Okonkwo strode through it majestically. He was a big man, suited and booted every inch the gentleman. A black limousine glided to a halt. Solomon bent forward to open the door, sliding elegantly into the back seat. Rusty desperately searched for a taxi. Two minutes later, he was in pursuit. Afternoon traffic in London can be slow, so his target hadn't got that far ahead. Ten-pound notes in the top pocket of his driver got Rusty a shortcut, and the gap soon closed to a manageable distance.

Rusty paid the rest of the fare as he got the driver to park near the apartment block. He crossed the road between stationary vehicles as the traffic started to build in preparation for the evening rush hour. Where was a postie when you needed one? He didn't have long to wait. A couple let themselves into the building; they were young and looked single. Maybe the guy had brought the girl from the office back for a 'quickie'? They were so engrossed in one another as they moved entwined to the lifts that they didn't notice the door didn't close behind them because of Rusty's right foot.

As the lift ascended, Rusty slipped into the foyer and called the lift. His luck held. No one else was coming home just yet. The lift doors opened, and he pressed the button for the top floor. Rusty checked the gun in his inside jacket pocket. He didn't plan on using it except as a frightener. He pressed the buzzer on the door to Solomon's flat. The door swung open.

"Come in, Mrs Pohan. I've been waiting for you," said Solomon Okonkwo, wearing only a towel. "Who are you?"

Rusty stepped forward and grabbed the cultural attaché. Despite being a big man, he was weak and no match for the trained SAS operative. Rusty kicked the door closed and bundled Solomon into the lounge, expertly zip-tying his wrists and ankles in seconds.

Solomon was shouting now. He demanded to know who the hell was in his flat. Rusty slapped a strip of duct tape across his mouth to shut him up and carried on with his preparations.

"Who am I? Why am I here? I'm your worst nightmare. It's time for you to pay for causing the death of Olabisi Promise Chukwu."

Solomon's eyes widened as Rusty opened the sash window to the fullest extent. He looked out onto the early evening traffic. As he turned back, he saw that Solomon's eyes widened even more. Rusty shoved him unceremoniously to the ledge. Then he cut off the ties with a knife, ripped the tape away and held on to the towel. Just a gentle shove was all that was necessary after that. Solomon screamed. The traffic still moved along at a steady pace. Nobody looked skywards, not at once, at least.

Rusty had already moved away from the window. He folded the towel neatly and put it away in the airing cupboard, and then he tidied up the flat and made his way towards the door. He paused and wondered whether to leave a note for Nurul Ruby Pohan. She wouldn't need to cook tonight; she shouldn't worry about the randy attaché anymore. He thought just a few words would suffice; something along the lines of 'Solomon has left the building.'

Sunday, September 23rd, 2012

After the Olympics, there were troubled times in the capital. Indeed, there were concerns across the country. Lights burned late into the night at Larcombe Manor. Nevertheless, the members of the Olympus Project and its agents vowed to continue the fight against terrorism, battle with organised crime, and fight for justice in whatever arena they deemed ripe for direct action.

When Rusty returned from disposing of Solomon Okonkwo, Erebus asked him at the Wednesday morning meeting whether everything had gone to plan.

"No problems whatever, Sir," replied Rusty. "Everything fell into place, you might say."

Erebus smiled. "You played your part well, Rusty. A few pedestrians were shocked when the naked former cultural attaché dropped in. But a vote of thanks must go to Giles and his team in the ice-house. They have created a series of transactions that show that Solomon Okonkwo withdrew significant amounts of his nation's funds to finance a serious betting spree. It's a toss-up who will uncover it first: the police or the High Commission. Either way, his death will be ruled a suicide. The poor devil couldn't face the truth about his attraction to the fillies."

"Oh, excellent, Sir," said Rusty. "I approve of that."

Among death, there's life; hasn't it ever been the same? In dark days at Larcombe, they decided that a criminal should pay the price for his crimes. Even so, there were still brief but enjoyable occasions when Annabelle Fox and Colin Bailey, now known to his colleagues as Phoenix, spent time together.

Their relationship had matured in the last few months. So late on this particular September afternoon, as they lay together in his bed, they planned a few days from the pressurised conditions they had suffered for so long.

After this year's absence, there was a Festival at Glastonbury in 2013 in late June. Soon, the tickets were going on sale. Athena traced a circle around Phoenix's left nipple with a long slender finger. Colin knew that this was a set-up for something he wouldn't enjoy. Colin listened. He said his piece.

"The prospect of a muddy field full of teenagers pissed up, drugged up and effing and blinding throughout the weekend isn't that appealing. Athena," he protested.

"But darling, Glastonbury is a highlight of the 'alternative season'. It's the place to see and be seen."

Colin stared at the ceiling. For the past couple of years, he had spent almost every waking hour avoiding people seeing him; he did most of his best work when invisible.

"Look," purred Athena, "there are plenty of luxury camping providers online. I've checked out a yurt package at around six thousand that will give us luxury showers and toilets. In addition, there's a private access road, gourmet restaurant, round-the-clock security, and extra goodies."

"Suppose you get custom-made wellies for that price?" grunted Colin. "SIX grand!"

The circling motion stopped. A sharp pinch left Colin grabbing for Athena's arm, and seconds later, he flipped her over onto her back.

"Are you sure I can't persuade you to come?" asked Annabelle Grace Fox as her long slender fingers moved further down his body.

Colin decided it was pointless to resist.

In due course, Athena would secure the tickets. Then, she would book the yurt. So, all things being equal, Annabelle Fox and Colin Bailey were going to be at Worthy Farm throughout the Festival weekend at the end of June 2013.

It was becoming imperative that Athena and Phoenix remained close. In the months since Erebus had lost his beloved wife, Elizabeth, he looked to have aged ten years. The old gentleman had been dropping heavy hints of his imminent retirement. Erebus travelled up to London on Olympus business on several occasions. Their leader returned to Larcombe early in the morning and was reticent on the matters discussed.

Several years before, he had indicated to Athena that he wanted her to be his successor. As the Phoenix became a prized asset of the Olympus Project, it was plain his position at the top table was inevitable. When Erebus realised that Athena and Phoenix had become involved, it sowed a seed in his mind. They would make a formidable pair, heading up affairs at Larcombe Manor after his departure.

When Olympus snatched Colin Bailey from the waters below Pulteney Weir in the summer of 2010, he heard of the Project's aims and objectives. Erebus had a vision. He had his family's wealth behind him. The half a dozen senior Olympus members who lived at Larcombe, whose true identities were hidden by their given mythical personas, contributed as much as they could afford. The amounts available for the Project were plentiful, but the scope of those initial aims and objectives was more far-reaching. Erebus told Phoenix that other silent partners shared the same beliefs, and their financial backing was essential.

Erebus had been the sole contact with these financiers over the years. It was time for him to convince them that Athena and Phoenix could assume responsibility after he had gone, and together they would bring their vision to fruition. Late-night returns from London suggested that this had not proved easy.

The day after Athena and Phoenix finally agreed on sharing a yurt next summer, Erebus chaired the usual morning meeting in the Manor house. Senior members and other attendees entered in dribs and drabs. The conversation centred on the gun and grenade attack last week in Manchester in which two female police officers died. Police caught their killer, but the agents were concerned about the ease of getting hold of weapons in the UK.

"At one time, this was unthinkable," Rusty said to Phoenix. "If it happened in the States, we'd shrug and accept it. But we would swear blind it could never happen here. Now it's as easy to get a gun as a morning newspaper."

As the last straggler took his seat, Erebus tapped the table to bring the meeting to order.

The first matter on the agenda concerned an incident near Banbury at the beginning of the month. Thanatos had prepared another lengthy report. Their eyes glazed over as he delivered it; Mondays were always a trial.

"Cropredy village is five miles north of Banbury in Oxfordshire. Every August, its inhabitants welcome an invasion of up to twenty thousand music lovers for Fairport's Cropredy Convention. Organised by the folk band, this outdoor extravaganza has been held annually since the 1970s. Cropredy Bridge on the River Cherwell was a major battle in 1644 during the English civil war. King Charles engaged the Parliamentarian army led by Sir William Waller. As the battle loomed, the villagers took care to protect the most valuable item in their church. If the Parliamentary forces won the battle, there seemed every chance the lectern would become part of a cannon. So the villagers hid it in the river to enable its recovery with ease. But when they went to retrieve the lectern, it wasn't there. So instead, the damaged lectern reappeared further up the river many years later."

"Who won?" asked Phoenix, trying to sound interested.

"It was a stalemate, but both sides sustained heavy losses. The local historical society was on their monthly expedition in the first week of September, looking for relics from the past relating to the Civil War period..."

"Am I going to enjoy where this story is going?" muttered Athena.

"Exactly," continued Thanatos, "they dug up human remains instead of the odd shoe buckle or fragment of a musket. It didn't take long for someone to realise that the body unearthed from the ground wasn't a Roundhead or a Cavalier."

"Heavens," exclaimed Rusty. "Are you saying they emasculated the poor bastard?"

Phoenix stifled his laughter with difficulty. Erebus looked down the table, peering over the top of his half-glasses.

"Children, please. Continue Thanatos, but can we dispense with the frills?"

Colin glanced at Thanatos; he had somewhat cruelly dubbed him, Alastor and Minos as the Three Stooges. Although on his arrival at Larcombe, they appeared to be 'yes' men, they seemed to be in awe of Erebus and jealous of Athena's relationship with the old man. They were overly wary of him too. After being closeted together since the Olympus Project began, the originals made it plain the newcomer needed time before being accepted into the fold.

Chris Rathbone, known as Thanatos, was in his midfifties now. Thirty years ago, he was a SAS sergeant working with the FRU in Northern Ireland. Thanatos had spent five years in deep cover as a mole in the UDA. What he experienced there left physical and mental scars. After a stint in Bosnia, his country abandoned him despite thirty years of serving his country with honour. His identity was now known to the IRA. They knew he had been supplied with the names of suspected members by his army paymasters and leaked them to the UDA. Despite informing them of his death threats, no protection had ever been offered to Thanatos by the MoD. The Olympus Project had been his saviour; Larcombe Manor was his safe house.

Colin knew, deep down, that Thanatos fought his demons daily. The lengthy reports, with the bells and whistles, were a way of occupying his mind, reducing the time for those horrors that he had witnessed and taken part in for his country to creep inside his head and send him over the edge into insanity. Colin resolved to show his colleague due respect in the future.

He and Athena would become the senior duo at Olympus HQ after Erebus retired. The others needed to consider them a valued part of the team. Thanatos continued.

"I'm afraid this body could stir up a hornet's nest, Sir. As you will recall, there was a lot of activity straight after the effective prison break we orchestrated. The chase continued across the country for weeks. The police found nothing. The media assumed that Muslim extremists released these prisoners, maybe even Al Qaeda itself. Our borders leak like a sieve, as we know, so the public was pleased to accept that a dozen men could disappear to a place of safety. More wander in and either find a job or sign on for benefits every day. So a handful going the other way was an easy pill to swallow. There was no possibility of anything relating to the prison break linking to Olympus. Any trace of possible CCTV evidence, the vehicle movements involved, and the vehicles themselves were gone. Other events in the weeks after the Olympics deflected attention from the problem until this happened."

"Have they identified the body?" asked Erebus.

"It was one of the clerics and a member of the terrorist cell the authorities caught after 2005. When our clean-up crews dispersed the bodies around the Midlands, they got over-enthusiastic, it would seem. So rather than follow the 'one body, one grave' principle we adopt, one crew hacked a couple up and buried them in a shroud like a jigsaw."

"What do you mean, a jigsaw?" asked Erebus.

"The head and legs of the cleric were in with the torso of the bomb-maker, Sir."

"Unbelievable," said Erebus. "Get Henry Case to sort out the buggers involved, and please make sure that our systems are updated and rigorously followed in the future. Don't we have Standard Operating Procedures for this method of disposal?"

"Of course," replied Athena. "I will see to that myself, Erebus. We must assume that the authorities now realise that the prisoners are dead. Why are they keeping this knowledge from the public? How did they handle things with the historical society at Cropredy?"

"If the police and the secret services know that nobody rescued them, then who do they think killed them?" asked Phoenix.

Erebus stood up from the table and walked over to the window. He gazed across the lawns towards the old stable block and the ice-house. As the others sat and waited for him to consider what steps to take, he thought of everything they had achieved over the past five years. The vision was still crystal clear in his mind. The organisation was sound. Any minor setbacks, such as this ill-advised desecration of their victims' bodies, would be dealt with swiftly, but it wouldn't damage the integrity of the whole operation. Thanatos was almost correct in his statement that nothing could be traced back to Olympus. Erebus resolved with a sad heart that the two loose ends that might potentially give the authorities a scintilla of a clue must die.

"Perhaps I can suggest an answer to your question, Phoenix," he said, returning to his chair at the head of the table. "I expect them to concentrate on organisations that have been vocal in attacking Muslims in this country. Several groups will come under scrutiny. As for Athena's question about news coverage, no doubt the authorities have closed things down tight, as they are wont to do, in the interests of national security. They don't want to spook these white extremist groups fighting against the Islamisation of Europe. They want them to carry on spreading their vitriol and remain unaware of their close surveillance. Do you have anything to add about the Sealed Knot weekend warriors, Thanatos?"

"Well, Sir, as I said earlier, they found the remains and contacted the police. The local free paper recorded the discovery in a single paragraph together with court appearances of a drunk driver and council tax defaulters. It didn't attract any great interest, hidden away in that manner. However, a few keywords proved enough for that first publication to be picked up by Giles and his team in the icehouse. They then put search routines in progress to track the forensic results when they became available. They identified the bodies and forwarded an email to the police. The message was intercepted and amended in due course. The police emailed the secretary of the historical association. They informed him that although the bones were human, as suspected, they had been buried for well over a century."

"The bodies have only been in there a few months. They didn't swallow that, did they?" said Phoenix.

"One imagines a few ramblers on a Sunday afternoon scavenger hunt find the sight of a decomposed body more than their stomach can handle," said Erebus. "Eyes would be diverted rapidly. I doubt they could account for what they saw to the police or a reporter if one got a whiff of a story. For the time being, Giles can keep the surveillance in place to see what comes of it. With the police forensics staff swamped with work, I doubt they'll follow up the lead. We might have dodged the bullet."

Thanatos had finished. Erebus looked at his watch.

He nodded towards Phoenix and Rusty.

"Perhaps you'll join me in the orangery in an hour, gentlemen. I have a matter to talk about with you."

Phoenix and Rusty left the room together in silence. They walked across the lawns to the stable block and their accommodation.

"See you in an hour then. Phoenix," said Rusty.

Phoenix went into his quarters, closed the door, and set to work on cleaning his gun.

Chapter Two

As Phoenix and Rusty entered the orangery, they found Erebus tending the ornamental plants scattered around the room.

"I hope you will look after these when I'm gone, chaps," he said. "I should hate to learn they just withered away."

"My Granddad had a greenhouse," chimed Rusty. "I used to help him in the summer holidays."

"This is an orangery, dear boy, not a mere greenhouse," snapped Erebus.

"Athena and I will ensure the plants come to no harm, Sir," said Phoenix. "I love this place. You have always invited me here for our meetings, and it's a place of solitude. It's good to escape from the Manor house or the other buildings and spend time here. Athena and I will use it as our base for quiet contemplation."

That seemed to appease the old gentleman. He smiled briefly; then, it was back to the grave matter in hand.

"In the folder on the table are the names of the two

clean-up crew operatives responsible for the faux pas at Cropredy. I have instructed Henry Case to interview the other crews. They will visit Larcombe over the next few days for a 'refresher' training course. It may involve visiting the place you refer to as 'Hotel California' to learn what procedures they followed when they disposed of their prisoners. But, again, I pray that we are only dealing with an isolated case."

"Dealing with, Sir?" asked Rusty, with a puzzled expression.

"Did I not make myself plain in the meeting?" asked Erebus.

Phoenix picked up the file and opened it. There were photographs and background reports on the two men. His mate looked over his shoulder, and Colin heard the sharp intake of breath.

When Colin arrived at Larcombe, he had spent many hours under Rusty's tutelage. Rusty had been a SAS veteran when selected for the first intake of the Special Reconnaissance Regiment in 2005. He had shown that his temper was as fiery as the colour of the hair on his head. Four years later, he fought with a superior officer, and they asked him to leave. In the past three years, Rusty had trained dozens of agents for Olympus here at Larcombe. That sharp intake of breath suggested that Rusty had trained these men or served with them in the SAS or SRR.

"Are there any questions?" asked Erebus.

"None," replied Phoenix.

"If it has to be, then I'm prepared to carry out your orders, Sir," said Rusty.

"No choice, I'm afraid," said Phoenix. "They screwed up. Bodies can't be left for anyone in power to find. Once identified, it would pose several uncomfortable questions. There will be a record of their being helped at Larcombe by the charity to cope with their PTSD.

"We must keep an acceptable level of detail," said Erebus. "The Charity Commission insist on it. Just recall what nightmares their last visit caused. We can't invite them here, as with the others that Henry Case will interrogate and retrain if they smell a rat and go to ground. It would be the devil of a job to find them if that happened."

"With training they received in the service, plus the upgrade they got here, then it will be a tricky job anyway, Sir," said Rusty.

"I trust the two of you can cope?"

The two friends looked at one another and nodded.

"With the right planning and attention to detail, we can work miracles, Sir," said Phoenix.

"Happy hunting; you have forty-eight hours. Any longer, and news of the other crews arriving here may filter back. The job needs completing before they get wind of what's happening."

With that, Erebus left. Colin and Rusty stayed in the orangery for a further thirty minutes devising a plan of action. Then they returned to the stable block to pack their things. Fifteen minutes later, they visited the ice-house and collected the required tools to finish their task.

Colin ordered transport, and just over an hour after Erebus started the walk back to the Manor house, the two agents were on their way towards the Oxfordshire countryside.

They arrived a mile from their target at two-thirty in the afternoon. On the trip up, Colin and Rusty went over the plan repeatedly. The pair developed strategies for each eventuality they foresaw. Colin knew that for Rusty, part of keeping his mind so active was to push any thought he was being sent to kill former colleagues to the furthest corners of his mind. Colin was calm. He didn't know the clean-up crew members. Erebus said they had to go. That was enough.

"I'll go ahead and put the first phase of our plan in place, Phoenix," said Rusty.

"Right," replied Phoenix. "I'll give you an hour. Let's synchronise our watches. On my mark, the time is 14.35. Mark."

"Check," said Rusty and got out of the van. He collected his kit from the rear and set off across the fields.

Colin sat in the van and waited. Finally, when the clock ticked forward to 15.20, he, too, left the van with his kit and set off at a brisk walk towards the target.

Al Stratton and Terry Wright-Jones lived in an isolated cottage on the outskirts of Great Bourton, just a few minutes up the road from Cropredy. So they had been ideally situated for the cleaning task when handed it. The bodies of the cleric and the bomb maker were retrieved intact from another Olympus safe house in Banbury. They had transported them through the village at night and planned to bury the bodies in the countryside.

Both men had been Sergeants in the SAS and served in Bosnia and Iraq. They had years of experience between them. When the black marks against their names for insubordination and unnecessary violence towards prisoners during interrogations mounted up, they found themselves surplus to requirements and back on 'civvy' street. After working for various security firms and debt collection agencies, always just staying one step ahead of the law, Olympus approached them.

While they trained at Larcombe, they received warnings that they were drinking in the Last Chance Saloon. Rusty and the other instructors had tried to break them, but they kept their noses clean throughout their training period. For the past three years, they had been used on various operations and, although surly and distant with their colleagues, they followed orders well enough. No black marks existed against their names in the reports that Rusty and Phoenix had seen.

The drink was their downfall. Stratton and Wright-Jones returned to the cottage on the night in question and went indoors. Their task had been to bury the two bodies, a half-mile apart, in areas with the minimum pedestrian footfall.

"Sounds like hard work, Terry, for two ragheads," said Stratton.

"Sod it," grunted Wright-Jones. "Let's have a drink first."

One thing led to another, as it often did with these two. Dawn was a distant memory before the drinking ended, with both men passed out in the lounge. But, the devil will make work for idle hands. When they awoke, hung over and irritable, they chopped the bodies up in the outhouse behind the cottage. They then planned to bury them on either side of the same field, three minutes from where they sat in the house.

"They can wave to one another," chuckled Wright-Jones.

"Fat chance," muttered Stratton. "We'll separate them. Then they'll know what it felt like for our lads to stand on an IED and get blown to kingdom come."

They filled the shrouds with parts from each of the mutilated bodies, and Stratton and Wright-Jones buried the remains on opposite sides of a field near Cropredy Bridge that night.

Colin looked across the open ground towards the cottage. Everything was quiet; it was undoubtedly isolated. There was no traffic sound anywhere. Just a few birds were singing in the trees to break the silence. Through his glasses, he picked out the outhouse. He could barely see the grill of an old Ford van parked to the side. Stratton and Wright-Jones were home.

A hedge ran the field's length to the lane in front of the cottage to his right. He needed to backtrack twenty metres and use the cover to reach the target by 15.35 when Rusty expected him to make his move.

He crawled backwards until he could safely hunker down and run towards the cottage under the cover of the hedge. Colin rechecked his watch. Fifteen thirty-two.

He stashed his kit under the hedge and put his SIG Sauer P226 into the waistband of his trousers. It felt cold but reassuring against his spine. He strolled up to the front door, knocked and waited.

Stratton opened the door. "What can I do for you, mate? Hang on, don't I know you?

Colin nodded. "I was nearby and wondered if you guys wanted to join me for a beer. I'm parked up the road and staying in the pub in the village tonight."

"That sounds great," said Stratton, standing back and inviting him to come inside. "Why don't we have a few beers? You can tell us what you've been doing. Phoenix was your name if I remember right? One of the blue-eyed boys at Larcombe. Met up with you on that prison break caper."

Colin stood his ground. He didn't want to go inside the cottage alone. However, there was no movement from inside the building. So plan A had been for Rusty to gain access from the rear of the house and take out whichever operative didn't answer the door. Colin would then dispose of the other man at the front when he was distracted by events behind him.

Colin heard a faint crunch of the gravel behind him and the unmistakable touch of cold steel on his neck.

"You'll have to do better than that, Phoenix," sneered Wright-Jones. "We spotted you ages ago. It doesn't take a genius to work out why you're here. Someone must have uncovered our handiwork. The old boy sent you to clean up, didn't he?"

Wright-Jones continued talking as Stratton patted Colin down and found the gun. He looked at it and turned it over in his hand. Then suddenly, he whipped his arm across Colin's face knocking him to the ground.

"We're going to take a short drive," said Stratton. "One way for you, I'm afraid."

"Move," growled Wright-Jones and shoved Colin forwards. Colin stumbled and fell again. Stratton pointed his gun at him, and the three men headed towards the outhouse and the old Ford van.

Colin experienced a sinking feeling. Plan A had long gone down the drain, and these two old hands had skipped several other scenarios in the playbook. What could he do? He was unarmed and with Rusty nowhere around. Had they spotted him as well? Was his best friend in the van? Had they killed him, or were they destined to die side by side?

Colin thought over the past thirty months working for Olympus. Athena's face drifted in and out of focus. His head was still spinning from the pistol-whipping Stratton dished out. With so much to live for, was this how it would end?

"Ah well," he sighed as he stumbled to the van's rear, and Wright-Jones opened the doors. "Nothing is ever forever, is it?"

Stratton shoved him towards the empty van, but Colin resisted. He wasn't getting in without a fight. Stratton tucked the Sig Sauer in his belt and grabbed hold of Colin, bundling him into the back and slamming the doors. Colin cracked his head on the bulkhead and lay there stunned.

He heard four muffled reports.

His head hurt; nothing made much sense. He curled up in a ball and waited for the van to pull away. He tried to think about making one last-ditch effort to save himself when they reached wherever these two planned to kill him and bury his body. What had happened to Rusty?

The van doors were suddenly thrown open.

Colin gathered up his strength and sprang from the van. Stratton and Wright-Jones lay in the yard, dead. Both had been shot in the back of the head. Exit wounds at the front destroyed any chance of their relatives viewing the body. The familiar smell of death that should have attacked his nostrils was not in evidence. All he could smell was the authentic smell of the country.

"Thank God for Plan Q!" said Rusty, who appeared by his side. Colin saw his teeth as his mate grinned at him but little else. Rusty was in full camouflage gear, his face blackened.

"Thought my number was up," shuddered Colin. "What happened?"

"I could tell as soon as I got in the neighbourhood that the cottage was an ideal spot. It's almost impossible to get close without someone spotting you, especially when well-trained like this couple. I had to use everything I'd ever learned to make my way undetected into the garden at the rear. I had to improvise. I burrowed into the compost heap near the back wall. It meant I was six feet from the van doors. Then I waited for your conversation at the front door. Terry came out and crept around the side of the cottage. I would break cover then and ride to the rescue, but I thought that might end up with a firefight. I didn't want to risk it. Sorry you got roughed up, mate. Once I knew they planned to take you off in the van to get rid of you, I stayed hidden until they put you inside the van. They were a few feet in front of me, walking towards the front of the van, when I stood up and took them out. They never suspected a thing."

"Thanks," said Colin. Although it was alien to him to show emotion, he wanted to throw his arms around his friend and hug him, but the stench was awful.

"First things first," said Rusty. "Let's get these two into the van. Then I'm going indoors to have a shower or two. A change of clothes and a beer will help. Maybe this pair has a stock of food in the house we can grab too. Then I reckon we watch telly and wait until nightfall."

Colin couldn't believe how Rusty could remain so cool.

"You knew these two guys; I got the impression you weren't happy doing this job when Erebus laid it out for us."

"They crossed the line, Phoenix. When they joined Olympus, they agreed to follow the rules. I might have been unhappy about the mess they made of disposing of the prisoners. I might have questioned that Erebus thought it serious enough to dispose of them. But they were prepared to kill you without a second's thought. I couldn't allow that, mate."

The two friends bundled the bodies of Stratton and Wright-Jones into the van. Later that night, they would be driven back to Larcombe to their final resting place in the crowded pet cemetery.

The two agents took showers and spent the evening in total silence. The food was prepared and eaten. They each drank a can of beer. The TV was watched and then switched off at the mains as midnight approached — no point leaving it on standby.

Rusty drove the old Ford through the lanes in darkness until they reached their transport. Colin followed Rusty back to the outskirts of Bath in the Olympus van. They swung between the pillars at the entrance to the estate at just after two in the morning.

At three o'clock, an electrical fire was instigated at the isolated cottage near Great Bourton in Oxfordshire. The fire burned swiftly. It's great living in the country, miles from anywhere, unless you need a fire engine. Unfortunately, before anyone noticed the flames and summoned the fire brigade, the blaze reduced the cottage to little more than a shell.

Tuesday, September 25th, 2012

"Back so soon, gentlemen?" asked Erebus as Phoenix and Rusty strolled into the morning meeting.

"Mission accomplished," said Rusty.

"Everything went according to plan, Sir," added Phoenix with a grin at his pal.

Henry 'Head' Case looked up from the reports he read.

"I think we may need to apply for planning permission for an extension to the pet cemetery if we have to bury many more bodies. As we speak, a work detail is in progress, ferreting away the two you delivered early this morning."

"Sad business," said Erebus, "when we have to bury two of our own. I'm afraid they were 'off-message', as they say in modern parlance, so we had no alternative. I believe we can draw a line under the Cropredy affair now and move forward."

Athena had not seen Colin since he left the meeting yesterday, so she was unaware of the near-death experience he had endured. He and Rusty's blasé comments when Erebus had spoken to them were to protect her as much as keep the full facts from Erebus. There was time enough to tell him what had gone on when he debriefed the operation later, almost certainly in the orangery.

"I don't suppose we missed much while we were away yesterday?" asked Colin.

Athena smiled.

"You couldn't have picked a better day to be off-site. The Avon & Somerset Police visited us."

"What on earth for?" asked Colin.

"They were looking for you, Phoenix," said Erebus. "Or more precisely, they asked after a troubled serviceman who raised a few doubts in the mind of one of the Charity Commissioners earlier this year."

Sir Julian Langford QC, known to his colleagues as Minos, the judge of the dead in the Underworld, took up the story. Another of the Three Stooges, Minos, was nearly sixty years of age. After a long career in the law courts watching criminals evade justice or receive softer and softer sentences for serious crimes, he had retired a disillusioned man. A family tragedy followed. His young son Harry committed suicide. He bought the drugs online as simple as downloading a CD onto his iPod. Minos joined Olympus after reading the advert placed by Erebus in The Times; he was a valuable and contented member of an organisation able to make a difference.

"You will recall the Data Protection Act raised a few issues concerning the personal information we hold on our people here at Larcombe. The Commissioners required us to complete a questionnaire, and then the ICO inspectors descended on us without warning for a review of our answers. The visit was said to be in an advisory capacity. They offered practical advice on how we might improve things should the need arise. Of course, we took our normal precautions when strangers visited us. The ice-house was locked down, and only a skeleton crew remained in the stable block. I did my utmost to show them that our records were in an exemplary state. If they looked out of the windows of this room, they would have seen a few service members tending to the flower beds or cutting vegetables from the kitchen garden. The whole picture we try to portray at times is what you would expect to see when lads return from the theatre of war suffering mental problems. They engage in a modest level of activity and exercise to complement the counselling they receive while the mind repairs itself. The interviews went well. We schooled the candidates we chose, and everyone kept to the script. They were poised to sign us off with distinction."

"Then I walked in and stuffed everything up," said Phoenix.

"I'm afraid it complicated matters, Phoenix. There's no denying that," Minos replied. "Rather than debriefing the Swindon mission as you expected, you realised the situation and collapsed in a heap. That allowed us to get you out and concoct a cover story. We avoided answering awkward questions about who you were and where you had served. We thought we had pulled the wool over their eyes. But, unfortunately, the senior Inspector chewed over events on the train journey north and, in due course, sent a report to the Charity Commission to cover his backside. They decided his concerns about what went on behind the walls of the Olympus Project were significant enough to call for further investigation. With the Leveson and Savile inquiries prominent in the news, it was inevitable in the current climate. So they invited the police to at least confirm this serviceman's identity and current status. Was this the right place for him? Had we mistreated him here even?"

Henry Case joined in at this point. "Minos and I met to talk about your case. Phoenix in the aftermath of the visit. We thought it politic to create a plausible persona for you that would satisfy the ICO if they came calling again. We have to keep sweet with the Charity Commissioners no matter what. We have kept the authorities and the public at arm's length for five years."

"So what happened yesterday then?" asked Colin, who had felt a slight chill running down his spine since he heard the police had been asking after him.

"Two officers arrived mid-afternoon without warning," said Athena, "a female Detective Inspector and a uniformed sergeant. They travelled across from the county force HQ at Portishead. These days it's where their Criminal Investigations people are based. They wanted to speak with you. During their advisory visit, they asked to interview the serviceman who fainted before ICO staff members. I called Henry Case, and he brought over the paperwork we had prepared."

"We informed them that Warrant Officer Second Class Garry Burns was the soldier they had seen collapsing. We said Burns was a veteran of several trips to Iraq. After he returned, medics diagnosed him with severe PTSD. Burns could still function and work from time to time, but there were several days a month when Burns got emotionally unstable. After leaving the military, he had spent several years having random erratic episodes, and his GP just chalked it up to his excessive drinking and temper issues. When Burns came here as a volunteer, we got him to cut back on his drinking and stopped him from fighting everyone in sight. He did things he was not proud of over there, as did many of his colleagues. We offered to counsel him on his mental issues and arranged weekly visits with a social worker. That social worker got him into sessions with a psychologist and quarterly sessions with a psychiatrist. Those sessions helped him find his way back. It was slow at first; several months passed before we built the trust that enabled him to share his experiences in a vulnerable and truthful way. It can be a real battle to enter willingly into therapy, open up to a stranger, and hope they don't tear you apart and judge you. Finally, after talking to others and taking drugs for depression, sleep disorder, and mood swings, we judged him to be 'relatively' healthy. The police learned that a virus caused the incident during the ICO visit. I showed the detective the MO's report on the matter. As he had entered the Olympus Project as a voluntary patient, we couldn't prevent him from walking away. We told them we preferred that he had stayed here, among friends and fellow service members who understood the hell he had suffered. But he was adamant he felt well enough to make it on the outside on his own. We said that he left Larcombe Manor to travel the world in July. We haven't received a card from him so far."

"How did this DI react to that?" asked Rusty.

"Difficult to tell. The woman was young, too young, I

thought to be a DL," said Henry Case. "She read through every scrap of paper we had prepared for his so-called personnel file. The DI asked for copies, which we provided. She asked for a specific date when Burns volunteered himself for treatment. She studied his ID extremely closely."

Athena tried to reassure Colin.

"Don't worry, Phoenix. We chose Garry Burns for a reason. He did serve in Iraq. Burns arrived with the first intake the week the Project opened for business. His records before he joined the Army at sixteen and throughout his time served will stack up when they check. He was with us until September 2010, when he went missing on a mission in West Africa. Burns was trying to track members of Boko Haram, and his handlers lost radio contact with his party. Nothing was ever heard from them again. Henry merely picked up the threads of his life here at Larcombe as if he had never left. You joined us in July and underwent training and facial reconstruction in your first three months with us. As far as that Detective Inspector was concerned, you were Garry Burns when the ICO inspectors visited."

"Wouldn't they spot the difference in our appearance?" asked Phoenix.

Henry Case stood up and walked over to a whiteboard. He placed photographs onto the board and secured them, one by one.

"This is Garry Burns with his mother and father at Barry Island, aged seven. This picture shows Private Garry Burns at seventeen in Rheindalen. Here we have Garry Burns again, with half a dozen other squaddies on a beach in Tenerife. He's about thirty in that one. When he joined us, we took this photograph for his ID card. He was thirty-eight years old in November of that year, which was 2007."

As 'Head' Case stuck that final photo on the board, even the antique clock on the mantelpiece seemed to pause; the likeness to Phoenix was incredible. Then, without saying a word, the intelligence head placed Colin's latest photograph alongside that of Garry Burns.

"Meet your twin, Phoenix," said Henry. "The surgeons made minor alterations to your features in September and October, perhaps unwittingly, maybe with a nod to a fallen comrade, but as you can see, the resemblance is uncanny."

"The police know how you looked on July 1st, 2010, when you went missing in the River Avon in Bath. You moved a few miles from the city to be with us, and we altered your features. Nobody you knew before that time thinks you are alive, let alone know how you look now," said Athena. She hoped her lover could see there was little cause for concern.

While this conversation was taking place at Larcombe, the young female DI reviewed her findings with her boss in the Criminal Investigations offices at Portishead,

"His paperwork shows that Burns had PTSD after his experiences in Iraq. Unfortunately, I couldn't talk to him as he had waited until his early forties to take a gap year. I expect he's trekking towards Machu Picchu as we speak with a bunch of people half his age."

"What did you do with the ID photograph?"

"I contacted the ICO inspector who raised the query and sent him a copy. He forwarded it to the colleagues he had with him on the visit to Larcombe Manor. Every single one of them gave him the same reply. 'That's the man I saw; I'm almost sure that's him.'

When I pushed the senior inspector to say whether he was one hundred per cent certain himself, he said, 'No, I couldn't swear to it. My colleagues agree. We think it's the same man, but we wouldn't want to swear to it in a court of law. Please remember; it was a long day. We had trawled through reams of paperwork and carried out interviews with officers of the charity and service members receiving help. Their stories were harrowing; we have no concept of the conditions we ask them to endure when we allow our politicians to send them off to such places. Then just as we were bringing matters to a close, the door opened, and this man entered the room. He stood there for less than five seconds, then collapsed in a heap. He received attention from two charity officers at once, and stewards came in to carry off the poor devil. I challenge anyone to say they were certain in those circumstances. If he wasn't the man in the photo you sent me, then he's his twin.'"

"That's as far as we've got, I'm afraid."

"Forget the ICO people; they can't help us any further," said her Chief Inspector. "Forget the charity, too, for now. Everything points to them doing a great job. Let's see if we can find this, Garry Burns. We can't afford to commit many resources to this; there's no evidence of a crime. Perhaps we can post a notice on the relevant backpacker sites, asking if anyone has seen him. Leave his photo on a few forums and ask him to contact us. I'm not sure what else we can do."

At Larcombe Manor, the morning meeting had finished. Rusty and Phoenix had then brought the elderly gentleman up to speed on the clean-up crew mission in the orangery. He was concerned about the tap-dancing they had resorted to finishing the job.

"My fault, chaps, I suppose," he said. "I should have given you more time to formulate your plans. How are you holding up, Phoenix? Is everything clear in your head over the police business yesterday afternoon?"

Colin looked at Rusty.

"Do you mind, mate?" he said. Rusty took the hint and left them alone.

"That detective paid particular attention to the ID photograph, Sir. She pored over it for several minutes. What did she see in the face of Garry Burns? Could she have thought that maybe Garry Burns reminded her of someone she knew?" said Colin. "I was in Oxfordshire yesterday afternoon, miles away from Larcombe Manor. How can I know that female Detective Inspector? Yet I'm positive I do."

"She identified herself as DI Zara Wheeler, and her colleague was Sergeant Toby Drysdale," said Erebus.

"There you go," sighed Colin. "She worked with my nemesis, Phil Hounsell. Hounsell and Wheeler were on my tail from Durham to Manchester and then to Bath. I kidnapped Hounsell's wife to get him to back off and allow me to travel freely to London. I had unfinished business. Everything went south when I got back. Instead of releasing her and disappearing as planned, I was running for my life with coppers on my tail. No doubt Drysdale was one of them. I remember Ms Wheeler well; no wonder she made DI at such a young age. She's as sharp as a tack. If she thinks there's any doubt about the truth of the story we gave her yesterday, she'll keep gnawing at it like a dog with a bone. That picture holds the key to the slight possibility of a cover-up job. Deliberate or not, my facial reconstruction leaving me with features so similar to Burns may well have given us a problem, not a solution."

Erebus had listened to Phoenix intently.

"You may be worrying unnecessarily, dear boy," he said. "When they left yesterday, they believed that Burns had gone to see the world. Where would they look for you if they peel away enough layers of the onion to expose you as being alive? Not here, just minutes away from the city where everyone thinks you died. They might try to trace Burns's movements and will come to a dead end. So I suggest you keep a low profile for a while. As for Burns. Giles may have to magic up a cover story in a few months; a tragic accident while swimming off the Great Barrier Reef could suffice."

Colin reluctantly had to agree; he was no doubt worrying about nothing.

Chapter Three

In her office at Portishead, DI Zara Wheeler stared at the photograph of Garry Burns, which she had pinned to a screen by her desk. Just who was it that Burns reminded her of from her past? It annoyed her, but she resolved to keep trying to remember. This dogged determination had got Zara to her present position, allied to her extreme intelligence. She reflected on her career since she arrived in the West Country.

Zara had been a DS in 2010 when she rushed south from Nottingham with DCI Phil Hounsell. They were pursuing a killer who had kidnapped Phil's wife, Erica. The then-young DS had been helping Phil ever since his short stay at Durham.

DCI Hounsell worked with SOCA in London and travelled north because he knew the victim and the story behind his case. He turned up in the murder room where the team had been beavering away without luck looking for clues. A child killer had been shot dead within an hour of being released from prison on parole. Phil Hounsell was convinced that Neil Cartwright's killer was the father of the girl he murdered. Colin Bailey had waited ten years to take his revenge on the life of his daughter Sharron.

The events of Saturday, July the first, 2010, will forever stay in Zara's mind. So much had happened in such a short time. Working with Phil Hounsell had been an eye-opener. Zara was a shy, reserved young woman back then, and despite her superior officer being married with two young children, she couldn't prevent herself from having feelings for him. She experienced sensations she had never had for a man before.

When she worked with the team at the Manvers Street station in Bath, clever detective work on her behalf had discovered the remote cottage where Erica Hounsell was a prisoner. Erica was released unharmed, and she and Phil reunited. Now calling himself Colin Owens, the killer was wandering around the streets of the old city when an off-duty female officer recognised him. She was with her mother, heading towards the Theatre Royal to watch a play. Shots rang out, and the officer was injured, but this allowed Phil, Zara, and her colleagues to close in on the killer and bring the hunt to an end.

Her boss had tackled the fugitive, and both men finished up in the River Avon. Toby Drysdale was a young PC working at Bath, and he had rescued Phil Hounsell from drowning in the treacherous waters under Pulteney Weir. Zara had needed to give Phil the 'kiss-of-life' to resuscitate him. It was a tough life, but someone had to do it, she thought as her cheeks reddened at the memory two years later. She looked around the office at Portishead, hoping that nobody noticed. How times have changed since then.

Bailey or Owens had drowned. Where the body ended up, who knew? Perhaps it made its way as far as the

Severn Estuary; more likely, it lay somewhere between Bath and the Bristol Channel in the underwater foliage and detritus that populates every UK river these days — caught up in a shopping trolley, perhaps? On the other hand, it could lie among the reeds waiting for the chance to pop to the surface and frighten an old chap fishing on the river bank.

Zara looked at that photo of Garry Burns. Was there a likeness? Was that what had been niggling at her brain? Burns was broader in the shoulder, fairer-haired and blue-eyed; he carried two stones more than the killer. The two men were roughly the same height and age. Even so, Burns didn't resemble the grainy CCTV image they had found from Aberdeen airport when Bailey returned to the UK from West Africa.

She glanced across the room at the back of Toby Drysdale's head. He had risked his life leaping into the river that day and later received a commendation for his bravery. Phil had been underwater, struggling with Bailey for several minutes. When he came up, he was exhausted. Toby had brought him ashore.

Another one of her young Bath colleagues, PC Idris Williams, and the other onlookers kept looking for Bailey. He never surfaced. No way he could have stayed under that long and survived. It was pointless to believe otherwise.

Zara unpinned the photograph and filed it away in a drawer; she intended to give the matter further thought another day. Unfortunately, her desk was full of urgent, up-to-date cases that needed her attention.

Later that day, she drove back to Bath from Portishead and arrived home. Strictly, it had been Mary Trueman's home, Phil's mother-in-law, but these days, it felt like it was her place. She fed the cats and poured herself a glass of wine while she wondered what to get herself to eat. Then she returned to reflect on those early days in Bath.

She remembered Phil's tense journey to Royal United Hospital in the ambulance. Debbie Turner had arrived earlier and received treatment for a bullet wound. Callum Wood, who worked with Phil Hounsell years before in Wiltshire, was by her side. Debbie's mother had undoubtedly kept an eye on the two of them, wondering whether she might need a new hat in the future.

Zara took her glass of wine and wandered into her bedroom. She opened the wardrobe and brought out the dress she had worn to Callum and Debbie's wedding early last year. It would be nice to have somewhere special to go, to get the chance to wear that again. She took care when replacing the dress, just in case.

Debbie will be on maternity leave soon. Zara wondered if she could get away with that dress for the christening. Zara doubted it. It meant another shopping trip for an outfit and shoes for the occasion when she could find time to get away from work.

Zara imagined Debbie might well opt not to return to work afterwards. She and Callum were both pushing forty. Phil always said that the two of them had been in love since he first met them in the late Eighties. She had to get herself shot before the silly sod told her he loved her. Zara returned to the kitchen and freshened up the drink in her glass.

"Do you think someone would declare their undying love for me if I got shot, Napoleon?" she asked her cat as he turned his head imperiously to acknowledge her presence. On the other hand, Josephine wasn't interested in what she had to say tonight and attended to her paws in front of the television.

Not long after Callum and Debbie had married, Mary

Trueman had shown signs of not being herself. Zara bonded with Mary right from the start. After Erica's kidnapping, they were thrown together at Phil's house with her two grandchildren, Shaun and Tracey. Once Erica had been released, staying here at Mary's was the ideal solution for them both. Zara needed a base in Bath or nearby, and Mary needed companionship after losing her husband, Bob, a few years earlier. The house felt empty when she was there alone.

Phil had left RUH and returned to work in London to tie up his loose ends with SOCA. Disillusioned with how things were going with that outfit, he promised Zara they would continue to work together. But, after clearing up four of five cases in one fell swoop with the Bailey business, he was owed a favour or two.

He was true to his word, and the authorities helped things progress. They had decided to wind up SOCA and replace it with a National Crime Agency in 2013. As a result, many former SOCA people returned to the provinces over the past year. Phil just happened to leave the sinking ship long before the rest of the poor devils. Dozens had left due to the ever-increasing lack of funding, others, naturally, feeling as disillusioned as Phil had left to do something worthwhile.

Phil moved to Portishead and was promoted to Superintendent shortly after. Zara had asked for a move to Manvers Street, Bath, straight after she returned to work. However, she discovered that despite Durham pleading for her return, her move was sanctioned by the middle of July. So it was only a few weeks before Phil set the wheels in motion to get her to join his team on the coast.

There were no more kidnappings and chases through the streets on Saturday evenings while stationed at Bath. But there was still plenty of fun to be had in the old Roman city. That summer, she had learned how to let her hair down and enjoy herself at last.

Toby Drysdale had helped. Phil had been right; he said that Toby fancied her when he lay in bed in RUH. Soon after that weekend, they went out for a few drinks. They had been to the cinema. After watching Bath playing Rugby at the Rec, they went for a meal. Then one night, it just happened. Toby and Zara became friends with benefits.

Zara had been glad they had slept together. It didn't change her feelings towards Toby, nor did it change his towards her, as he admitted. They were just best friends. She was always quiet and attentive, and her elderly parents had never let her mix with boys that much when she was a teenager. At university, she wanted to get the best degree she could, and the antics of most of her fellow undergraduates were beyond her comprehension. So she kept herself apart and didn't socialise that often.

Her superiors recognised her intelligence and application in her early police career and marked her for rapid advancement. She was going places. That alone would have been enough to alienate most of the 'plodders' filling most police stations. But her shyness and odd mannerisms led to people seeing her as a figure of fun. So Mouse was a nickname unkindly applied by one of the underachievers in the squad room at Durham who picked on her.

She blushed easily and wrinkled her nose as she pushed up her glasses. Zara didn't fit in with the lads or girls who behaved like the lads. When she was in Bath, the atmosphere felt different. They were a smaller unit and more friendly. It's always tricky for coppers to mix with the public. A police officer is always on duty. You have to hold something back even when you're not, so it's easier to mix with colleagues; they understand.

Toby understood the situation. He was in uniform and still a constable then. Zara was a DS being fast-tracked for better things. Toby knew his place. They both knew in the throes of their passion that love and marriage were out of the question. So they saw each other only occasionally. Every once in a while, it led to sex. They both wanted it; they both enjoyed it. Nobody got hurt.

Zara stopped reminiscing and looked at her empty glass. She decided she had better start getting that food. This wine on her empty stomach had begun to make her sentimental.

As she prepared a few things she found in the fridge for a quick salad, she recalled drinking on an empty stomach the night Idris Williams left Bath. Then, early in 2011, he returned to the valleys to rejoin the Powys Rangers or whatever they called the force in South Wales. Zara had transferred out of Bath to rejoin Phil Hounsell and his team at Portishead by that time.

She had finished work late, as usual, and rushed back to join the old gang in one of the busy pubs in the city. Everyone had more than a few drinks that night. Toby got into a taxi, legless. Somehow, Idris persuaded Zara to go back to his flat. She was in no condition to drive home. After another large glass of wine, she and Idris collapsed into bed at four o'clock.

The sex was incredible - as much of it as she could remember - and Zara lost the inhibitions she had with Toby. Everything was always tender and comfortable with her best friend, as it had been since that first night when he discovered how innocent she was. But Idris got the shock of his life! Zara took the lead and did things she never dared do with Toby. Zara imagined that he had a big grin on that plain round face for days as he tended to his new flock over the Severn Bridge.

She had crept out of his flat at eight o'clock and found her way home to Mary Trueman's. She never saw or heard from Idris again. Mary hadn't even asked where she'd been. Mary wanted to know if she had seen Bob picking the beans for dinner in the garden. Zara had been so hung-over it barely registered. Over the months, Mary's grasp on reality slackened, and Phil and Erica agreed that a care home was the best place for her. Since then, Zara had lived in Mary's old house alone.

She took her patched-up evening meal through to the lounge. First, she encouraged Napoleon and Josephine to budge so she could at least share the sofa. Then she decided there wasn't much point leaving what remained in the bottle. So she topped up her glass again.

Zara tried to watch something on the television, but nothing suited her mood, so she switched it off and let her mind wander. The wine took firm control now. She giggled as she remembered going to work the Monday after Idris had left. Phil Hounsell and the team were picking up the threads of yet another domestic abuse case, and she had sat across the table from him.

There was always going to be a connection between them. The rest of the team knew the history. Zara couldn't help looking at her boss that morning and wondering what he would think of how she had behaved last night. Her relationship with Toby Drysdale was common knowledge. So Phil was well aware that the innocent young girl who sat on the bed next to him in that Manchester hotel had disappeared long ago. She wasn't so innocent now! She was just miserable; the job and the people you work with do that to you as time passes.

In the first few months at Portishead, several gut-wrenching cases were handled. Her promotion to DI followed a series of successful prosecutions based on the efforts of her and her team. Zara knew it had been worth the hours they had put in for the poor women and children involved. Sometimes though, she wanted to curl up in a ball, have a good cry, and shut the world out.

Zara needed to find someone she could come home to every night and love unreservedly and know they loved her in return. Not Toby, bless him; he was her best friend, but he wasn't the one. If only Idris had been at Durham! If her sexual awakening had occurred well before she met Phil Hounsell, she would have ripped that towel from his body in Manchester and feasted on him there and then. Things might have been so different if she had given him a night to remember.

God, she was pathetic! She slammed the empty bottle into the recycle bin, stacked her dirty crockery in the sink, and went to bed. She crawled under the duvet, curled up in a ball, and had a good cry.

Monday, November 1st, 2010

Phil Hounsell looked up from the report he was studying.

"Good morning, Zara. Did you have a good weekend?"

"Hello, Phil, not too bad; I did some clothes shopping. Toby and I went to the cinema on Saturday night."

"What did you watch? Any good?"

"It was 'Never Let Me Go'; Toby has a thing for Keira Knightley."

"I guess the rest of the time; you did the same as Erica

and me; eat, drink and sleep. At least, for as long as the kids allowed us."

Zara nodded. Any time off became precious when the pressure was on, as it had been since she set foot here at Portishead. Translated, you were so mentally tired precious little got done.

When the rest of the team had gathered, Phil updated their latest case.

"This is our latest victim," he began. "Laura Barrie is twenty-three years old. The attack began at just after two in the morning last Sunday. Laura and her partner, Troy Green, thirty-eight, had returned home from a nightclub in Bristol. An argument broke out on the pavement outside their apartment. He accused his girlfriend of making eye contact with several young men at the club. She denied it; he let his fists continue the discussion. Then, as you can see from these photographs, Green launched a ferocious attack on Laura. She was left with a severely swollen face, chipped teeth, clumps of hair pulled from her scalp, cuts, bruises, and scratches on her body. Witnesses from the block of flats and passers-by tried to intervene, but Green threatened them with violence. Throughout the attack, Laura Barrie begged her partner to stop."

"This is her statement to the officers who attended," Phil continued." I was on the floor, I begged Troy to stop, but he just laughed. I was confused. I didn't know what was happening. I thought he was going to kill me.' Green dragged her from the pavement and attempted to get her inside their apartment. Detective Constable Isaac Haynes noted that on arrival, Laura was seriously injured and terrified for her life. However, the quick actions of the members of the public, who contacted us, helped save her. Laura had gone to the hospital and received treatment. When she was fit enough, they interviewed her. At first, she was reluctant to speak out as she feared reprisals. However, DC Haynes and a female colleague who specialises in domestic violence cases encouraged her to make a statement, and, in due course, she gave testimony against Green in court. The officers' reassurances certainly helped sway this girl around to doing the right thing. That worked in our favour because Ms Barrie learned a few things about her partner."

"This is what she has since added to her first statement," Phil concluded. 'I found out he did it before to other women. But they never went to the police. They were too frightened of what he would do to them.' Laura Barrie is one brave young lady. We must ensure she gets the support she needs until the trial."

"What are we looking at here, Sir?" asked one of the Detective Sergeants on the team, Angela Chambers.

"Well, intent to cause grievous bodily harm, for a start. If we could persuade other victims to come forward, there might be a stronger case. I don't think there'll be much of a problem getting a conviction unless the CPS and the courts screw up matters. Think of a number between five and seven; that should be a reasonable sentence to expect."

Zara Wheeler leant back in her chair.

"Thoughts, Inspector?" asked Phil Hounsell, conscious that this mannerism usually indicated a deep and meaningful insight to share with the team.

"Just a few, Sir; I've only been here at Portishead for a short time, but we seem to have more than our fair share of these attacks, don't we? Not every one of them turns out as well as this one seems to have done. For us, at least, not poor Laura. In September, we had Carole Beech, who had separated not long before from Levi Beech, the father of her six-year-old daughter Daisy. Carole had been in an abusive relationship for five years. Beech reacted by snatching Daisy from school and threatening to kill her if Carole didn't return to him. After two weeks, Carole got her back when the courts forced Beech to give custody. They detailed his restricted access to his daughter, but he pressed Carole for a total reconciliation. He couldn't accept that she didn't want to be with him anymore. Carole Beech was due in court to ask for a permanent residency order on September 15th, ensuring that Daisy lived with her. Levi Beech entered the family home the evening before and stabbed both Carole and Daisy in the heart. Her sister found the bodies when she arrived at nine o'clock the next morning to drive them into Bristol."

Zara looked at her hands folded in her lap and added.

"I talked to her sister Mandy last week."

Phil looked up. Everyone around the table was familiar with the case. It had been one of the most harrowing scenes those attending officers would ever face. The mood around the office had been sombre for days.

"Did something prompt that meeting, Zara? Beech is on remand awaiting trial; everything is OK, I hope? I thought that was put to bed weeks ago."

"I followed up on my own time, Sir. Her sister was devastated by the deaths. I promised to keep in touch. Mandy could never understand why they never assessed Carole as high risk, even though the neighbourhood police were called out time and time again because of Beech's volatile behaviour. He had been reported to the police on seventeen occasions over five years. Concerned neighbours reported suspected assaults when they saw Carole with cuts and bruises. They reported late-night disturbances, shouting, and screaming from Carole and the daughter. It was common knowledge on the estate that Beech carried a weapon. She reckons the authorities failed her."

"We have to be careful not to get too involved, Zara," her boss said gently. "It will mess with your head if you get too close."

"I know that Sir, but in a few areas we cover, no systems exist for sharing information on women and children at risk; in those areas with systems, they repeatedly fail. We recorded those seventeen reported incidents in the end, but none of the related services knew of the dangerous escalation in violence. No doubt you can guess why? Cutbacks have led to a massive backlog of inputting data. Since Carole and Daisy died, several incidents have been added to our records."

"Let's park this for now, Zara." said Phil, "this is a massive subject. I admit it warrants our attention, but we must concentrate on our current cases. I think you and I should consider the bigger picture at another time. If we need to co-opt anyone from other agencies, we can do so. So let's switch our attention to the ram-raid attacks on the jewellers along the M5 this past month. Where are we on that?"

Zara remained seated; she looked at the floor. The ghosts of Carole and Daisy Beech drifted across the carpet. She needed to focus. They did have successes. They did get criminals banged up now and then. It seemed they dealt with a never-ending stream of cases similar to the Beeches. If only it happened in dysfunctional British families, they might get on top of things. Instead, the government seemed powerless to stop the flood of Europeans, Africans, and Asians arriving in the region. That tsunami never showed any sign of stopping; the problems mounted daily. She knew how that little Dutch boy must have felt with his finger in the dyke.

The day's work ground to a halt with no progress, and the team left the office. Zara stared out her window as her colleagues left on foot or from the car park. They would scatter across the Avon and Somerset region to rejoin friends and families for a few hours of respite.

"Penny for them, Zara?" said Phil as he stood by her office door, leaning against the door frame.

"Sorry, Phil," she replied, "it's been a bad day. I was out of order this morning."

"You need a holiday. Take a break and recharge the batteries. This domestic violence stuff can get to you. Look, Erica and I would love to have you over for dinner one night. The kids love to see you; you know that. Maybe we could fix something up for this weekend?"

"I'm seeing Toby," Zara said, then added, "look, there's nothing serious with Toby and me. We're not moving in together or anything. I don't want to let him down. We're just going to the rugby. Then out for a beer."

"Okay point taken; we're both grateful for you staying at Mary's place. It was terrific for the two of you until her dementia took hold. You were our babysitter at the end of the phone too, which was great. I'm just concerned that you're there alone a lot these days."

"I'm fine; I've never felt unsafe there. It's a lovely, quiet spot."

"Too quiet, perhaps; it's not your security that's the worry. You're a young, single woman, and you should be amongst people more. Erica and I wouldn't be upset if you moved into a flat in the centre of Bath or Bristol or even out here on the coast in Portishead. It might do you good to have company on your doorstep to help take your mind off what you're dealing with daily."

"I'd prefer to stay where I am, Phil," said Zara firmly. "The cats and I are happy enough where we are. I have several days of holiday owed me, though, and you're right. I need a break. Perhaps I'll check something out online tonight when I get home. Can we meet tomorrow to discuss the thoughts I bored you with this morning?"

"Yes, miss," said Phil, grinning.

Why do I let him do that, Zara thought. When I go off on a tangent, Phil chews me out in front of my colleagues. One minute he tells me he's concerned for my welfare like a father to a wayward daughter. The next, he makes my heart flip with a daft comment and a smile.

They left the car park in convoy, and Zara followed Phil back to Bath. She flashed her lights at the back of his Lexus as she turned off towards home. He waved a casual hand and was swallowed up by the traffic.

"Seven nights in Tenerife, and I fly from Bristol next Tuesday," said Zara, poking her head around Phil Hounsell's door the following day.

"Happy days," said Phil. "I wish I was coming with you."

Zara blushed and pushed her glasses up her nose. Why did she still do that?

"How's your timetable looking today, Sir?" she asked, changing the subject to avoid dreaming of lying on a beach next to her boss.

"Let's meet for lunch and continue our chat into the early afternoon. I must be away for three o'clock to meet the Assistant Chief Constable; other than that, I'm yours after twelve."

Zara was sure it was deliberate, him teasing her that

way. He was in one of the happiest, most robust relationships she had come across in the force. So many marriages fell by the wayside. They broke because of the nature of the work, the unsociable hours, and the stress. Yet Phil and Erica's marriage had remained rock solid despite everything.

They met in the canteen at noon and found a quiet corner. As Phil and Zara picked at their food, Zara unloaded her thoughts on her boss. Phil realised that Zara had been holding on to a heavy burden for a long while. Letting it out would help her regroup and find her way back to being the sharp, intelligent go-getter he had uncovered at Durham.

Phil listened intently and marvelled at Zara's grasp of the topic. When he was in RUH recovering from his ordeal, they held hands when Erica arrived. He had promised Zara that he would make sure they continued to work together. So what about this quiet, shy little thing made him so protective? Zara was still only seven stones, wringing wet just as she had been the first day he clapped eyes on her. She and Toby had done the deed; that was plain to see on their faces the Monday morning they returned to work, even if they imagined they had gotten away with it. He wasn't a copper for nothing.

The rumour mill even offered the possibility of a brief fling with Idris Williams, but Phil didn't buy into that. It sounded a step too far for Mouse. Phil suddenly recalled their conversation in the hospital. He'd forgotten that. What with being in London for a while, then Portishead, he hadn't been back to Manvers Street, where the lads in the office dubbed him Cat that day because of his giant leap to grab Bailey.

Cat and Mouse had been his and Zara's moniker when

they worked together. But, deep inside, did he always see them joined at the hip?

Chapter Four

Zara played with her food. She could tell that her boss was distracted. Phil had asked what the problems were with the current system for assessing risk. She said those who assessed risk had a poor understanding of the factors contributing to an increased risk. It had always been hard to do accurately and relied mainly on the subjective judgement of people who weren't domestic abuse specialists.

As he stopped daydreaming and returned to her, Zara wiped her mouth with her napkin, sipped at her coffee, and tried again.

"Did you hear of the DASH form they introduced last year?"

"Naturally. Although it was rushed through before we had things in place to carry it out, we had no time to organise training. So the people at the sharp end didn't know how to get the best from it or even understand what the form told them. But, hey, it's better than we had before, which was nothing."

"DASH aimed to get consistency in identifying risk,"

said Zara. "The questions map certain risk triggers: Pregnancy, conflict over access to children, the victim finding the nerve to walk away. These flashpoints can cause an abuser to increase the frequency and severity of abuse. A properly completed form will tell us if a woman is in danger."

"Often, the woman withholds pertinent information, though," added Phil. "They're scared of losing their kids, with social services hovering."

"If they had referred Carole Beech to agencies for a protection plan, things might have turned out differently."

"You don't have to convince me, Zara; I know how damaging domestic abuse is across many areas. Stack up the number of deaths. Add on the estimated fifteen billion pounds cost to the UK economy. Then factor in that a quarter of our violent crime statistics are domestics; it's a nightmare. God knows how many kids are living in abusive households."

"Consistency of decision-making is vital," said Zara. "If we get the risk assessment right and refer the high-risk people, we stand a chance of reducing abuse. In addition, I'd want us to train our front-line officers to be more proactive than reactive."

Phil nodded but sighed.

"Our officers are expected to be a jack-of-all-trades during periods of austerity such as these. Do you know what you get if you're Jack? You're a master of none. It's hard to find the time and resources. Cast your mind back to what you said regarding the complaints records; it was weeks in arrears. We'd attended the funerals for Carole and Daisy Beech before the computer records even caught up to show the hassle that Levi caused them."

"Doesn't it make you want to give up, Phil?" asked Zara.

"Don't start me off on that road, Zara," he said grimly.

Several times over the past couple of years, he had wondered what he was doing. The current 'police service' was light years away from the 'police force' he had joined. They had rooted out many of the old practices. The corruption problems were a thing of the past, for the most part, thank goodness. But many criminals stuck two fingers up to the law and continued to prosper.

Lawyers, bankers, and criminals were the Big Three winners in our society.

"When I see the ACC later, I hope I get the chance to outline our concerns. I've been doing background work to show I've been listening to you. Although Carole Beech told us Levi threatened to kill her and Daisy several times, each incident was treated in isolation. They never considered that the danger to the daughter was independent of the risk to her mother. That needs to change. I'll do my best, Zara, as always,"

The two colleagues sat in quiet contemplation for a few minutes. Neither of them appeared to want to be the one to get up and leave.

"If I don't see you before you go, have a great time next week. Enjoy yourself, but most of all —relax and forget work," said Phil, getting up and giving her shoulder a gentle squeeze.

"Thanks," she replied as she felt the warmth of his hand through her jacket.

Detective Superintendent Hounsell left for his appointment with the ACC; Detective Inspector Wheeler returned to her office and tried to concentrate on her open cases.

There was plenty of crime in Portishead and the surrounding area to keep her occupied. She read from the first file in a pile on her desk.

Many years ago, in an earlier life, Ken Lewis was

married. He left school, joined the Navy, met a girl in a port, and settled into domestic bliss. After leaving the Navy, he drifted from one dead-end job to another; the marriage had long since foundered. Today his health was shot to pieces. Alcohol was the main contributor to that, and his mental state was frail.

The report and Ken's story contained within it was not related to those elements of his life, except to say, without a doubt, contributed to his vulnerability. He became an easy target for exploitation. His problems appeared to have exposed him to an existence that most people living in 21st-century Britain naively believed had been consigned to the history books.

Ken Lewis said he was held captive by a family of travellers. In his statement, he claimed that his home was a ramshackle hut in a field; body and soul, he belonged to this travelling family. His treatment was appalling. The food was left on a plate by the door to the hut. In return, he worked laying paving stones or asphalt on people's driveways, whatever the weather.

Ken, now in his late fifties but looking older, was found wandering along the side of a slip road leading to the M5 in late September. He was picked up by a police vehicle on patrol. He was a rambling, incoherent wreck. The first port of call for him was a hospital for a check-up.

A nurse who treated him on arrival saw bruises over the whole of his body and head lice. In addition, he showed signs of malnutrition. The poor devil hadn't been able to wash or shower in months. For the past five weeks, he had been a patient in the psychiatric wing of a hospital in Taunton.

Zara found it hard to believe that slavery, abolished in Britain two hundred years ago, still existed. However, if the data in front of her was valid, then the practice of domestic servitude was virtually endemic.

"How can this happen in what we consider a civilised society?"

Angela Chambers overheard her comment as she passed by her office door.

"Something interesting, Ma'am?" she asked.

"Parliament passed a Bill recently that set aside a specific day for Anti-Slavery Day. Any clue what date that is?"

"No, Ma'am," replied Angela.

"The eighteenth of October, two weeks ago. I missed it too. I read about Ken Lewis, the chap Traffic found near the M5 several weeks back. He claimed to have been held captive, working for scraps, for years by a family of travellers. I understand we've identified them, but because we don't know Ken Lewis's location, it won't be easy to make any charges stick. Moreover, because he has mental problems, getting him to give evidence will be virtually impossible."

"The government introduced new anti-slavery laws weeks ago, Ma'am, making it an offence to hold someone in 'servitude' or requiring them to perform forced or compulsory labour. I read something on that a week or two back. The scale astounds me; how can something terrible happen around us, and we don't notice it? What does that say about us as a police service, let alone as a society?"

"Come on in, Angela; close the door. Look, you were in the meeting the other morning when DS Hounsell, with justification, chastised me over the domestic violence case I handled. He said I was letting it affect me. He was right. I ate, slept, and drank the Beech case for weeks. Nothing else got through the wall I built up around myself. Since that story broke, I've been ignorant of many things in the big, wide world. In the end, what justice will we get for Carole and Daisy? He'll get six years, possibly, and a voice warning me not to count my chickens is gnawing away in my head. One little slip by us in the evidence we put together, or one little slip by the CPS on disclosure, a slippery defence counsel or a weak-minded judge—Levi Beech will be free. Someone lost a daughter and a granddaughter; someone lost a sister and a niece. Count the things they'll miss: birthdays, proms, graduations, weddings, babies, holidays together, just a night playing bingo. Where's the justice in six years, Angela? Tell me that."

"Phil Hounsell has said this to you, Ma'am; he certainly keeps saying it to us all the time. 'We have to work with the system we've got, it's not perfect, but we can't have vigilantes roaming the country dispensing their form of rough justice.'"

Zara Wheeler threw her head back and laughed loudly for the first time in a while.

"Sorry, Angela. Well, it's good to know that something I've said is stuck in his head. Back in Bath, I said that to him when he was in RUH after his dip in the river. Phil came to the idea that this guy Owens did us a favour. We know that he disagrees with modern policing and soft sentencing. He thought the world was better without the sixteen criminals Owens or Bailey killed, and he had done society a favour. Phil almost considered turning a blind eye."

"I think most officers have felt that way at one time in their career," said Angela. "I'd better let you get on with your work; I hear you're off on holiday soon?"

"Tenerife on Tuesday," sighed Zara.

"Don't do anything I wouldn't do, Ma'am," whispered Angela as she got up to leave, then added brightly,

"I'll see you when you get back. After that, things might have changed; who knows?"

Zara looked at the stack of files on her desk, needing her attention. 'Fat chance,' she thought. Zara daydreamed for a while. Maybe she could meet someone on holiday. Not for a long-term relationship, just mindless sex. She wondered whether she had changed so dramatically from the timid creature from her Durham days. Could she imagine sitting at a bar, spotting a likely candidate, and walking over to them? Could she make it understood that she didn't plan on letting them go until after breakfast?

"Fat chance of that," she laughed.

It was dark, cold and wet when she flew back into Bristol Airport. The sunshine had made a welcome change, and Zara caught up with the reading she had been putting off for far too long. Her evenings had been the sex-free zone she anticipated. That didn't mean there were no men eager to spend time with her or good-looking young men on the beach or in the bars and restaurants.

It was just that, as she didn't take holidays abroad as often as her colleagues, she was unprepared for the harsh realities of November in the Canary Islands. Moreover, the average age of the men in her hotel was seventy, and they were married.

Meanwhile, the good-looking young men on the beach were gay. She passed the bars and clubs where the young guns enjoyed themselves. Finally, she decided against the nightly bingo and what passed for the senior citizens' in-house entertainment in their all-inclusive package. Zara bought a cheap bottle of wine from the local supermercado and took it to her room each night. She was bored and itching to get back to work.

Zara found her car in the airport car park and drove

home to Bath. She planned an early night and an early start in the morning. She planned to sit at her desk by eight o'clock.

"Welcome back," said Phil Hounsell. He arrived at the office at his usual time. Zara had been in for an hour. The stack of files was no smaller. The fairies hadn't been while she was away. She had thought the same last night when she opened the door to Mary's house. The mess she had left behind when working late had trimmed her preparation time to make the flight out to a minimum.

Before she could think of cooking herself a meal, she needed to change the bedclothes, tidy the kitchen and put the mail in a prioritised order. In the end, she had emptied her case, gathered up her dirty clothes and loaded the washing machine before ringing for pizza delivery. Then she had to wait the forty minutes it took the young guy to get from the centre out to Mary's place on his scooter. While she waited, Zara got the hoover out and gave the house a well-deserved clean.

"Have I missed anything exciting?" she asked as her mind switched back to work mode.

"Batteries recharged and ready to go, I see," said Phil with a smile. "Straight past the small talk and back to business as always. A raid is in progress, as we speak, out near Burnham-On-Sea."

"It's not what you would call Dodge City, Sir. What's occurring?"

"If you want to be in on the action Inspector, you better come with me," called Phil as he headed for his office. Zara grabbed her coat and trotted after him. It felt more like the good old days.

"This raid is a follow-up to the Ken Lewis affair you looked at before you flew off to the sun," Phil told her. They were making the half-hour drive along the coast to the seaside resort of Burnham-On-Sea.

"I never imagined we'd get any change out of that case, Phil," said Zara. "Ken Lewis was messed-up. The Kelly family have long memories. Finding anyone to stand up in court and testify would be impossible. Members of the Kelly clan have been around in this corner of the West Country for a century. What changed?"

"A nurse at Musgrove Park called last Wednesday to say that Ken was experiencing a period of lucidity. She was speaking off the record but wanted someone to get a statement from him sharpish. She didn't want his abusers to get off scot-free. So someone went in from Taunton police station. The officers 'conned' the doctors that they had popped in on the off-chance to see how Ken was progressing. It bought them time with Ken; he gave us enough clues to determine where they held him. It's coming up on the left. It looks as if our search teams have got their hands full. What a bloody tip."

The property looked empty and unloved; it was an old-style bungalow built in the 1930s with a carport to the side. In it stood a Ford Transit that looked like it hadn't moved since the 1970s. Ivy grew out of the radiator grille. Phil parked his car and went to the boot.

"I remembered to stash my boots in here before I left home today. I threw Erica's in, too, because I knew you wouldn't have any, first day back and everything. They might be big for you. Better than tramping around these fields in those shoes, though."

"My hero," Zara said and was glad to be able to pull on the boots. Phil strode off around the back of the bungalow to where most of the action had taken place. Zara struggled along after him.

"Update, please, Sergeant," called Phil.

DS Nick Frobisher spun around at the sound of his voice.

"Good morning, Sir. I didn't expect to see you here," replied the young copper, who Zara remembered worked out of Portishead.

"I need to keep you young beggars on your toes," said Phil.

"We've got a lot of things to plough through, Sir. We've found the place without a doubt. Ken Lewis was one of several people kept here by the Kelly gang. Several may be with other gangs now. There's not so much work around here in the winter. We removed the men we found here at six o'clock when we raided the place. They kept them in the sheds and caravans you can see dotted around the field and set them to work on block paving or asphalting driveways across the county; they did general labouring when they weren't doing that. A few accused the family of assaulting them; there were a few marks and bruises in evidence. One word out of turn, complaining of a lack of food or dry bedding, resulted in punches and kicks."

"What did you find in the bungalow, Nick? Is there anyone at home?"

"No, Sir; the guys we found were waiting for a van to arrive to take them off to work in whatever town the gang procured jobs for them. It's difficult to hide these many police vehicles. So we had to hope the van arrived and could hang around long enough for us to apprehend the driver and any passengers. I'm afraid we haven't seen anyone. I expect the activity spooked them, and they've reported back to Kelly Senior. We're hunting down the next likely site on the list of places they could be staying. We'll get them sooner rather than later."

"OK, Nick, we'll let you get on with things. What about inside the property itself?"

"Had to effect entry. So you'll find people from UKHTC indoors. They are collecting evidence to help with a prosecution."

Phil and Zara plodded back up the field towards the bungalow. Phil wondered if he had met the officers in London; the Human Trafficking Centre had been integral to SOCA while he worked there.

"Trafficking is normally associated with prostitution, people smuggling, and organised crime," Phil said to Zara. "Not with the Irish gipsy laying your new patio."

As they reached the front of the property, they could see what remained of the front door. Police vans and a couple of leylandiis hid it from where Phil and Zara parked at the rear of the property.

"Lucky we brought our big red key," said Phil as they eased their way past the splintered wood into the hallway. The two UKHTC staff were strangers. After the officers introduced themselves, the female, the senior partner, described what they had discovered so far. She outlined how it fitted in with the work they carried out countrywide.

"There are thousands trapped in hovels similar to this," he told them, "doing things they don't want to do. We need to help get them out of their situation and stop others from being sold into slavery—there are almost fifteen hundred enslaved people in the UK. But, of course, those are only the number of people we have located. The true scale of the problem could be much greater. Fifteen hundred is certain to be the tip of the iceberg."

"Slaves found at travellers' sites, such as this one, are

tramps, drug addicts, care-home runaways, illegal immigrants, fugitives, and ex-convicts," her colleague continued. "We're talking of a largely forgotten horde of non-persons. The gangs of travellers arrive in their vans early in the morning. They scoop these stragglers off the streets and from the hostels. Then they get whisked away with the promise of a day's labour. They rarely see money: a can or two of lager and food scraps. Most of the men your people released here today were held against their will, forced to work for at least twelve hours a day for food and a bed."

"It's been well-known for a while that this is how several members of the travelling community make their money," added the female officer. "The State benefits these men were entitled to were paid directly into the Kelly bank account. We found evidence of this, plus correspondence that shows that the authorities knew the men were here. They believed the Kelly family looked after their welfare, but I doubt if anyone bothered to check. The Kelly family is constantly on the move. It's in their nature, so if anyone came to call in office hours between nine and five, odds on they found the place deserted."

Phil and Zara listened to their depressing story. Finally, at least Ken Lewis might get a degree of justice. When eventually arrested, the Kelly family faced false imprisonment charges and any other charges that UKHTC could lay at their door.

"Oh, by the way, we found passports too," said the female officer, "although they look iffy. I reckon you've several illegals in amongst the guys you removed to a place of safety earlier. Do you want to follow up on that?"

"Leave them to us," said Phil. Then, turning to Zara, he added, "we've seen enough. It's all good stuff — the clock's ticking for the Kelly family. I know we cover a big patch, and they know most of the hidey-hole's on it, but we'll root them out. So let's get over there and interview these suspects."

Zara collected the passports from the female UKHTC officer, and she and Phil Hounsell went outside to the car. After storing their dirty boots and getting their shoes back on, Phil drove them to Portishead.

"These interviews can be tricky, Zara," said Phil.

"Stating the obvious again, Phil? Well, you wouldn't expect the authorities to make it simple. We need to find interpreters for a start. We'll have to watch every word in case we infringe on their human rights, no matter how they got here. The system works against us at every turn."

"Blimey, Zara; I thought a week's break might cheer you up, but you're even more cynical than before you went away."

"We must stick by the law, Phil, which means we're already up against the clock. When we get back, we need to uncover the nationality of these two suspected illegal immigrants and chase up interpreters. It would be good to check these passports to see if the UKHTC officer was right to be suspicious. One thing we don't know is the condition of this pair. They may have needed hospital treatment. By the sound of it, even if they presented with a relatively clean bill of health, they will be thirsty and starving."

"We'll interview them in the staff canteen if it speeds things up, Zara," joked Phil.

There was no sign of a smile on the face of his colleague. Phil pulled into his parking space in front of the Portishead HQ and decided he'd better play these next few hours wearing his serious head. Zara was right about watching your step when dealing with these sorts of cases.

An hour later, they found an interpreter for a Romanian

guy whose passport said he was forty-four, but whose features and physique placed him closer to sixty-four. As for suspect number two, he was a Nigerian whose papers said he was fifty-two. Within seconds of seeing him, Phil realised that his English was better than most UK teenagers; unfortunately, they couldn't shut him up, and everything he shouted related to hellfire and damnation. Phil scanned through his passport to see if he was a preacher of an obscure denomination, but it described him as a mature student. His given name was Sunday, however, so that felt right.

Phil took Zara to one side. He wanted to have her with him as he conducted each interview.

"A female officer in the room might help to make them feel less threatened. The poor beggars have had a right ordeal. There is no point in us playing 'good cop, bad cop' and trying to force information out of them. Let's tread softly and see where it leads. The more comfortable they are, hopefully, the longer it will be before they demand to see a brief."

"Right you are," said Zara. "That makes sense. I'll get tea, coffee, and sandwiches brought across. I'm not playing 'mother', but it will ease the tension."

"Makes sense; okay, who do we start with, Anton Dumitrescu or Sunday Aronu?

"Best get the interpreter doing something useful, or she'll be looking at her watch, wondering if she'll be back in the office by clocking-off time."

Anton Dumitrescu came in first and shuffled towards the seat as he looked around the room. He looked like a frightened shadow of a man. Then, as Phil asked the interpreter to tell him who he was and why he was at the police station, there was a knock at the door. A young female PC entered, pushing a trolley.

"The refreshments DI Wheeler ordered, Sir," she said, then left the room.

Phil noticed that Dumitrescu stared at the trolley; he didn't seem to notice the attractive young female officer.

"Tell Anton to help himself," said Phil Hounsell to the interpreter.

The suspect's eyes widened; it was clear he was ravenous. He grabbed the food and stuffed a packet of biscuits in his jacket pocket in case the trolley disappeared. The interview was off to a good start. Phil coaxed Dumitrescu through the process with his usual calm professionalism.

The interview with Sunday Aronu was a different matter altogether. The big man was a borderline fruitcake. He blessed the food before taking a bite and refused coffee as it was 'the Devil's potion'. Phil was desperate for a mug of coffee but made do with a cup of weak tea, which he hated, to avoid offending Sunday. Zara watched Phil's discomfort with every sip and stifled a chuckle.

Two hours later, the interviews were at an end. Phil and Zara returned to his office to look at their gathered information.

"Much as we expected," said Phil, looking dejected. "Dumitrescu has a forged passport; he came into the country by hiding in the back of a lorry transporting tyres and then ran off into the night in Wolverhampton eighteen months ago. He was picked up off the streets by a traveller's gang operating near Redditch and then sold to the Kelly family a year ago. Since then, he has been kept in dreadful conditions and forced to work wherever they sent him."

"What he told us gives us more evidence for our case against the Kelly gang when we track them down," said Zara. "Earlier this year, the Coroners and Justice Act created a new offence of holding another person in slavery or servitude or requiring them to carry out forced or compulsory labour. Until this Act came into effect, no single offence covered the crime in full; this recognises forced labour as a crime on its own—these men's statements make it easier to bring a prosecution."

"Sunday Aronu was different, though," said Zara. "I'm not sure on what planet he is. His passport is fine as far as I can make out, but an expert might show otherwise. It appears he arrived in September 2004, stating he had a place at a theological college in London. That course should have lasted two years. Instead, he overstayed way beyond the time his visa expired. He doesn't seem too clear on why he ended up in a hostel, except to say he thought that God would provide. So in the end, the Kelly gang provided for Sunday Aronu for the last three years."

Phil looked up at the ceiling as if searching for divine inspiration.

"So, where does that leave us?" he asked.

"There are two ways of dealing with illegal immigrants, Sir. The Border Agency can handle the administration, or we can move forward via criminal proceedings. However, in general, even if criminal proceedings cannot go ahead, a person may remain categorised as an illegal immigrant as far as the administration is concerned. This is because they can still be subject to deportation or removed by the Home Office under the relevant sections of the Immigration Act 1971."

"Is there any knowledge you don't have stored away in that massive brain of yours, Mouse?" said Phil, shaking his head in astonishment.

Zara blushed and wrinkled her nose.

"I can quote the relevant act, Sir, but does it help? Neither of these two has committed an offence we wish to pursue through the courts. However, they were offended against and as illegals; either by 'entering without leave' or 'remaining beyond the time limited by leave', then it's best to hand it over to the UKBA to deal with, isn't it?"

"Yes, Miss," said Phil. "Let's get these two on their way then. Can you get hold of the Southern regional office and arrange for a collection?"

Zara looked at the clock.

"Nothing will happen today now, Phil. We'll have to put them up for the night. I'll ring through and see if they can do a pickup first thing tomorrow."

Phil shrugged. A bed in the cells was light years better than the conditions they had suffered for months, so a good night's sleep, breakfast in the canteen and then they'd be off in the morning on the journey towards deportation. Ah, well, you can't have everything.

Chapter Five

Zara went back to her office and made the call. The UKBA official noted her request and promised to call back in the morning. So, after a long and fruitful day, Phil and Zara drove back to Bath and their respective homes in convoy.

Zara arrived back at her desk bright and early the following day. She waited patiently for the call. Dimetrescu and Aronu had been fed and watered, ready to leave. She dropped in to see them in the custody suite. They were resigned to their fate but had no complaints about their treatment since yesterday.

Only one thing concerned Dimetrescu. Did he have to hand back the packet of biscuits? Zara suggested he share them with Sunday Aronu. She bought a bar of chocolate from a vending machine and handed it over to the Nigerian. Sunday blessed it, broke it in two, and gave half to the Romanian.

When she walked back into her office, the phone rang.

Two minutes later, Zara slammed the phone down and stomped across to Phil's office.

"Good morning Zara; I take it someone's rattled your cage?"

"Unbelievable!" she cried. "Bloody unbelievable. The Border Agency say they have no one available. I told them we were up against the clock with these two and couldn't charge them with any criminal offence. The bloke dared to say, 'Not my problem! It's the cuts, love, and we're short-handed.' So I asked him what he expected me to do with them. He said unless we wanted to hold on to them for an offence, then we may as well let them walk!"

"What a crazy, fucked-up system," exploded Phil.

Everyone in the office looked up and listened in on their conversation now. Nobody would stand up and say their superiors were mistaken. They knew this to be an everyday occurrence. Anton and Sunday walked to the carpool, and a driver dropped them at the town centre. He left them with a wave of the hand and a good luck wish.

In his office, Phil Hounsell and Zara Wheeler still fumed. Was it ever worth the effort? There must be a better way.

As any policeman will tell you, life goes on. DS Hounsell and DCI Wheeler, or Cat and Mouse, didn't have long to wallow in self-pity. Other cases lay on their desks. Other tragedies waited to unfold.

"Did you know this Armitage fellow, Sir?" asked Zara one morning, showing Phil a brief obituary in a police magazine.

"He was stationed in London with SOCA while I worked there, Zara, but I wouldn't say I knew him. Armitage was rotten to the core. I kept as far away from his circle of friends as possible. Not that he had that many friends, except in the criminal fraternity. I heard he got killed."

Zara read pieces aloud from the article, "DCI Richard Armitage was discovered by his playing partner on a Lewes golf course - on a late October afternoon; he had been shot at close range - no eyewitnesses - few leads to follow."

Phil said, "I laughed at the comment saying, a valued friend and colleague we will sorely miss. But, the truth is they were glad to see his back. That's one less rotten apple in the barrel."

"Their investigation centres on his drugs gang connections. Armitage planted narcotics on gang members and blackmailed them for large cash donations to make evidence disappear. One of these gangs probably put a price on his head," continued Zara.

"It was a professional job, whoever carried it out, from what I heard," said Phil.

As the weeks ticked by, the daily grind continued, but just after the New Year, the team received two bits of good news.

Every member of the Kelly gang was under arrest. They wintered in a site near Cheddar Gorge. Nick Frobisher and his 'snatch squad' paid them a very early morning call. Despite spirited resistance from Kelly Senior and his wife, they bundled the gang into the police vans and returned to HQ before breakfast.

"Excellent," Phil Hounsell enthused. "That gets 2011 off to a good start. Now it's up to the courts to get a good result."

Zara checked back through her paperwork.

"With the evidence we gathered, they'll struggle to get out from under this one. 'Employment of Illegal Immigrants - Criminal proceedings are appropriate in cases where the employer has deliberately and knowingly breached the law.' Tick. 'An offence has occurred when an employer employs a person knowing that the employee is an adult subject to immigration control; also where the employee has not obtained leave to enter or stay in the UK. Or the employee's leave to enter or stay in the UK is not valid, or has ceased to affect.' Another tick."

"Remind me; what are we talking about here? Please tell me it's a big number."

Zara smiled. "Don't be stupid, Phil; it's just a slap on the wrist as usual. But, still, together with the imprisonment, abuse, and exploitation of the British nationals that we released near Burnham, they will be put away for a while."

"We haven't uncovered any more sites where they might have been holding people, have we?" asked Phil.

"Nick Frobisher collected paperwork at Cheddar that indicates the Kelly gang sold on their labourers. They would be hiring again in the spring, I imagine. They found a large sum in notes in a safe in Kelly's caravan."

Phil decided the good news warranted a beer or two after work to celebrate the prospect of a minor win. So most of the team joined Phil and Zara in a pub by the Marina. There were several soft drinks in the order he gave over the bar because it wouldn't do to have anyone getting pulled over for drunk driving later.

Angela Chambers collected her gin and tonic and sat by Zara Wheeler.

"These things usually come in threes," she said.

"Sorry," said Zara, "what do you mean?"

"Well, we've received two bits of good news today. First, Anton Dimetrescu sent the custody sergeant a postcard from Ostend. He's back across the Channel and working in the kitchens of a five-star restaurant. Anton's got a flat and everything."

"Is he still illegal?" asked Zara.

"Oh yeah, but he wanted to thank us for the way we helped him. Nice of him, don't you think?"

"I suppose the third good news would be to learn that Sunday Aronu has found what he was searching for."

"Never a whisper since he left us, Ma'am, I'm afraid," said Angela.

The bar soon filled with men who wanted to watch football on the big TV screens. The police officers had their corner to themselves, but gradually numbers dwindled as people drifted off to family, and commutes demanded their time.

"Ready to make tracks back to Bath, Zara?" asked Phil.

Angela nudged Zara gently. "Why not spend the evening here in town? Go for a meal and find a bar without those sports-mad Neanderthals. What do you say?"

Zara looked at her lemonade and lime. Nothing exciting waited for her at home. Napoleon and Josephine would cope for a few hours.

"Go on home, Phil," she said, "Angela and I are hitting the town."

Phil drank up, waved a hand, and left the pub.

"Right, let's find somewhere decent for a bite to eat," said Angela, knocking back her drink. They left the pub just as the game started. Zara didn't think anyone noticed they had left. Angela Chambers knew her way around Portishead. They had only walked for a couple of minutes before she guided Zara into an Italian restaurant. Zara hadn't eaten as well in ages. She wasn't sure how she would manage to drive home now; Angela insisted that the food deserved to be accompanied by a good bottle of wine.

When they came outside into the night air, Zara shivered. Angela led them to a small side street and into a quiet bar. Zara sat at a table in a booth near the fire. She spotted

Angela chatting with two girls at the bar, then returned to the table with two large glasses of wine.

"Looks as if I'm getting a taxi," said Zara.

"Why not stay at my flat?" said Angela, sitting beside her.

"I don't want to cause you any trouble," said Zara. The wine and the log fire in the hearth made her uncomfortably warm. Angela's head leant towards her, and her perfume was exotic.

"It will be no trouble," whispered Angela and brushed a stray hair from Zara's cheek.

"What are you doing," asked Zara.

"What I've wanted to do ever since I set eyes on you, Zara," said Angela. She kissed Zara gently on the cheek, then on her lips. Zara tried to push Angela away. Instead, Angela kissed her more deeply, her tongue parting her lips and forcing its way into her mouth. Zara relaxed and savoured the experience. It was the first time a girl kissed her; it felt different. It was enjoyable, but did she want to experience more than this moment of affection?

"Angela," she said, finally pulling away. "I'm sorry, this is wrong. I'm straight. I've never had feelings for a girl. Sex with Toby has been great, and although we're just friends, I still want to find a man to settle down with one day. I'm a single girl, but not because I'm gay or confused. What the hell? Everyone knows I did it with Idris Williams. If you had been there that night, you'd have no doubts that that's what floats my boat.

Angela looked crestfallen.

"I'm sorry, Ma'am, the drink gave me the confidence to kiss you." she sobbed. "I've always known, but I've not found anyone I truly fancied. I come to this bar to talk to other girls, to be among girls who understand, but I've never done it with anyone yet."

Zara sighed. "I still have the problem of how to get back to Bath."

"Please stay at mine, Ma'am; I promise it will be okay."

"Only on one condition. Please call me Zara, not Ma'am, when we're out socially. We can still be friends, Angela."

Angela cheered up somewhat. The two colleagues drank up and left the bar. Angela's flat was a five-minute walk away. Zara slipped her arm through her Sergeant's, and they strolled amiably along the pavement and into the apartment block. Angela let herself in and asked Zara if she wanted a coffee.

"Yes, please, black, no sugar," she grinned. "I don't want to be hanging in the morning when I walk into the office."

After they drank their coffee and chatted about everything except the kiss in the bar, it was time to sort out the sleeping arrangements. There was an awkward moment when Angela led Zara into her bedroom. Zara stopped by the door.

"Have my bed, Zara," Angela smiled. "I'll take the couch. So you'll be perfectly safe."

"You'll be freezing," said Zara. "We're both adults. If I can borrow nightclothes, we can share the bed."

Ten minutes later, they lay under the duvet, trying to keep to their side of the bed.

"Goodnight, Zara," whispered Angela. "Sweet dreams."

Zara wondered if Phil Hounsell knew that Angela preferred the company of girls. Did he think something might happen if he left her alone in that bar? Maybe that's why he asked if she was ready to get off home. Why did Phil always come into her head? What gave him the right to be protective of her? He was married. Why did she still think of him and 'might-have-been'?

She blinked back the tears that followed. Angela slid closer and put her arm on her shoulder.

"Hey, what's the matter, Zara," she whispered.

"Nothing anyone can change, Angela," she groaned and snuggled into the comfortable bed with the warm body of her colleague wrapped around her. Sleep was a long time coming. She listened to Angela's gentle snoring as the clock ticked around into the small hours before her eyes finally closed.

They showered, drank coffee, and shared a slice of buttered toast in the morning. All done in silence. Zara knew that comments would follow if people saw them arrive at work together. If a team of detectives couldn't spot her wearing the same clothes as yesterday, they had a problem. Zara hoped they might avoid Phil Hounsell for at least a big part of the morning. Maybe she could find time to pop home at lunchtime to change.

"Penny for them, Zara," said Angela.

"We both have secrets, Angela. No one will hear a word about yours, I promise. I hope you find someone soon and if you come out, then fine, that's your choice. I have a secret, too, that I don't want to become public knowledge. So you have to swear you won't breathe a word to a soul."

Angela walked around the table and held Zara close.

"Get it off your chest, girl. It will do you good if it's eating you up; I won't say a word, I swear."

"When I met Phil Hounsell in Durham early last year, I was a virgin. Nothing happened in those weeks we worked together. Toby Drysdale was my first."

"Okay, so what's the big secret?"

"I want to be with Phil Hounsell. I want him so much it hurts."

"Oh! Is that it? Everyone knows you two are hot for one another. We thought you'd been at it like rabbits across the country. We believed that the thrill of the chase for that killer was making you both horny."

"What do you mean hot for one another? Phil's married with children, and Erica is a friend. I live in her Mum's house. I babysit Shaun and Tracey. He doesn't fancy me; he mustn't."

"Well, it's plain he does; it's just the opportunity that's missing. If the right opportunity presents itself, then he'll go for it. Come on; we've got to get to work."

They left the flat, made their way towards HQ, and then strode into the building. Sod what anyone thought. They knew full well what was what; that was what mattered.

"Morning, ladies," called Phil Hounsell, "will Portishead ever recover from the hammering you gave it last night?"

"You should have stayed," said Zara, more brazenly than she ever thought possible, "you might have learned something; we both did."

Phil Hounsell decided that discretion was the better part of valour. He didn't want to get involved. Two young, unattached female officers out for a night on the town, even the quiet seaside town of Portishead had become alien territory to him these days.

Erica had collared him as soon as he walked through the door last night. The euphoria surrounding news of the capture of the Kelly gang had fooled him. His idea of a quick trip to the pub to celebrate backfired. It had meant getting home too late to go to a meeting at the junior school where Shaun started later in the year.

Phil groaned as he recalled Erica letting him know the score.

"I can tell where you've been; I can smell it on your breath. So here I am, rushing around after finishing work at the building society, picking the kids up from playschool, bringing them home, and getting their tea. Then I get everyone showered and dressed, ready to leave. We sat there in the front room, like lemons, waiting for Daddy to arrive home, and where did you go? Down the pub! Where on your list of priorities does this family come these days, Phil?"

His contrite apology had not been too welcome. He trotted upstairs to Tracey's room and quietly opened her door. She was fast asleep. When he checked, Shaun was also asleep across the landing. Phil had made his way downstairs, feeling the temperature drop every step.

Erica sat engrossed in one of her TV soaps.

Phil had wandered into the kitchen to find his dinner in the microwave. He heated it and sorted out a lap tray and cutlery. When Phil sat down, she muted her programme. He thought that, with luck, the ice maiden was melting. A glance at the screen showed a commercial break. He wasn't out of the woods yet.

"Did everyone on the team go to the pub or just the two of you?" she asked.

"As many as could make it," he replied, ignoring the implication, and tucking into his steak pie. "We've had a good result today. We rounded up the Kelly gang at Cheddar Gorge yesterday morning."

"Couldn't you have called?" she asked.

Phil had been going to answer when the programme

restarted, and the mute button was depressed. He realised the conversation had ended and carried on eating his dinner.

Sometimes being a copper meant long hours; Erica understood that. She appreciated the situation only too well after their years together. It wasn't easy with a young family. Phil wanted to spend time with Erica and the kids, but work took up most of the time when their children of five and three were awake. So he always arrived home well after they went to bed. They tried to make it up on the weekends. They did as many family things as possible to compensate. But the strains and stresses of the week meant that he was exhausted as often as not.

Phil Hounsell felt each of his forty-five years as he looked across the office at Zara Wheeler and Angela Chambers. He couldn't keep up with these young ones anymore. What happened to that little 'Mouse' he met less than twelve months ago? These days she was a party girl and no mistake. He watched as she worked at her desk. Zara looked up, sensing that someone was watching her. He smiled at her self-consciously. She blushed and smiled back. Then she moved her chair so her head was behind her computer monitor.

Phil puffed out his cheeks; what was the matter with him? He had work that needed to get done. He needed to tidy up a few things from his backlog and get off early today. Fences needed mending at home.

The days got longer, and the clocks, at last, sprang forward. Police work can be humdrum and predictable in a county that is, for the most part, rural. There were major incidents from time to time in Bristol, Bath, Yeovil, and Taunton. But Phil Hounsell and his team kept busy without the excitement that murder or an armed robbery brought.

Not that they welcomed that level of crime when it landed on their doorstep. Even so, countless cases of road rage, domestic violence, petty theft, and drug offences were frustrating and predictable. Burglaries, criminal damage, and computer fraud filled Phil's officers' time well enough but without the buzz of a serious crime.

As for the annoying little idiots who tied up hours of police resources with anti-social behaviour, Phil thought they should get conscripted into the army at sixteen. "Not just for eighteen months like in the old days of National Service," he told his closest friends, who he trusted not to run to his superiors to complain about him being 'so beastly'. "No, they should stay in for twenty-two years. Then, they'd come out with a trade and respect for authority that'd turn them into model citizens."

In early March, his ACC had called him into her office. He imagined another bollocking for not singing from the same hymn sheet as the rest of her clones. But instead, it was another sparkling initiative from the architects of the modern police service.

The force launched an online crime tracker to give the public access to information extracted from its systems. The website aimed to help cut the time people spend waiting for police officers to call them back to deal with their enquiries, as they would receive an automatic update by email or text. In addition, victims of crime could now send messages back to the investigation team and catch up with progress.

"There's a gap in the market for the bookies here, Ma'am. So the victims could view the odds against ever seeing their stolen property again?"

"That's a very cynical view, Superintendent. No one wants to be the victim of a crime. But, if you are, then you want it to impact your life as little as possible. This site gives people more choice on how they are updated and with a better service."

"Sorry, Ma'am, but the available resources would be better spent on officers on the beat to deter the burglars in the first place. Then, when we catch them at it, if we lock the offenders away for longer, we reduce their capacity for nicking stuff for a considerable time.

"This is a more positive approach, DS Hounsell," the ACC twittered on. "It is a more enlightened, streamlined, and efficient method of combining policing with modern technology."

"I'm sure it will go down well in certain community areas, Ma'am," said Phil.

As he left the ACC's office, he knew she believed these initiatives were popular with the public. Still, she only had connections with a small section of the public: the upper classes and upper-middle-class Daily Mail readers who held a somewhat extreme view of today's criminal. Phil was still close enough to the real world to recognise the criminals in the region who laughed their heads off at such initiatives. It didn't affect their activities one iota.

Finally, in June, the Kelly gang were due to appear at Bristol Crown Court. Phil Hounsell and Zara Wheeler made arrangements to attend as often as possible. They wanted to see them face the enormity of their crimes and bring justice to the dozens of men they treated worse than dogs.

DS Nick Frobisher was to be there every day. He had worked tirelessly on the case, checking and double-checking through the evidence and ensuring they had closed every loophole tight; nobody wanted the Kelly gang to escape punishment because of a technicality. Nick didn't want a slippery defence counsel ruining the hours of work he and his colleagues invested.

The first couple of days went well. Nick's efforts looked to be paying dividends. He hoped that in the face of the evidence piled up against them, the accused - Seamus Kelly Senior, his wife Siobhan, and their sons Patrick and George - would plead guilty. Unfortunately, their defence was obstinate to the last: they merely hired these men for casual labour. They couldn't have known details of their standards of personal health or housekeeping.

Seamus and the boys claimed they only saw these men at work and were satisfied with their efforts. Siobhan Kelly said that she kept passports and papers for the workers as they claimed they didn't have total security in their homes; she owned a safe, so it was natural to offer to lock their valuables away for safekeeping.

When questioned about the massive amounts of cash, the four became evasive. Seamus Kelly said, "We're travellers; we don't trust banks. But, over the years, it must have mounted up."

Nick Frobisher rang into the office each morning and kept the team at Portishead up to date with proceedings.

"It should be over by tomorrow," he told Phil. "If you're coming over to see the fun, you'd better hurry."

Phil called Zara into his office, "We're off the Crown Court in the morning. I'll pick you up first thing; pack a bag; we'll stay over and help Nick and the others celebrate. I can't wait to see the faces of the Kelly family in the dock when they get their sentences."

"Nick thinks it will be over tomorrow, then? That was quick."

"Tomorrow or Friday," said Phil, rubbing his hands.

Angela Chambers caught Zara as she left for home later that afternoon.

"Off to watch the final stages of the Kelly case then?" she said and gave Zara a nudge.

"Yes," replied Zara, "it will be a real boost for us to see them go to prison; we get so few headline wins these days."

"Remember what I said, Zara; if the opportunity arises, go for it."

Zara hadn't given that a thought. Phil had said 'pack a bag' just in case they stayed over, but you would hardly call the trip from Bristol back to their homes in Bath a trek. Her head was in a spin as she drove home. After a restless night, Zara got up, showered, and dressed. She packed a bag with a change of clothes and her night dress and toiletries. The doorbell rang.

"Ready, Zara?" asked Phil, casually wandering into his mother-in-law's house, "Where's your bag? I'll carry it out to the car."

They drove into Bristol and parked in a multi-storey car park. As they walked to the courts, Phil said, "We'll leave our bags in the boot. We can book a B&B for tonight if necessary. I don't think I can keep up with you younger ones these days, and no way am I driving after a few beers celebrating with Nick Frobisher."

The defence counsel tried everything possible to muddy the waters and convince the jury of the Kelly family's innocence. They were fighting a losing battle; the prosecution evidence proved overwhelming. The jury was sent out and returned in just over an hour. They recorded guilty verdicts on each indictment.

In his infinite wisdom, the judge delayed sentencing until the following day. Then, he asked for any mitigating circumstances to be brought before him so he might come to his decision.

"Well, that's a pity," said Phil. "I hoped to see that Kelly family banged up today."

"Guilty on every count, though, Sir," said DS Frobisher. "We couldn't have hoped for better. The jury didn't waste time; they saw our compelling evidence, despite the defence counsel's shenanigans."

"The gang is going for a meal and a drink in that great Italian place in Corn Street," said Nick Frobisher. "Why not stay over and celebrate?"

Nick dragged Zara along with the rest of his team while Phil returned to the car. He retrieved their bags from the boot and booked them into two single rooms at a guest house on St. Nicholas Street. He joined them in Corn Street after his colleagues had already demolished one round of drinks. Four hours later, after a terrific meal and more wine than was good for them, plus a few liqueurs, they tottered out onto the cobbled pavements.

Nick and the other young police officers headed unsteadily towards their digs. Zara and Phil reached their B&B in minutes. Phil collected the two keys, and they stumbled into the lift. Zara waved her key in front of Phil's face.

"Wasting police funds, Superintendent?" she slurred.

Phil looked at Zara. If only she'd stop swaying in front of him; was it her swaying, or was he drunk? Finally, the lift doors opened, announcing their arrival on 'Level Two'.

"Level Two." Zara mimicked the recorded voice and giggled. She grabbed Phil's arm and moved towards her door. As Zara tried to slide the key card in, Phil's face brushed her cheek. She turned toward him, and they kissed. They got the door unlocked and fell into the room.

Zara led him to the bed and gently pushed him backwards. He brought a hand up and cupped her tiny breast through her top and bra. He slid his hands up and slipped off her blouse, letting it fall to the floor. She kissed him again, her tongue invading his mouth, and Phil knew he was lost. He slid his hands over her back and unhooked her bra, sliding the straps down her arms and casting the bra aside. She pulled him close and removed his shirt so Phil could feel her tiny bare breasts against his chest. He began caressing her, planting soft kisses on her neck, and moved to her left nipple. A gasp escaped her lips.

Phil's other hand stroked her through her panties; her wetness told him she was as lost as he was. He continued to kiss her as she squirmed beneath him. He knew it was wrong but hadn't he always known that this would happen? Hadn't he wanted this? Zara pushed him off, and, at first, he feared she was coming to her senses. Instead, she straddled and smiled at him as her hands unbuttoned his trousers. Zara removed everything, including his shoes and socks. She kissed her way along his stomach.

Her tongue licked the tip of his erection, and then her lips wrapped around him, and he moaned as she took him in fully. He reached down, grabbed her by her arms, and pulled her up, kissing her. He flipped her onto her back and removed the rest of her clothes. Zara groaned as Phil slid inside her. She wrapped her legs around his body, and her hips met him thrust for thrust. For them, time stopped as both became lost in their frantic lovemaking.

Later, as they lay together and their breathing returned to normal, Zara cuddled up to her boss. Finally, after over a year of aching for him, she had got what she dreamed of almost every night. Eventually, Zara fell asleep in Phil's strong arms.

Phil lay wide awake, staring at the ceiling.

Finally, he said, "That was wonderful, but it should never have happened. It can never happen again, Zara."

"It was fantastic, even though we were both drunk," she giggled and slid on top of him, kissing his nose.

"I'm married," he said, pushing himself up on his elbows. "I love my wife and children. We've always had this sexual tension between us, knowing the other one of us wanted something to happen. Getting drunk just encouraged us to let those feelings get the better of us. It happened; it was great, but madness."

Zara stayed where she was and tormented him, moving against him.; well aware his body was going where his mind told him not to go. She enjoyed this new power she held over a man. Zara had enjoyed how Phil made her feel and wanted that pleasure again. Right this minute, if possible. She wasn't Mouse any longer.

Phil eased her body away from him and climbed off the bed. He dressed and found the door key to his room.

"I'll see you in the morning, Zara," he said and left her alone and empty. Not for the first time, she cried herself to sleep.

Chapter Six

Phil Hounsell woke early. He hadn't slept well, and he felt terrible. Phil stood in the shower, praying that the hot water washed away the memories of last night. He had let Erica down, let himself down.

As he towelled himself dry, he thought of Zara Wheeler. She didn't deserve that, either. They both knew that last night was inevitable ever since they met. It had been great for him, and he knew how much she had enjoyed it. People in the adjoining rooms must have known, too.

Why did he have to be such a heel and burst her bubble? It happened. What difference would it have made if they had spent the night together? It was the old chestnut about being pregnant: you can't be a 'little pregnant'. You are, or you're not. He became an adulterer when he entered that bedroom, whether he left after an hour or eight hours.

It's too late to think of that now, he thought. I must face Zara in a minute. At least I'll have to try to repair the damage and salvage a working relationship. They were due in court for the sentencing later. He dressed and made his way downstairs for breakfast. He just hoped that he could manage to eat something. As he walked past Zara's door, he resisted the temptation to knock.

When he entered the small restaurant, only a handful of guests sat at the tables. Zara was nowhere in sight yet. Nobody looked up when he walked to a table. Instead, everyone's eyes turned towards the TV set on the wall tuned to the local BBC news. A reporter stood in a familiar spot. What on earth!

"DS Angela Chambers responded to an attack by a mugger on customers outside the Nat West Bank in the High Street when the mugger stabbed her. The emergency services received calls from two members of the public shortly after the young policewoman came on duty at 7.00 am. Eyewitnesses informed the police that a man had just withdrawn cash from the ATM. He had been stabbed in the back by a young man wearing a hoodie. DS Chambers attended in a marked police car with another officer when attacked. Police are still trying to find out the exact sequence of events. A witness reported seeing a delivery driver stabbed, too, as he tried to prevent the man from escaping with the stolen money."

Phil sat in his chair, stunned. The reporter turned to a middle-aged woman and asked her to describe what she'd seen.

"The police arrived," said the lady, "and the female officer came at him from behind the delivery van and shouted. 'Put down the knife. Put down the knife.' The man turned around and stabbed her several times in the neck. She fell to the ground. The policeman fired a baton round and then used a Taser to stop the man and arrest him. It was a war zone; three bodies and a young man twitching on the floor in handcuffs."

"Thank you," said the reporter, turning to a familiar face in a Hi-Viz jacket. It was the Chief Constable.

"Chief Constable, this must be a terrible time. Do you have any update on the officer's condition you can pass on to us? Also, how serious were the injuries to the other two men?"

"Such events highlight the dangers police officers face daily on the front line protecting the public," the Chief Constable replied. "I cannot give you any news on the police officer, but I can confirm that our officer used a baton round and Taser electric stun gun to restrain the knifeman. In addition, we have arrested a man on suspicion of attempted murder. One of the injured men, a 65-year-old local man, is in a serious but stable condition. The second man, a 28-year-old driver from Bristol, is receiving treatment for minor injuries."

The reporter thanked the Chief Constable, wrapped up the report, and handed back to the studio. Phil wanted to get the latest news; he couldn't hang around for the next update in thirty minutes. He should tell Zara what had happened.

Phil went up to her room. He got no reply. He checked at the reception; her room key was there. Zara had already left for the courts.

Zara Wheeler woke up at seven o'clock with a start in a strange bed with a headache and no nightdress. Last night came flooding back to her. She'd enjoyed a magical hour of sex with Phil, and then her world had come crashing around her. She wanted to use the bathroom and have a shower, but she didn't want him to know she was awake. She couldn't face seeing him; not yet.

Zara lay there thinking back to last night until she heard him moving around the room. She crept into the bathroom.

Zara couldn't wait any longer. A few minutes later, she listened to the lift. He had gone for breakfast. That was her cue to shower, get dressed, and pack her bag. Breakfast could wait; she wanted to get to Corn Street to sit with Nick Frobisher and the team. A good result there might help to soften the blow.

Zara walked into the Crown Court building. It was bustling with people, but she sensed an odd feeling about the place. Something terrible had happened, but what?

DS Nick Frobisher sat on a bench outside the courtroom with his head in his hands.

"What's up, Nick? Do you have a hangover?" she asked.

"Haven't you heard," asked Nick, surprised to see her on her own. "Where's the boss?"

"He's still at the guest house, tucking into a full English, I expect," replied Zara.

Nick stood up and hugged Zara to him.

"Oh, Zara, it's terrible. Angela got stabbed this morning."

Zara pushed her colleague away; she couldn't understand what he was telling her.

"What do you mean, stabbed?" she cried.

"A bloke mugged a guy at an ATM in town, knifed him when he refused to hand over the cash; a bloke delivering to Gregg's had a go at him and got injured too. When Angela and Frank Darby turned up, she approached the guy with the knife, and he ran at her and stabbed her in the neck several times. Frank tasered him and put him on the floor."

"How's Angela?" Zara asked, praying that her friend would make it.

"I've just seen the Chief Constable on TV. No news yet; it'll be back on in twenty-five minutes. I've phoned HQ. They won't or can't comment. Everybody is in pieces."

The clock ticked on. There would be no chance of finding a TV and watching the following news summary before the court was in session. Nick and Zara entered the room and sat together. The young constables out with them last evening were already there, their faces grey, partly from the night before and partly from the shock of the morning's news.

Phil Hounsell arrived just as the judge entered. Phil slipped into the seats reserved for his team and sat at the end of the row. He tried to catch Zara's eye, further along, next to Nick Frobisher, but she avoided his gaze. He thought he deserved it. One of the young coppers whispered to him that she knew the latest; Nick had told her when she arrived. Phil wanted to get this sentencing lark over and get outside for the latest news.

The judge took his own sweet time going through the information in front of him. He seemed relaxed and cheerful. Phil imagined the old beggar's wife must have relented last night for the first time in months. Then he cursed himself for thinking of sex again. It only reminded him of his problems. His daydreaming was interrupted by a surprised gasp from the bench beside him. He heard a whoop of delight from the dock.

The stupid old sod went the way of so many of his colleagues.

'We mustn't be too harsh on them; they have such difficult lives to contend with.'

The judge imposed fines Seamus Kelly could reasonably afford, and Seamus, Patrick, and George Kelly received the minimum custodial sentences possible. Considering the time they had been on remand, they would serve little more than three months. In addition, Siobhan Kelly received a fine and a community service order.

The Kelly family members in the public gallery clapped and cheered when they weren't pissing themselves with laughter. Kelly Senior and his sons went to the cells, but the decision robbed them of any chance of wiping that supercilious smile off their faces.

Nick Frobisher was fuming. "Where's the justice in that?" he asked. "We have twenty-eight days to appeal; surely we can do better than that?"

The stony faces of the prosecution and the CPS suggested otherwise. Nobody could believe so many hours of work got devalued so off-handedly — what a system, what a shambles.

Phil Hounsell and his team collected outside the courtroom and discussed what to do next.

"Let's get back to HQ and find out what's happening there," he said. "No point hanging around here. We'll debrief this fiasco when our heads are clearer."

As they spilt out of the Crown Courts onto the pavement, reporters and camera crews were everywhere, shoving microphones in their faces.

"Do you have any comment on the sentencing?"

"What message does this send to the public?"

Phil stuck to 'No Comment' for every question and shepherded his team away from the commotion as quick as possible. Then, the media's attention suddenly switched to the doors of the Crown Court.

Phil paused, expecting to see members of the Kelly clan hoping to celebrate their patriarch's lucky escape with a mindless rant on live TV. Why was the Divisional Commander here?

The police colleagues moved closer to listen to his interview.

"The incident lasted around ten minutes between the

emergency calls and DS Chambers's stabbing. DS Chambers was taken by ambulance to a hospital, but I can confirm that she died of her injuries shortly after arrival. The other two victims of the attack are receiving treatment for their injuries. They are not life-threatening. The death of an officer is always a tragic event, and I offer my deepest sympathy to the officer's family, friends, and colleagues."

Phil, Zara, Nick, and the others stood in shocked silence; a reporter continued speaking to the camera.

"Colleagues have been left traumatised by the killing of DS Chambers, who was wearing a stab-proof vest. She loved her job and was a dedicated member of the police force. Unfortunately, dedication to duty cost Angela Chambers her life."

Another channel was reporting a few yards away. They heard a young female's voice.

"Angela Chambers lived alone in the town of Portishead. Her parents and her two brothers live in Exeter. She joined the force in 2004; senior officers paid tribute from Portishead HQ. The Assistant Chief Constable told us, 'Angela was a great girl, and she was a valuable team member, just doing the job she loved, and as someone who loved life.'

Zara felt hot tears on her cheeks. Nick Frobisher put an arm around her shoulders to comfort her.

Nick had tears in his eyes, too. Zara recalled the night in Portishead when Angela kissed her, coming out to her as a lesbian. She and Angela had moved past that and become good friends. She knew that only a few weeks ago, Angela had found someone.

Angela had rushed into her office on a Monday morning to tell her the news. They met on Saturday night at a club in Weston-Super-Mare, and 'it happened at last.'

She was so excited and happy. Why did life have to be so bloody unfair?

Zara could still hear the woman's voice chirping away in the background.

"Her family is traumatised and understandably upset and angry. Angela Chambers came to work, and her parents expected her to phone home this evening, and she now won't do that. Meanwhile, in other news, at the Crown Court today, Judge Erskine-Mathers is accused of extreme leniency in sentencing a travelling family. They were found guilty yesterday of the false imprisonment of a group of homeless men who they kept in terrible conditions and forced to work on jobs in the area."

Phil Hounsell wasn't listening; he needed to be back at HQ. Zara was still being comforted by Nick Frobisher. Phil nodded to Nick, suggesting he should look after her and bring her back to Portishead. He hurried back to the guest house, collected his things from reception, and walked to the car park for his car. The drive to the coast was lonely. The same as the rest of the team, he felt wretched.

"Come on then, lads," said Nick. "We'd better make tracks back to work. Zara, Phil has gone on ahead. You can ride with me."

Zara continued to sob quietly and just nodded her head.

The mood at the station was utter despair — another life lost from the thin blue line. When Zara returned to her office, she noticed Phil's door closed. He wasn't anywhere in sight. When she inquired, she learned the senior officers were with the ACC.

Zara couldn't settle at her work. She wanted to get into town to the High Street to see where her friend and colleague died. Instead, she found Toby Drysdale in the corridor, looking lost.

"Toby, are you free for a while?"

"Supposed to be going out in ten minutes on patrol. Why?"

"I want to go there."

Toby squeezed Zara's hand.

"It's awful, isn't it, Zara," he said quietly. "Are you sure you want to see where it happened?"

"Yes," she replied.

"Meet you in the car park in ten, then," said Toby, returning to the squad room.

The two friends drove into town in silence. Toby parked the car, and they walked past the bakery and towards the bank. Forensic officers still examined the crime scene. They were numbering items lying on the ground. A tarp shielded what Zara imagined was the spot where Angela's neck wounds bled so profusely that they proved fatal.

Just beyond the police cordon on the other side from where she stood, Zara clung to Toby. She saw that bouquets had accumulated at the base of a street lamp.

"I don't think I've ever felt so wretched," she said. "Why is life so cruel?"

Toby knew there wasn't much to offer in consolation. They would need to pull together to get through this. Time will never erase the memory of their colleague. They could only keep working to keep the public safe and try to do their jobs to the best of their ability when they apprehended the criminals, then pray the authorities gave the police the resources and support they needed to bring them to justice.

Toby had been on the job long enough to know the first two parts lay within their compass. Unfortunately, the last part was a different matter altogether.

He had learned what happened with the case over which Nick Frobisher sweated so much blood. No matter how hard they worked, no matter how many officers made the ultimate sacrifice, as Angela did, if the government kept cutting funding and the legal system kept favouring the criminal over the victim, they were fighting a losing battle.

Monday, June 20th, 2011

The funeral of DS Angela Chambers took place at noon.

The crowds in the city centre applauded as soon as the hearse bearing her body came into view. Hundreds of police officers travelled across the West Country to pay their respects to their fallen comrade.

The funeral cortege edged through Exeter. Members of the public in the packed cathedral awaited them. The service was transmitted to hundreds of mourners outside in the warm summer sunshine.

The Assistant Chief Constable, DS Phil Hounsell, DCI Zara Wheeler and other fellow officers from Portishead HQ followed the procession.

Horses from the force's mounted unit drew a funeral carriage. DS Chambers's coffin was shrouded in black cloth; her police helmet lay at its foot.

At noon, chimes from the cathedral marked the start of a two-minute silence.

Angela Chambers's family entered the cathedral. Her mother, Kathy, her father, Chris, and brothers, Steve and Robbie, sat together with other family members.

The cathedral choir sang 'Abide with Me' as the coffin entered, carried by six senior officers.

Chief Constables and senior officers from forces across England and Wales were among the congregation inside the cathedral. Whether family members, the public, or police officers, mourners wiped away silent tears. Hymns were sung, poems were read, and people remembered Angela's thirty years of life.

Her family said she wanted to make a difference and did a job she loved.

Fellow officers described her as always smiling, with a great outgoing personality.

Her Chief Constable spoke of her dedication to serving the public.

'We will miss her. We must never forget our colleague's great sacrifice. DS Chambers was born at the Royal Devon & Exeter Hospital in 1981, attended Exeter School and went to Plymouth University before joining the force in 2004.'

The family followed the coffin to the crematorium for a private service.

In Bristol, Ashley Crookes, twenty-three, of no fixed abode, was remanded in custody and accused of DS Chambers's murder. He faced a further charge for the attempted murder of two other men involved in the incident in Portishead.

Two months later, in the early hours of the morning on Tuesday, 9 August, vandalism and looting erupted in Bristol in response to similar events occurring elsewhere in the country. Again, the police and fire services turned out in force.

DS Phil Hounsell was at home in Bath with his wife, Erica. Their children, Shaun and Tracey, were asleep in their beds. A couple of miles away, in Erica's mother's house, DI Zara Wheeler sat at home alone.

The days preceding the funeral of their colleague had been tense and emotional for everyone on the staff at Portishead HQ. The day of the funeral was traumatic; everyone spent the days that followed grieving and healing.

For Phil and Zara, an awkwardness existed in their working relationship that had never previously been there. It was strained, certainly. On the other hand, it was cool and artificially professional. Whichever way you found to describe it, it couldn't last.

Zara spent most evenings at home with a bottle of wine and her cats. Toby Drysdale persuaded her to go out with him now and again, but the friends with benefits were now strictly just friends.

Nick Frobisher dropped in once or twice in the first week or two to talk. He lived in Weston and was engaged to a primary-school teacher; they planned their wedding for next Easter.

Zara had talked with Angela's mother after the short service at the crematorium. Only family and half a dozen close colleagues attended. Kathy Chambers slipped her the phone number of Freya Garroway, Angela's new girlfriend.

"Freya was in the cathedral, Inspector, but she couldn't face coming here. Angela told me what a good friend you were to her. Perhaps you would keep in touch with Freya? I think she'll need a shoulder to cry on, too; we all will."

Zara waited a month before she called Freya. After she explained who she was and why she had called, they agreed to meet. Zara suggested the same quiet bar she and Angela visited in Portishead. Freya knew it; they met one evening after work and shared a few drinks and a few memories.

Zara saw what attracted Angela to Freya. She was petite but athletic and dressed more like a young boy than a girl.

Zara noticed that Freya got several admiring looks from the adjoining tables. Freya was still grieving for her lover.

"It was her first time. I had been 'out' for a few years. So we hit it off straight away. We planned to move in together; it felt right, you know?" Freya leant forward with her arms crossed, holding her sides as if her stomach hurt. "I fall asleep at night, just holding the pillow she slept on, crying into it. I haven't washed it yet; I can still remember her perfume if I try hard."

"I miss her too, Freya," said Zara, "she was a good friend. If you ever want to talk, ring me."

"Cheers," said Freya. "I'll do that; you're OK, Zara." Freya leant across the table awkwardly and held Zara for a second, kissing her on the cheek.

When they went their separate ways later that evening, they promised to keep in touch. Zara hadn't heard from Freya, but she hadn't called her either.

When Phil Hounsell arrived home after the murder, Erica was waiting to console him. She knew he would be hurting after losing one of his officers; they permanently closed ranks and pulled together when such a tragedy hit the force. She had kept up to date with the breaking story, like many thousands of others in the region.

"Hello, darling; you must have had a terrible day. I'm so sorry," she said, throwing her arms around her husband and holding him tight.

He had laid his head on her shoulder, "So am I, darling; so am I."

In the Hounsell household, the days leading up to the funeral were predictably solemn. Erica didn't want the kids to be under Phil's feet when he came home at night, so she packed them off to bed early.

On Saturday morning, she left him to brood while she

went shopping and then spent the afternoon lazing in the garden, watching the kids play. Phil finally wandered out to sit in the sun with them for an hour at four o'clock.

"Did you realise that Angela Chambers was gay?" asked Erica.

She had discovered this from Zara earlier in the week when she rang her to see if she could babysit the kids on Saturday night. Zara said she was unavailable. Erica convinced herself that Zara was free but didn't want to come over. Zara had changed the subject and rambled on about being worried about Angela's new girlfriend. She wondered how she was coping.

"I wouldn't be much of a detective if I couldn't spot the clues," Phil had replied abruptly. "She and Zara were friendly."

Erica had looked at her husband. He must think I dropped in with the last shower, she thought. Zara had nothing in common with this Angela Chambers on that score. He knew that, so why would he suggest the two of them may have been more than friends?

She wasn't opposed to some detective work herself. But, when Phil came home on the day of the murder, her intuition told her something felt wrong. Why did he arrange an overnight stay in Bristol to be present at the Crown Court for that case? That had sounded strange at the time. He could have been home for forty minutes, if not sooner.

Erica had seen Phil in the bedroom that night when he stripped off his shirt. It was only a tiny scratch, on his back, just below his shoulder blade, but he tried to keep turned away from her so she didn't see it.

Erica put two and two together. Phil was trying to steer her away from Zara as a threat. Zara kept her distance from them, yet she had been a close family friend since she moved south.

The funeral had come and gone; the atmosphere remained. Zara kept herself to herself. Phil was throwing himself into his work and getting home late. The kids didn't appear to notice, and Erica's weekends had been bearable. The kids enjoyed the days out Phil insisted they went on.

Erica visited her mother every day, whether Mary Trueman knew she was there or not. It kept her away from the simmering tension at home. As August began, just as the weather often behaved during that month, the pressure rose; there was a gathering storm. Sooner or later, that storm had to break.

The violence in Bristol started in the early hours of the morning of the ninth of August. Masked gangs of youths threw bricks in the streets and set cars and bins alight. The aftermath of the trouble was visible in the morning as fire crews still worked to make the area safe. Smashed glass, fragments of bricks, and charred rubbish littered the streets.

Police had to counter the rioters rampaging through the city as one hundred and fifty young rioters caused disruption. However, when Phil Hounsell and Zara Wheeler arrived at work later that morning, the ACC brought them up to speed at once.

"This began in London at the weekend. I don't know the rights or wrongs of that incident, but it was a flashpoint that sparked trouble across the country. I can understand peoples' frustrations with what's happening in the country. Peaceful protest is one thing, but this is different. We warned the public to stay out of the city centre last night as our fellow officers tried to bring the situation under control. There was damage to shops and vehicles. In Cabot Circus and out in the suburbs, shops were looted. We prayed that this disorder did not come to Bristol. Plenty of units are on duty, ready to respond if required. The primary concern is keeping people safe and minimising disruption to residents, motorists, and local businesses. Our duty to the wider community is to do everything to calm things down, restore order, and prevent criminality. Our resources here are on standby to help wherever we are needed. I'm sure you will understand the need to follow the popular mantra - Keep Calm and Carry On."

After the update and the pep talk, Phil Hounsell and his team returned to their offices. Other cases needed investigating. The ram-raiders had struck again. Two more jewellers were replacing plate-glass windows and stock trays worth tens of thousands. The gang travelled via the motorway network from London or the Midlands and picked off targets like shooting fish in a barrel.

"If we can spare someone," said Phil with a laugh. "We could study CCTV images to see if the same vehicles travelled on the M4 or M5 on either side of the raids."

"They might just as easily be from South Wales," said Zara Wheeler, "or even Manchester."

"Let's keep positive, shall we, team?" said Phil. He was conscious that Zara's demeanour had quietened since Angela's murder. However, he used that event as his datum point rather than accepting that his reaction to the night they spent together was the real reason behind her negative nature. Things were still unresolved between them.

Sitting at his desk late in the afternoon, he wondered whether to drop in on Zara on his way home tonight to clear the air. His phone rang. It was not good news. The CPS had decided it was not in the public interest to appeal Judge Erskine-Mathers's verdict in the Kelly family slavery case.

"Terrific," thought Phil after putting the phone back. "The latest score in the football: the Villains one, the Blues nil. It's the same as being on the terraces at St. Andrews; nothing changes."

He looked at the calendar. "It's not worth the effort now, as they'll be out in a month."

With a heavy heart, he picked up a stack of files and worked his way through them. It would be a late one tonight, that was for sure. Relations at home remained frosty; he was happier working here even if few positives were available.

In Bath, Erica Hounsell was on a mission. She dropped the kids off at a friend's house for tea and headed towards her mother's house. She hoped to arrive before Zara got home. Erica and Phil both had keys, so they could come and go as they pleased.

Zara rented the place alone after her mum went into the home; paying visits without warning had never been required. But Erica wanted to get to the bottom of that scratch. She needed to know what happened the night before Angela Chambers's murder.

She had her suspicions. When Zara entered the room to find her sitting there waiting, she was confident that her face would give her the proof she needed. The drive was empty when she stopped opposite the house.

Erica turned the car around in the driveway and parked a hundred yards back up the road. Minutes later, she sat indoors, in familiar surroundings, with a cup of coffee in her hands. Two cats were scrutinising her. She waited.

Thirty minutes later, she heard the sound of a car on the drive.

The door opened, and Zara Wheeler walked into the lounge.

"Hello, Zara," said Erica.

Zara's face betrayed her, just as Erica had imagined. She blushed profusely; she could not look Erica directly in the eye, and the tears were only seconds away.

"I'm sorry, Erica," was the best she could manage.

"How long has it been going on?"

"It hasn't. I mean, it was one drunken night. That's no excuse, but there was never anything before or since. There never will be. Phil thinks it was a stupid mistake."

"What about you, Zara? What do you think? Was it a mistake?

Zara slumped in a chair; she didn't know what to say. No way had it been a mistake! It was what she'd dreamed of almost since they met. What did she think? She thought Phil had decided he needed to behave as if they hardly knew one another and stay professional rather than confront the feelings he'd shown her that night. Neither of them faked it, that was for sure.

"We were drunk, Erica; we made a mistake."

Erica finished her coffee; she walked through to the kitchen. Zara followed her.

"What are you going to do now, Erica?" she asked.

The front door opened. Zara turned back into the lounge to see Phil Hounsell in the doorway, holding a large bottle of wine.

"We need to talk," he said.

Erica opened the kitchen door further so Phil saw she was there. His face was a picture.

"I'll bring us three glasses, shall I?" she asked.

Chapter Seven

Wednesday, May 2nd, 2012

Zara Wheeler had enjoyed another great weekend. On the twenty-first of April, she accompanied Toby Drysdale on another platonic day out. It marked the twenty-fifth anniversary of the old Roman city gaining World Heritage Site status.

The weekend just gone had been a feast of rugby. Toby and Zara watched an Under-20s match on Friday night. Two games contested by Medics from various parts of the country on Saturday and Sunday was the mini-rugby festival. It was not the best rugby for Toby to enjoy, but terrific fun and the clubhouse bar was open, so it made for a good weekend.

Monday and Tuesday hadn't been great. Zara suffered the effects of the alcoholic weekend but felt 'chipper' again by Wednesday morning. Zara was certainly getting around the force's patch of late. She was in Yeovil. Zara and several colleagues ensured that everything on this leg of the Diamond Jubilee Tour went as smooth as silk.

Hundreds of people turned out to cheer the Queen and the Duke of Edinburgh as they arrived in Yeovil. The last time they visited Somerset was ten years before to mark the Golden Jubilee. The royal couple had toured stalls at the Jubilee Country Fayre earlier, and while Zara watched, the Queen presented official name tags to two police horses. Harry Patch and Jubilee were on their best behaviour.

Zara watched ten minutes later as the royal couple, safe inside in their car, drove serenely away towards Crewkerne. They would soon reach the Town Hall, where they became someone else's problem. Zara was heading back to Portishead. Then she wanted to get home and put her feet up. There was far too much standing around on these Royal tour duties for her liking.

As she joined her colleagues to climb aboard the transport, taking them back to Portishead, Zara reflected on the past nine months. That large bottle of wine that Phil brought hadn't been big enough. They sat in Mary Trueman's lounge, and the whole sad story spilt out.

Erica soon accepted that Zara had told the truth regarding the one-night stand. Both women were in no doubt that Phil was desperate to save his marriage. However, Phil and Zara could see Erica would make him work bloody hard for it. After her second big glass of wine, Zara could tell she needed to fetch fresh supplies from the fridge.

It had been a long night, the aftermath of which proved oddly calm. Erica and Phil started the reconstruction of their marriage. So far, everything appeared to be going well.

Zara and Phil saw each other at work from time to time.

However, duties kept them apart, as often as not, by his design instead of by accident. Their relationship was fragile when they got thrown together, but it had remained intact so far.

Zara had imagined she would need to find a new home. But Erica rang her a week or two after that emotional night to say she could stay as long as she wished. She could continue to rent her mum's place, but they agreed to sell it to her if she wanted to make an offer.

Mary Trueman would never return there to live, and the money could be needed to finance her care. So Zara decided the time had come to put down roots.

For six weeks, she had been a homeowner with a mortgage. After that, she felt more of a grown-up, but she was still single and searching for a person to share her life with. So as the coach passed the turning to Weston, all she had to look forward to tonight was feeding the cats, a quiche, and salad with a bottle of wine. Then she would read up on the extra duties she was destined to be policing for the Olympics.

Less than three weeks later, everyone was back on the buses. They were off to Taunton, Yeovil, Glastonbury, Frome, and several smaller towns en route. Their last duty before the Torch Relay disappeared into Wiltshire. After that, there would be a brief respite, then back to their patch. At least it was someone else's job to follow the torch through Bath and on to Bristol.

Zara and her colleagues saw Will.i.am in Taunton. One of the young DCs who had been at the Crown Court in Bristol told her who he was. Zara was none the wiser. It had been an early start, and the relay got underway just after six o'clock. It was going to be a long day.

Zara hadn't enjoyed working so much for ages. The weather was gorgeous, the crowds vast and well-behaved, and there wasn't a hint of trouble. They returned tired but happy to Portishead just after three o'clock.

The next team of officers was leaving for Bath on the bus to receive the runners back into the county from Bradford-on-Avon. Zara's day had finished, so she drove back to the city. The traffic was horrendous. Every car park was full. She got home, parked the car, and caught a bus to the centre.

She spotted Jason Gardener in Milsom Street and cut through the crowded streets to watch the runner in the Royal Crescent, where she was only a month ago with Toby. The blue skies and the Bath stone looked exquisite. For Zara, it seemed the end of a perfect day.

Phil Hounsell hadn't been with either of the teams today. Instead, he had been at Portishead with senior officers putting contingency plans together for the Olympics' impact on the force area. They were ensuring that they could respond if any disturbances occurred, such as over-enthusiastic drinkers or flare-ups at open spaces that planned to have giant screens transmitting the significant events. Another item on the list was the itinerary for the Queen's visit to Bristol in November.

After a warm day cooped up in the office, Phil got home early, something he had done much more often since last August. Erica and the children were ready and waiting to go into town.

"Daddy," shouted Tracey, "are you coming?"

"Yes, darling," said Phil, "we're off to see the Torch Relay."

Phil, Shaun, Erica and Tracey walked into Victoria Park

and headed towards the noise. The streets in the centre were full of people. People hung out of office windows on the upper floors — balloons and bunting were on view everywhere. Yet, there wasn't a frown in sight. On the contrary, everyone's face wore a smile; it was catching. Erica and Phil watched the procession as it passed them, wrapped together in a warm embrace. Shaun and Tracey clung to their parents for dear life. It was scary but fun.

"There's Auntie Zara," screamed Tracey.

Shaun and Tracey called out to Zara, who was just over the road on the opposite side of Milsom Street. No way she could hear their little voices above the clamour.

"How has she been?" Erica asked Phil.

"I can't remember the last time we talked, in all honesty," he replied. "We've been scattered around the County of Somerset with the extra duties this summer."

Erica watched until Zara disappeared into the crowds.

"Oh, that reminds me," said Phil. "Callum rang this morning. Debbie's expecting."

"Oh, that's fantastic news, Phil," cried Erica. "We must get a card to send them on our way home."

Callum and Debbie Wood, Erica thought, now there was a pair of lovebirds. Who thought they would ever get together?

She thought of the spectacle they had just watched. If only Zara Wheeler could find someone. Live together, get married, whatever to remove that niggling doubt. It was still there, deep inside her, that even though Phil was back on the straight and narrow now, Zara might still carry a torch for him. What was it with bloody torches?

Most of the late spring and early summer consisted of dodging the showers or more prolonged outbreaks of rain.

But, true to form then, the Queen's Jubilee weekend saw frequent downpours.

A lot of her colleagues were on duty. Still, Zara Wheeler braved the rain with Toby Drysdale in Victoria Park on Tuesday, June the fifth, to celebrate the Diamond Jubilee. A major celebration was held there with a stage with two giant screens standing at the bottom of the park's natural gradient. It allowed the public to picnic while they watched the Jubilee celebrations in London.

While Zara and Toby strutted their stuff, Phil, Erica, and the kids returned from Weston-Super-Mare. They had spent the weekend there, enjoying the events in the Winter Gardens. The kids loved the live music, the bouncy castle, the face painting, and the games. The wind and rain diminished the excitement for Phil and Erica, but the kids loved it.

When Zara returned to work, there were no happy, smiling faces in the office. This was partly due to the weather; there wasn't much respite from the lousy summer weather. On top of that, a growing list of internal problems mounted for their police service. Handling a death in custody in the south of the county led to accusations of corruption. Another incident saw a man of colour arrested and charged with offences, including possessing an offensive weapon and threatening to kill. However, he had likely been the victim of a racial assault by an unruly mob of white neighbours, if truth be told.

As June eased into July, Phil Hounsell found himself with the task of spearheading an attempt to challenge police behaviour and attitudes that, consciously or otherwise, sanctioned hate crime. In addition, his ACC handed him the unenviable task of salvaging the disaster of an internal inquiry that revealed officers' complete ignorance of the force's hate policy. Phil looked at the sad story and wondered why the dirty jobs seemed to come his way these days.

This revelation didn't help the public to grow to love their police service. It was just another brick wall between the police and the people they served. It became bigger every day. Phil drove home to Bath that evening and told Erica that he was sick and tired of battering his head against a brick wall.

"It's what you've always done, Phil," she said. "What else could you do?"

"They get more job satisfaction stacking shelves in Tesco," he moaned. "The trouble is they've got me by the balls, and they know it. I must protect my pension and suffer it for a few more years. I can expect a few more rotten jobs such as this one. Picking over the flesh of fellow officers hung out to dry is a job I detest."

"Well, haven't they asked for it?" asked Erica.

"Maybe, but I'm saying that the young, thrusting, fast-tracked officers never get tarnished by working on these cases. Instead, they get off-loaded onto the dinosaurs."

Erica moved from her chair to sit on her husband's lap. She hugged him.

"Whatever you do, Phil, you do it well, so they know they'll get the job done properly. As for the future, whatever you decide to do, I'll support you. As for the present, what do you say to an early night?"

Phil looked at his wife and then at his briefcase with the files on the case he had brought home to work on later.

"Yes, please," he replied.

In the Hounsell household, things were improving. The following morning, out on the Somerset levels, things went from bad to worse. Flash flooding had left cars stranded and roads under water. A storm overnight resulted in two weeks' worth of rain falling on a small stretch of countryside in less than fifteen minutes. Schools were closed, and properties were evacuated because of the threat of floodwater.

Zara Wheeler and Toby Drysdale travelled to Shepton Mallet. They were there to lend a hand in warning householders along the banks of the River Sheppey to stay tuned to local radio for an update on the situation.

Zara stood chatting to a guy from the Environment Agency when a reporter from BBC News grabbed them both for an interview. The poor bloke from the Agency had been on the spot for hours.

The best he could muster was a clichéd 'Our teams have been hard-pressed this week. However, we are doing everything we can to contain matters and prevent them from deteriorating.'

The reporter asked Zara if the police could give any advice to their viewers.

"It's important that people should not try to drive or walk through the floodwaters," she said.

As she uttered the words, Toby shouted for her.

Zara apologised to the reporter and ran to their car.

"What's up?" she asked. "Thanks for rescuing me. I felt a prat doing that. I can never think of what to say."

"It sounds as if someone should have listened to your advice," Toby replied. "They've spotted a car in the river half a mile away."

Toby and Zara sped towards the scene of the accident as fast as conditions allowed. Zara noticed the TV crew loading stuff into their van and knew they would soon follow.

The fast-running River Sheppey looked uninviting. A

neighbourhood police constable ran towards the car when Toby stopped.

"The car must have been travelling along this minor road at speed late last night. They must have tried to cross the bridge with the torrential rain and the flash floods. The force of the water took them through the wooden fence and over the side. The car remained partly submerged for ten hours. It's higher in the water than it should be. It must have caught up on a tree or something that swept downstream earlier."

"Are we looking for just the driver?" asked Toby as he got out of the car and, shrugging off his coat, headed for the waters.

"Toby!" shouted Zara. "You can't go in there; it's running so fast you'll be swept away."

"Get the rope from the boot of my car, mate," Toby called to the young PC.

"Okay," he replied, "I've got rope too in my vehicle. Maybe we can set up a human chain; it's not that far."

Toby tied one end of the rope around the trunk of a willow tree.

"What's your name?" he asked.

"Dave," replied the young policeman. "I suppose I should tell you before we go any further - I can't swim. I'm not afraid of the water, though, so I'll have the end of this rope around my waist. If you two can attach yourself to my line, you can try to get out there to see whether it was just the driver. Rescue isn't on the cards. We're only counting the number of dead after this length of time in the water.

Zara and Toby looked at one another.

"We haven't carried out a risk assessment, and the Health and Safety implications of this are horrendous," said Toby, trying not to laugh.

"I didn't sign up to push a mouse around on a desk," smiled Zara. "Just be careful."

They kicked off their shoes, threaded the rope through their belt loops and, as the TV crew arrived on the scene, they entered the water.

The water was fast-running; they soon found that the water current ran twice as strong underneath the surface. Toby turned back towards the bank.

"We need to move upstream," he called to Dave. "We'll secure your rope to a tree further up, and then we'll go in from there. If Zara and I can get as far out as possible, as soon as possible, we'll let the current take us towards the car. Stopping might be painful, but we can assess the situation, and then you can pull us ashore. Just shout to one of those TV people to help you take the strain."

They were soon ready. The two friends ran into the river and struck out for the centre. It was a struggle, but they got far enough so that the river carried them to the submerged vehicle. They both grabbed hold of the car and clung on for dear life. Toby took a deep breath and ducked under the surface. Fifteen seconds later, he came up spluttering,

"There's a baby in a child seat suspended upside-down in the back. Her head is out of the water. I can't tell for sure, but there's a chance she's alive. The driver didn't make it, though, I'm afraid. Whether she drowned or died in the crash, I can't tell."

Zara's heart sank. That poor child, losing her mother so young. She edged around the rear of the car, hanging onto the bumper.

"Where the hell do you think you're going?" shouted Toby. The rope tightened. They had no leeway.

Zara shouted to Toby to follow her.

"The water is less powerful this side," she yelled. "Maybe I can get the door open."

"We don't have enough rope," said Toby.

"It could be locked," said Zara. "I'll use your baton to smash the window. Then, if I can open the door, I'll detach my belt and go inside the car."

"That's crazy, Zara," said Toby, handing Zara his baton.

"We can't wait, Toby; if that baby's alive, we need to act fast. If Dave's right and there's a blockage keeping the car high in the water, the force of this floodwater could shift it."

"Exactly," said Toby. "Putting you in even more danger. What if it gets swept away?"

"I'll be on the telly," she called out, grinning at her best friend while detaching the belt that secured her to the rope. On the riverbank, Dave prayed. The sound man who volunteered to help with the line smiled benignly.

"O God, our help in ages past, our hope for years to come, our shelter from the stormy blast, and our eternal home. Yeah, I've done Songs of Praise. We always turn to religion at times such as these, don't we?"

"Bugger religion," said Dave. "The bloody paperwork to fill in if this goes pear-shaped is worrying me."

In the water, Zara felt numb with cold. She steeled herself for what was needed next. Two sharp raps with the baton smashed the glass. She cleared as much glass as possible and struggled to open the door. She had been right; it was more straightforward with the downstream door. She clambered into the interior. The water was a foot below the baby's head. Was it rising or falling? She checked the baby's pulse.

Her fingers had frozen now, and she was getting tired. She wasn't sure. The baby didn't react to her touch, but it wasn't stone cold. So there might still be a chance.

Zara tried again. There was something there, weak but steady. She moved her hand across the baby's face to free her from the child seat. She was sure she felt a whisper of breath on her hand; she hoped her imagination wasn't playing tricks on her.

Zara had seen Erica getting Shaun and Tracey in and out of the car when their relations had improved. It always looked so simple.

She wondered how Erica might have coped with a seat upside-down in a few feet of water.

"What's happening, Zara?" asked Toby, concern evident in his voice.

The seatbelt clips suddenly released, and the child dropped into Zara's arms, just above the river water's surface.

"She's free," cried Zara. "I'm bringing her out."

"Wait for me to get as far around as possible to help, Zara," shouted Toby.

Zara held the child's head out of the water with her right arm and slipped her left arm through the broken window. She was exhausted. Toby reached out and just managed to stretch enough to put a strong arm around them both.

"Dave," he shouted, "haul us back."

The two men on the bank took the strain. It lasted for only fifteen seconds, but it seemed like forever. Several pairs of hands helped them ashore when they scrambled up the slippery bank.

Zara didn't hear the emergency services arrive because of her concentrated effort, the noise of the water, and her thoughts of that poor little mite hanging there for ten hours. Finally, the baby was levered gently from her frozen hands and rushed to an ambulance wrapped in a space blanket.

Toby, too, resembled a competitor after completing the London Marathon. She looked at the crowd gathered around her; she could hear voices and applause. Zara could see the sky; the world was spinning. Dave, the young constable, caught her as she collapsed.

The sound man heard a noise and looked towards the submerged car. Then, with a groan and a scraping of metal, it broke free from its invisible captor under the surface. It careered rapidly downstream and finally smashed into the stone parapets in the centre of the next bridge across the Sheppey.

The fire engines set off in pursuit. Unfortunately, the baby's mother had to wait before her body reached dry land.

Zara came around briefly in the ambulance.

"How's the baby?" she managed to ask.

"It's touch and go, but she's got a chance, thanks to you," said a female paramedic.

Zara closed her eyes. A baby girl. She was so small and vulnerable, alone with her dead mother on a night like that. Life can be so cruel sometimes.

At the hospital, the staff took over from the ambulance crew. They kept warming the baby gradually, bringing her body temperature back to normal. Finally, an hour after Zara arrived, she sat up to drink a warm drink. She was shaky but on the mend.

A head appeared around the curtain of the cubicle. Dave, the young constable, had arrived.

"How are you feeling, ma'am?" he asked.

"Getting there, thanks," she replied weakly. "Any news yet on the baby?"

"Nothing concrete," he said. "You know what they're like. The little tot had been there since midnight. Mum dressed her well enough for a short trip in the car in the middle of summer, but ten hours is a long time. They say she's eighteen months. Still, while there's life, as they say."

Toby was Zara's next visitor. He looked somewhat better than she felt.

"Are you okay?" she asked.

"Don't worry, Zara," Toby replied. "I love the water, remember? Although this time, it will be you that gets the headlines."

"If I don't get carpeted for going against those instructions they give us - about going into dangerous situations without the proper authorisation and back-up."

"That camera crew captured every second of the rescue. Every country in the world will have shown it by tomorrow. Of course, the bosses might shout at us for getting stuck in without considering the danger. But the public will see the truth. You were a bloody hero. Thanks to you, the little girl has a fifty-fifty chance of making it."

"Well, I'll get back to Shepton, I guess," said Dave, thinking he was surplus to requirements, as the two best friends stood holding hands.

Toby hung around while Zara's condition continued to improve. They both grabbed some food later in the day, and a good night's sleep should finish her recovery. Toby kissed her on the forehead as she drifted to sleep; he found a nurse and asked if he could visit the baby to check on her progress.

"She's still holding her own," replied the nurse. "They recovered the car and her mother's body this afternoon. Her family know. The little girl is called Grace.'

"Can I see her?" asked Toby.

"Her grandparents are with her now. The mother's

parents that is. It's hard to understand how so much tragedy can fall on just one family."

"How do you mean?"

"The father served in Helmand and was severely wounded when Grace was three months old. They airlifted him back to the UK and admitted him to Queen Elizabeth Hospital in Birmingham. Kerry, the mother, drove backwards and forwards a couple of hundred times until he died of his injuries in February. After surviving that, she dies on a local road, she knows like the back of her hand. There's no telling, is there?"

"None whatever," said Toby, resting a comforting hand on the shoulder of the nurse. "OK, I'll be back in the morning to see my colleague. I hope we can drop in to see Grace before we leave."

"I'm sure her family will want to thank you both; Grace is all they have left now."

Toby left the hospital and made his way home. In the morning, he dropped into Zara's house to pick up a few things he thought she might need. Toby knew the hiding place for the spare back door key. However, it was the first time he had used it. When he reached the hospital, he found Zara sat up and irritable.

"The doctor says I can leave," she muttered. "My clothes are wrecked and...."

"Steady on," Toby said, "the cavalry's here. I picked up the essentials for you. Clean underwear, jeans, and a sweatshirt. It might be basic, but it will do the job until we get you home. I brought your toiletries, too, so you can face the world with a smile."

"Oh, Toby, you'll make someone a wonderful husband."

Zara threw her arms around his neck and kissed him.

"Someone's feeling better," a voice boomed from behind

them. The Assistant Chief Constable had turned up for a visit.

"Oh, sorry, Sir," said Toby. "Good morning."

"Could you leave us alone, please, Drysdale," said the ACC. "I need to talk to DI Wheeler."

Zara sat back on the bed. The ACC sat opposite her on a chair.

"That was a very foolhardy thing you did yesterday, young lady; as the senior officer, you should have waited until we decided how best to move forward. You know the procedures we have to follow. Fortunately, the outcome was successful, but we could have lost two, even three, officers yesterday. The press and the public will want to praise you to high heaven for your actions. They are waiting outside the hospital for their pound of flesh. Make the most of your fifteen minutes of fame. Going forward, this won't do your career any favours; it may scupper your chances of the accelerated promotion we anticipated. The force only rewards team players, DI Wheeler. No place for loose cannons, no matter how worthy the cause."

"I wish to get dressed now, Sir, if I may," said Zara angrily. "I want to visit the baby to check on her condition before I leave. The press can wait. As for my career, it will be what it will be. I shall continue to work hard, serve the public, and help lock up criminals. If that isn't what the police are for, then, going forward, there should be a rethink on what's important."

The ACC left her alone. Zara got dressed with tears stinging her eyes. Stupid man! How could anyone abandon a baby in a car in fast-running water until someone who never got their hands dirty completed a risk assessment?

She found Toby in the corridor. He brought her up-to-date with Grace's progress and her family situation. Zara's heart went to the little mite she had held in her arms yesterday. When they reached the ICU, Zara saw a middle-aged couple sitting by a bed.

"That's Grace's grandparents," said Toby. "Kerry's mother and father."

Zara walked into the room. The two heads turned towards her, and the man stood up and thrust out a big hand. His wife hugged Zara and led her over to look at Grace.

"She's doing well now," said the woman. "She's a fighter, is our Grace. She's going to make it."

"Just glad I could help," whispered Zara. She took hold of two fingers of Grace's left hand that poked out from the bedding that kept her snug and warm.

"We can't thank you enough," said Grace's grandfather.

"We're so sorry about Kerry," said Zara. "Can I come back to see little Grace later?"

"Of course you can, dear."

Toby and Zara left the couple with Grace and wondered when they would find the time to grieve the loss of their daughter. Life was so cruel. Toby asked one of the nurses if there was a way to escape the media circus at the front of the hospital. They told him to bring his car to the ambulance bay, and ten minutes later, he and Zara slipped away unnoticed.

The ACC had been right. The media circus was in full flow. The film of the river rescue was everywhere. Zara spent a few days driving from studio to studio for interviews. Her picture appeared on every front page. Her hand was sore from shaking hands with people on the street and signing autographs. She and Toby got invited to open fetes, received free theatre tickets, and were even photographed with the Bath Rugby team. For a few weeks, she became the nation's sweetheart.

Her superiors couldn't resist the public clamour for too long, and the Chief Constable presented her with her commendation. The Queen's Gallantry Medal was the reward she received for her actions. Then, as the Olympics became the primary focus of the world at large, Zara Wheeler slipped into the background without a fuss. Her fifteen minutes appeared to be at an end.

In September, she bumped into DS Phil Hounsell at Portishead. They hadn't seen each other in weeks. "Terrific job, Zara," he said. "I'm so proud of you."

"Thanks, Phil," she replied.

"Shaun and Tracey yelled at the TV every time you came on. Auntie Zara's on telly again! Come and see. They miss you."

"I miss them too. I've been visiting little Grace at her grandparents too. She made a full recovery."

"Good news on every front, then," said Phil.

"The ACC warned me my career might stall or come to a full stop because I ignored the guidelines. I've just seen him; I'm off to Larcombe Manor, outside Bath, on a fool's errand. The Charity Commissioners reported an odd occurrence when they visited last. A soldier with PTSD collapsed."

"Shock, horror, what do they expect?" said Phil. "That's a charity; I take it?"

"The Olympus Project run it; this is another pointless exercise I'm due to be sent on going forward, as they say, these days."

Zara left for Bath, and Phil Hounsell watched her walking away. Absence makes the heart grow fonder, someone said. Keeping their distance as they had done for weeks hadn't dimmed the flame much as far as Phil was concerned. Despite things between him and Erica being great these days, Zara could still get to him.

Phil Hounsell tore his gaze away from the receding figure of the nation's sweetheart and returned to his office. He buried his head in yet another lengthy set of statistics. Figures that masked they were losing the big battles on the streets. It almost cleared his mind of the memory she stirred of that night in Bristol. It almost cleared, but not altogether.

Chapter Eight

Wednesday, November 14th, 2012

At Larcombe Manor, the police follow-up to the Charity Commissioner's concerns and eliminating any trace of the Cropredy mission were both distant memories.

There had been the occasional flurry of activity since, but Erebus referred to the period as a phoney war. He knew that the ice-house continued to gather intelligence in bucket-loads every day. Even if only a tiny part resulted in Olympus agents getting sent into the field.

Yesterday morning, they sat through Minos's update on Thursday's forthcoming first elections for police and crime commissioners. The new commissioners took office in a week, replacing the existing police authority framework. Minos had given his report with his renowned attention to detail.

"The core functions of police and crime commissioners are to secure the maintenance of an efficient and effective police force within their area. Also, to hold the Chief

Constable to account for the delivery of the police and crime plan. Police and crime commissioners control the police fund (from which policing of the area is financed) and raise the local policing precept from council tax. Police and crime commissioners are responsible for the Chief Constable's appointment, suspension, and dismissal."

Athena decided that enough was enough.

"Have they thought this through? We are forty-eight hours away from the event, and I suspect that only a small minority of the public is aware of the fact. Who do they think will bother to turn out to vote? Everything about the tone of the rhetoric used on this only reinforces the status quo. It may be proper that the police are held accountable for their actions, but don't they realise that the British public wants action, not words? Words like 'giving the victims a voice' are dodging the issue. Harsh sentencing and eliminating the loopholes that let career criminals escape justice are the words the public wants to hear. When will they get the message?"

"Of course," added Phoenix, "that means they can continue to be as ineffective as ever. Our Chief Constable will only get worried if he gets caught giving a young female PC a good seeing-to on the photocopier."

Erebus chuckled.

"I think it safe to assume that no matter how successful this new set-up proves, we will still be required to sweep up the mess. I agree with Athena's interpretation. This move won't change the criminal agenda one iota. The government is committed to further cuts in funding so that police numbers fall. This election is to cost around four million. The new structure will cost substantially more than that to support a year. It appears to be little more than an extravagant whim. It is something I imagine the Home Secretary dreams will be popular However, items coming to us from Giles and his people in the ice-house will give us a big drain on our resources. Thank you, Minos, for your contribution. I think it's time for Alastor to come under the spotlight."

Major Michael Purvis, formerly with the Blues and Royals, had come to Olympus after his wife died during a burglary at her parents' home. Unfortunately, they never caught the culprit, stealing to fund his drug habit. Alastor, the Greek God, was the avenger of evil deeds, specifically familial bloodshed.

"I need to bring you up to speed on the growing menace from the Middle East. As Erebus will explain later, we have a heightened risk of a terrorist attack on mainland Britain. This time it is from jihadists emanating from the IS strongholds themselves."

Alastor ran through the initial background report.

"In late 2009, ISI transformed significantly. The Islamic State of Iraq planned to seize power in the central and western areas and turn it into a Sunni caliphate. What once was an organisation dominated by foreign individuals now became increasingly dominated by Iraqi citizens. The US military reported in 2010 that eighty per cent of ISI's hierarchy had been killed or captured. Their new leader, Abu Bakr al-Baghdadi, beefed up the group's leadership by appointing former Ba'athist military and intelligence officers who served during Saddam Hussein's rule. Many of these men spent time imprisoned by the US military. One of them, a former colonel, Samir al-Khlifawi, known as Hajji Bakr, had become the overall military commander overseeing the group's operations. He spent time at Abu Ghraib prison. He met al-Baghdadi there. The civil war which erupted in Syria last year allowed them to build a safe base near a small town north of Aleppo. From there, he intended to help organise the capture of parts of Syria by ISI, which, in turn, was to become their base for invading Iraq. A series of assassinations occurred within ISI after al-Baghdadi took office, and al-Khlifawi organised these. This purge wasn't ideological; it was to emphasise power."

They received the news in total silence. There were no comical quips from Rusty or Phoenix; the message was plain but incomplete. What extra information did Erebus have on ISI? How was Al-Khlifawi, or Hajji Bakr, involved in the potential terrorist attacks on these shores?

Phoenix and Rusty didn't have long to wait to find out. The others received a summary report from Erebus. He nodded to his two most trusted agents. Then, he indicated they were heading for the orangery.

A steward delivered refreshments from the Manor house when they were seated, showing that their stay would be a protracted one. Then, after he left, Erebus began.

"Can you help me, gentlemen? It has come to our attention that migrants camped outside the French port of Cherbourg are now targeting Irish ferries. They plan to stow away there because of the lack of passport control in Ireland. The journey begins at Cherbourg, where passengers show their passports before driving onto the Oscar Wilde ferry bound for Rosslare in the Republic. French port officials look at their documents but do not always ask to look at the boot of a car. Nor are vehicles subjected to any other scrutiny. Sixteen hours later, the Garda made a short passport check in Rosslare before waving the vehicles through. Rosslare is the last border stop before these migrants can take advantage of a short sea crossing to Wales. The Republic and the British Isles are parts of the Common Travel Area, so travellers crossing borders do not have to show identity documents. There is little or no sign of immigration control at the ferry terminal in Rosslare, where the journey to Fishguard commences. Often up to forty cars and a handful of lorries are onboard a ferry. Once the boat has docked, a marshal waves cars aboard. There may even be no sign of any police or security presence. Our investigations have shown that officers have more than enough to do with freight checking and anti-terrorism matters. Finding time to check individual passengers is beyond their purview. They appear to rely on ferry staff to alert them to the possible presence of illegals, but they aren't experts at spotting possible offenders."

"Terrific," snorted Rusty. "So the Welsh coast is leaking like a sieve, too? It's Liberty Hall right across the UK these days."

"We have uncovered intelligence on four potential travellers. That leads us to believe they are potentially more dangerous than a few kitchen helpers on their way to a handful of restaurants, Rusty," said Erebus sternly.

"Seek and destroy, Sir?" asked Phoenix. He was itching to get into the action.

"You are correct, Phoenix. These four need getting rid of with extreme prejudice, or whatever our American friends used to say."

"Understood," said Phoenix.

Rusty grunted to show he was now on the same page.

"In the file in front of you are photographs, histories, and everything pertinent we have on your targets. I must stress that these four must not leave Wales under any circumstance. Indeed, I should sleep easier if they made it no further than Haverford West."

"Can I take it that these four have connections to Hajji Bakr?" asked Rusty.

"They come from an extreme faction of ISI, making

them ultra-dangerous. Fanatics will go the extra mile to achieve their goals. Whatever target they have selected for their attack, we can rest assured it will aim to strike terror into the hearts and minds of everyone living in the UK. That's why we must take them out as soon as they land on British soil."

"Are we likely to meet any security forces on the same trail, Sir?" asked Phoenix.

"I doubt it; Giles is monitoring ports and airports as usual. The authorities have got it in their heads that the threat comes from Calais. They may uncover unfriendly traffic from that source, but our intelligence points to Fishguard as the 'hot spot' over the next couple of days."

"I haven't spent much time in West Wales," said Phoenix, "but I believe the transport systems are better than average. There are important industrial centres nearby: Milford Haven and Port Talbot. On the other hand, the roads may be more rustic near the coast. If these guys manage to get onto the M4, we'd be up the proverbial without a paddle. So we have to develop a plan that traps them inside a steel ring around the Fishguard terminal, and then we can arrest them. How many agents do we have available, Sir?"

"Apart from you two, do you mean? Only two, I'm afraid. We can't spare anyone else. Dexter and Vincent are standing by, awaiting your call."

"Oh, that's fine," said Phoenix. "I feel more comfortable now that I know they're on board. The four of us should be able to cope without too much sweat."

Kelly Dexter and Hayden Vincent had worked with Phoenix earlier this year on the Swindon mission. He had heard they had been in on the Weymouth beach job too, and, in both cases, they proved themselves to be excellent agents. The couple lived together in Shrivenham and were one of many teams that doubled up as clean-up crew or agents on missions with the Olympus Project.

"I'll leave you now, chaps; you have plenty of reading material to plough through and then the planning stage to tackle. Just be aware that Giles will contact you as soon as the four devils we're hunting board a ferry at Rosslare."

"Does that mean we know they've left Cherbourg and are en route to the Republic, Sir?" asked Phoenix.

"We are tracking their movements from Belgium to France and then to Ireland, Phoenix; they are somewhere in that region. Pinpointing where is proving tricky. But, rest assured, we will do our utmost to find them."

Erebus paused as he made to leave and return to the main building.

"Good luck, lads; come back safe and sound."

Rusty gave Phoenix an old-fashioned look after the door closed behind their leader.

"Blimey, the old man's getting soft, isn't he? Either that or we're up against nasty dudes this time, mate."

"Let's have a look at these reports then, Rusty. Then we can prepare for whatever they throw at us."

"It's difficult to know where the next threat is going to be, isn't it, mate?" said Rusty.

"It doesn't get any easier. So, let's see what intelligence Giles and his team have gathered on these terrorists," said Phoenix.

Over in the ice-house, Olympus had the best equipment available for intelligence-gathering, allied with the extraordinary skills of people such as Giles. As a result, they were more likely to spot a potential threat to national security than any official UK authorities.

According to Giles, a frantic search was underway for four suspected IS jihadis. The men had been holed up in Belgium and planned to sneak into Britain via Ireland and Wales to launch a terrorist attack. French police scoured the ports for the alleged fanatics. The men left the Middle East towards the end of October and travelled overland to Europe. So far, they had evaded capture. The French police dossiers included photographs, descriptions, details of their alleged crimes, and instructions to the officers on the ground that indicated their risk level was 'extreme'. They should approach with caution and effect arrests as soon as possible.

"We've thought for a long time that IS jihadists would try to smuggle themselves into Britain through Calais to launch atrocities," muttered Rusty.

"Creeping around to the side door and coming in through West Wales is sneaky," said Phoenix. "According to this intel, the French believe Cherbourg to be their exit point, not straight across the Channel."

Rusty smiled grimly. "As the old man might say, 'they don't play with a straight bat, old chap'."

Phoenix continued to read. The French appeared to have up to forty elite-unit officers overseeing the migrant camps near Calais. Their presence was designed to prevent infiltration by jihadists and combat the people-smuggler gangs who stow migrants away on ferries and trains to the UK. These officers were part of the Brigade Mobile de Recherche. The BMR had a close liaison with the French intelligence agencies.

"They keep insisting they are successfully stopping suspected terrorists. Since we haven't had an outrage on

British soil perpetrated by terrorists who have popped over on a day trip, possibly that view is correct," said Phoenix. "The bombers we encountered at the Olympics were homegrown. There are signs of escalation in the overall number of migrants there. As well as the established camps, loads of so-called refugees from Africa and the Middle East gather along the motorways leading to the ferry port. Every night we've seen TV footage of blokes trying to clamber onto lorries or running to hitch a ride on the Eurostar. They do whatever it takes to get across the Channel to get to our streets paved with gold."

"Paved with benefits, you mean," said Rusty. "I can't see the attraction, mate, can you?"

"The genuine migrants haven't been living in the lap of luxury, Rusty, be fair," replied Phoenix. "But no, I don't think I'd be in a rush to get here. Not while things are the way they are. As for the IS threat, they warned they would flood Europe with fighters posing as migrants. The open border policy is an absolute joke. These bastards want to destroy our way of life. We need to wake up, snuff out the threat, and get back to controlling our borders effectively. If we don't grasp the nettle, then, later on, we're asking for a heap of trouble."

"So while the government plays the role of an ostrich, we play the role of the British lion, is that it?"

"Par for the course, Rusty," said Phoenix. "Let's get cracking on making sure these four don't reach those streets they believe are paved with gold. I think it's time they received a one-way ticket to the promised land, don't you?"

Rusty flicked through the data they had received.

"Let's consider this, Phoenix. It says here, '2000-2500 British ISIS militants are now in the UK and prepared to launch deadly attacks. Security sources say MI5 and anti-terror police monitor thousands of terror suspects in mainland Britain. Most live in London, but many live in Manchester and the West Midlands. Security sources say the number of home-grown jihadists willing to launch attacks in Britain has grown massively in the last couple of years due to the rise of ISIS. Britain faces its most serious terrorist threat since 9/11 and has foiled several attempted attacks in the past year. Most people who try to become involved in terrorism were born and brought up here. They have come through our education system and concluded that their birth country is their enemy. According to this, the number of violent suspects classified as Al-Qaeda supporters monitored by security services has jumped significantly. Just a month ago, we raised our terrorism threat level to be substantial. Oddly, there was more of a threat of terrorist violence in NI from Irish Republican sources. It strikes me they underestimate the ISIS threat. We've got thousands here already; then this bunch of fanatics is arriving shortly. We have to assume these others know they're coming, surely?"

"It's possible," said Colin. "What are you thinking?"

"We might not see any spooks or anti-terror cops in Wales, but we might bump into a few hundred of their sympathisers. That could be tasty."

Rusty slid the initial reports to one side and concentrated on the photos and descriptions of their four targets.

"If I were them, I'd have a vehicle waiting to pick them up as soon as they set foot on Welsh soil. Then they could be past Cardiff before we know what happened."

"We need to be on our toes," said Phoenix. "Let's look at who we're up against, Rusty."

The known histories that Giles and Henry Case had collected made for fascinating reading. The four men due to arrive on the shore of the UK were 'hardcore' extremists. After the time they spent in Syria, they were battle-hardened. Their mission was never going to be a picnic; that explained Erebus's concerns.

Imran Nawaz, a 26-year-old computer sciences graduate from the University of Westminster, was born in Kuwait but grew up in London. He had been under surveillance by MI5 and on a no-fly watch list for two years. But in the spring of 2011, Nawaz escaped the UK undetected. He slipped out of the country in a lorry with the help of associates from a criminal network.

Another terror suspect, Mohammed Khawaja, under even tighter surveillance through a Terrorism Prevention and Investigation Measure, was thought to have escaped with him. Khawaja, 28, born in Somalia, jumped off a bus in Lewisham on Good Friday, 2011, and then vanished.

Intelligence services were understood to have investigated the possibility that Khawaja left on the same lorry as Nawaz. Khawaja had attended terror training camps in Somalia. He was known to be raising funds for al-Qaeda.

The network was now much more significant than previously thought, making it much harder for security agencies to keep tabs on its various strands.

The other two men travelling with Nawaz and Khawaja were Hassan Ashiq, 34, a nightclub doorman, and Jamshed Saswar, 41. Saswar, a father of four, grew up in Aston. His wife still lived in Smethwick in the West Midlands

Ashiq and Saswar entered Ethiopia in 2010 and were arrested in 2011. However, they escaped and returned to the UK only two months before Nawaz left London to fight his jihad.

"Interesting," said Rusty, "if sparse. Slippery beggars, aren't they?"

Colin looked at the photos of the four men, committing their faces to memory. It was true. They had little detail to explain what these four had been up to since leaving these shores. But slippery or not, they must find and deal with them swiftly.

The two agents stayed late into the night going over their plans. A phone call in the morning could send them into dangerous territory. Not Wales per se, you understand, but any place with extremists lurking, looking for trouble, was dangerous territory.

Kelly Dexter and Hayden Vincent arrived at Larcombe Manor at first light. Rusty and Phoenix shared breakfast with them in the staff canteen. Thirty minutes later, they were up to speed and descended into the armoury to meet with Bazza and Thommo. These two agents dragged Colin from the water two years ago and were a comedy double-act most of the time. However, even they appreciated that the mood was more subdued on this job. Each of the four agents had a kit bag with every conceivable piece of equipment they might need. Agents Longdon and Thomas were excellent at their jobs.

"We've counted the items into the bag, Rusty," said Pete Thomas, the serious veneer finally cracking.

"We expect to count them back in, minus a few rounds of ammunition, in due course," said Barry Longdon.

"We'll do our best not to lose anything, lads," said Rusty.

Two vans had been requested from the transport pool and stood fuelled, ready, and waiting by the stable block. Rusty and Kelly Dexter jumped into the driver's seats. They were up and away!

Two and a half hours later, they arrived in Carmarthen. They had safely negotiated the M4 until its end and began tackling the most rural roads that populated this little corner of the principality.

There had still been no contact from Giles in the ice-house, so they went for a meal at The Butcher's Arms.

"Very nice, too," said Kelly as they left the restaurant to finish the last leg of their journey. A tortuous forty miles that would take an hour and a half lay ahead. With only two arrival times to worry about with the ferries, they knew their targets hadn't been on the lunchtime ferry. The next one was due at midnight. They could only watch and wait.

In the ice-house, Giles and his team were being extra-vigilant. That was because there were so many possible ways for the terrorists to gain entry into the country. So while their intelligence told them that these four were crossing from Cherbourg to Rosslare, then Rosslare to Fishguard, they had to be ready to switch the point of attack at a moment's notice.

They hacked into various CCTV feeds that told them who was involved in the ports; so far, they could find none of the four targets. Henry 'Head' Case had an 'inkling'. It was one of those little ideas that creep into your head unannounced. Views that with no supporting evidence become the only thing you can consider. Henry was adamant Fishguard was significant because it gave the terrorists a three-hour run into Bristol. The Queen and Prince Philip were due to visit the city on Thursday, November the twenty-second, one week away.

"It follows, old bean," he said to Giles, who was less convinced, "just as night follows day. Her Majesty is at the Palace most days this week, with inaugurations and the odd dinner on the agenda. They are off to the Albert Hall tonight, but it can't be there that they are targeting, or we'd see bodies on the ground by now."

"So next Thursday, the pair of them will be in Bristol; the whole day, give or take?" said Giles, believing that Henry might be onto something.

"Well, a day for those two nowadays means six hours tops. But yes, they will go right across the city for little visits. Then they plan a gentle walkabout if the weather's fine."

"If the weather's fine. That will be a miracle after the summer we've experienced, Henry," scoffed Giles.

In Cherbourg, the terrorists made their way towards the ferry terminal. Nawaz and Saswar were the first of the two pairs to travel. They had formulated their plans in Belgium and crossed into France at the weekend. They stayed on the outskirts of Paris until they were ready to move.

Khawaja and Ashiq were still in Brussels, catching the ferry in two days. However, they were conscious of the need to stay apart for as long as possible throughout the planning stage. Nawaz and Saswar were catching tonight's sailing to Rosslare. They were to arrive in the mid-afternoon on Friday. The nightclub doorman, Ashiq, had booked his passage as a foot passenger; he was travelling alone.

Nawaz was younger, good-looking, and intelligent. He waited for four hours at the terminal to buy his ticket. The queue did not justify this delay. Nawaz waited for the right person to arrive. A young Irish student, travelling home for Christmas after working in Amsterdam for nine months, turned up with a large haversack. Imran Nawaz sweet-talked the young girl; his charming exotic way captivated the innocent colleen. He offered to carry her bag if they could share the experience of the sea trip. It was his first time at sea; he was nervous. She met him that evening; they planned to board the ferry together.

The Rosslare ferry left on time, and the first two terrorists were en route. They had been unchallenged.

Chapter Nine

Friday, November 16^{th,} 2012

Mohammed Khawaja and Jamshed Saswar left the second-floor flat where they had been staying in the early hours. They were soon driving away from the Molenbeek district of Brussels, enabling them to hide in plain sight.

The prospect of a seven-hour drive to Cherbourg did not faze them. They had suffered far longer journeys threading their way from Syria through Eastern Europe to Belgium. The border crossing would be simple enough.

They endured the hassle of toll roads and frequent roadworks on the A29, knowing they neared their goal with each kilometre. They stopped every couple of hours in France to rest. They made sure no one followed them. If challenged, they had no weapons for police or security services to find; no suicide belts were deployed on this leg of the trip.

The two men were friends on their way to a family wedding in Waterford. The clothing in their cases in the car's boot supported this claim. The other casual clothes were nondescript: ideal for strolling in any spare time on either side of the ceremony. Of course, they were perfect for blending into the crowds in a British city too, but the two terrorists didn't imagine anyone questioning them would make that leap.

Their arrival in Cherbourg, having made the trip without unscheduled delays, was perfectly timed. The booking Imran Nawaz had arranged earlier enabled them to drive onto the ferry with minimal fuss. The boot of the car had a brief inspection. Mohammed and Jamshed received a lengthy sullen stare from a security guard, but they were safe on board in minutes.

Neither man was a good sailor. Eighteen hours aboard a ferry was the least attractive part of their journey. However, the sight of the ferry port of Rosslare on Saturday afternoon was welcome.

Jamshed drove the car off the ferry. They headed towards Waterford, but a few minutes later, they turned off and headed towards a small white cottage on the outskirts of Kilrane. They parked the car at the rear of the property, hidden from the road. The back door unlocked. Jamshed and Mohammed entered.

"Assalamu alaikum," said Imran Nawaz and Hassan Ashiq.

"Wa alaikum salaam," replied Mohammed Khawaja and Jamshed Saswar.

"I trust your trip was uneventful, brothers?" asked Nawaz.

"We had a rough crossing, but we will recover soon," replied Khawaja.

The four men prepared themselves to talk, plan, and

pray. Tomorrow they would receive the call that told them when they crossed to Wales.

In Haverford West, Kelly Dexter and Hayden Vincent rested. They had been in contact with Phoenix and Rusty, who sat in their van one mile from the ferry terminal in Fishguard. Everything was quiet.

In the ice-house, Giles and his team pored over reams of intelligence. They were searching for phone messages, e-mails, CCTV footage, or something to offer a clue to the terrorist whereabouts. Then, late on Saturday evening, there was a breakthrough. The Belgian Special Forces Group had raided a flat in Molenbeek, a district of Brussels. They were acting on a tip-off. Shots were fired, and an SFG member was wounded. They arrested two suspected terrorists; one didn't make it to the hospital alive.

"Henry," called Giles, "it looks as if the birds have flown."

Henry Case trotted across the room. He looked at the information and nodded.

"Right; inform Phoenix and the team that their targets are en route to Rosslare. If we can't find them at Cherbourg, we'll have to keep an eye on an alternate crossing point. Start re-doubling our efforts in Ireland to pinpoint where they are and when they plan to travel."

Phoenix and Rusty received the update from Giles as they moved positions. Rusty was driving the van into High Street.

"I fancy a curry, Phoenix; let's try the Taj Mahal," he said.

Phoenix stretched; he hated hanging around, waiting for the action to start.

"Suits me," he replied. "Hold on, Giles has something for us."

He read the message. "Curry it shall be then, Rusty; Giles says our guys are either en route or in Ireland. They'll let us know which ferry they took. We're okay until midnight, at least. Let the other two know what's happening while you order me a sea bass hakka with trimmings."

"No worries, mate," said Rusty.

Time passed slowly but in pleasant surroundings. The food was excellent, and the two agents left the restaurant in a happy mood, despite the cold and the enforced wait. Over in Haverford West, the agents from Shrivenham were making out in the van. It takes all sorts.

Not much happens in Kilrane on a Sunday morning. Fair to say that not much happens any day in Kilrane, but the quiet solitude suited the four occupants of the small, rented cottage. The call they were waiting for came just after salat al-maghrib.

"Collection will be at the same time on Tuesday evening."

"Why are we hanging around here for so long?" asked Jamshed Saswar.

"The longer we are in England, the more time the security forces have to find us, brother," replied Imran Nawaz. "We will land as arranged, then move to Bristol in readiness to send a message to the British people. It's a message they will never forget."

"Who waits for us in Wales?" asked Jamshed.

"A friend," Imran replied.

Salma Begum grew up in East Anglia, where her father was a consultant surgeon. At school, she was intelligent and focused. Salma enrolled as a medical student of Medical Sciences and Technology at the University of Westminster. She dropped out after three years and followed another path. Salma Begum was twenty-six and married to the ISIS cause.

Her father had enjoyed various sports as a young man. Above everything, he had a love of water sports. As he grew older, the fruits of his labours as a consultant surgeon allowed him to develop that passion for speed. Salma Begum had often partnered with her father in powerboat races in the North Sea from eighteen. As a result, Salma became an extremely proficient driver in her own right.

As university beckoned, she spent less time with her father and less on the water. As her radicalisation increased, her distance from her father and her family lengthened, but those skills she had gathered on the choppy waters of the North Sea were not lost forever. The colleagues she met in the next few days soon discovered how valuable she could be.

At dawn on Monday, Salma Begum drove her ten-year-old VW Passat away from her flat in King's Lynn for the final time. She headed towards Peterborough and then cut across the country; she stopped near Rugby for breakfast. Then Salma returned to the slow, quick traffic dance to start a new week on the M42 and M50. She wasn't sorry to get to the M4 and trundle along in the heavy traffic until she reached the Welcome Break a few miles from Swansea.

Salma found a parking space away from the buildings with vacant spaces around her. She sat in her car and waited. It was just before one o'clock.

A van drew alongside and edged forward into the parking space before her and to her left. The trailer behind the van contained Salma's pride and joy. She smiled as she glanced to her left and saw its magnificent lines.

Without a word, the van driver got out, unhitched the trailer, and drove away. Salma eased the Passat into the vacant spot and got out of the car. She attached the trailer to the tow bar on the Passat. It was time for a cup of tea and maybe even a bite. Salma was ready for the next stage of the mission.

An hour later, Salma drove out of the car park with care and headed towards Tenby. She was just another boat owner moving their craft to a safe harbour for winter or a young woman with spare time on her hands going to enjoy the last hurrah before winter. Either way, her cargo raised no suspicions. The trailer received the odd envious look but nothing more.

Her craft was a small, fast boat designed with an extended narrow platform and a planing hull to reach high speeds. The craft had two powerful engines with more than 1000 combined horsepower. It could typically travel at over 80 knots in calm waters, around 50 knots in choppy waters, and maintain 25 knots in an average five to seven-foot sea. In addition, it was heavy enough to cut through higher waves, although at a slower pace. For the task that lay ahead, it was the ideal choice.

Salma had learned from her father that the so-called cigarette boats, dating from the 1960s, owed much of their design to craft used in offshore powerboat racing.

During that decade, this model had been used by drug smugglers to move drugs across the Caribbean to the United States. The accommodation was minimal; it could cope with the five passengers it was due to carry. In addition, the small low cabin under the foredeck was much smaller than a typical motor yacht of similar size.

Boats of this design are difficult to detect by radar except on flat calm seas or at close range. They are stealthy, fast, seaworthy, and difficult to intercept using conventional craft. Ninety minutes after leaving the motorway service station Salma Begum approached Tenby but turned off the main road and headed for a quiet beach.

Tenby Harbour, the jewel in Pembrokeshire's crown, sits in a central position in the Georgian town which has become the country's most popular tourist destination. As its Welsh name suggests, this 'little fort of the fish' attracts thousands to the glorious beaches surrounding it. Salma knew that moorings in the harbour were available up to a maximum size of twenty-one feet. Salma's craft was half as long again. They had looked at other options. They couldn't risk leaving her four colleagues exposed for too long in the town of Fishguard or travelling the roads that led east towards their target.

Driving south out of Tenby on the A4139, she threaded her way through Penally and Lydstep. A quiet country road then took her right to Manorbier. From the village, she followed the signs to the beach car park.

Getting the men from Ireland to the boat might prove a tricky obstacle, but Salma and Imran Nawaz had devised a cunning plan. As the sun sank lower in the sky, another day ebbed away. Salma prepared to spend the night in the Passat with her precious transport secured behind her.

In the summer months, Presipe is a little gem. Huge crags of fossil-rich red rock jut out towards the sea to form private coves and slips of sand. Salma knew from her holidays there as a child that the sands on the beach were secluded. It was so quiet that if she ventured out on this November Monday night, she was sure to find it untouched by any footprints other than her own.

Tuesday morning dawned. The weather in Southern Ireland, West Wales, and, indeed, most of England was dreadful. A very wet period began as a succession of low-pressure systems developed in the Atlantic and moved to the UK.

Persistent, heavy rain affected many places and caused widespread flooding and landslips, with southwest England being the most affected. Winds were strong, and gales were forecast, warning that uprooted trees could cause structural damage.

In Kilrane, the four terrorists huddled together in the small cottage and wished the day would pass quicker. Instead, they were eager to start the next leg of their journey.

Over in Wales, the four Olympus agents had spent a restless weekend wandering and waiting to confirm when their targets sailed.

Rusty leant against the wind and struggled towards the Pendre Inn. He had parked his van next to Kelly Dexter's in the town car park in Fishguard. He met the others in a warm bar, with the prospect of real ale and good food. This job could be tedious with hanging around, but it had its perks.

Phoenix ordered drinks at the bar when he walked through the door. Several pairs of local eyes followed his every step. English visitors had never been ultra-welcome in these parts.

"They'll know me again," said Rusty to Kelly and Hayden as he sat with them at their table. Phoenix brought over the drinks.

"Tuesday evening, and no news yet," sighed Kelly.

"I hate playing the waiting game," muttered Rusty.

"Tell you what," said Phoenix. "So am I. Let's assume until we get confirmation they've set off that they have travelled tonight, tomorrow morning, or whenever. We'll do what we planned each time as a 'dry run'. It will keep us sharp.

"Great idea," said Hayden Vincent. "You had better enjoy that pint. We'll be off to the ferry port as soon as we've eaten to meet the ferry at half-past midnight. Now, pass me the menu. I'm starving."

A few hours earlier, in Kilrane, a removals van had pulled into the driveway of the small white cottage. The driver parked beside the building. Imran Nawaz came out to greet him.

"Are you ready to leave, brother?" he asked.

Imran nodded. The driver opened the large double doors at the rear of the van. It was stacked from floor to ceiling with furniture. He clambered into the back and called to Imran.

"Get your friends out of the house now. We must move fast. We need to unload a few items; you will see the hiding place we have constructed for you."

Imran called the others. Ten minutes later, pieces of furniture had been removed, revealing a gangway to the side leading to the back of the van. As soon as Mohammed, Hassan, and Jamshed were in a small cavity at the rear, surrounded by furniture, Imran and the driver replaced the furniture. After that, Imran was confident nobody would suspect that three fugitives had stowed away inside as they closed the doors.

"Keys?" asked the driver impatiently.

"Sorry, brother," said Imran. "They're in the cab."

"Have you made sure there's nothing left in the cottage?" asked the driver as Imran returned with the car keys. Imran assured him they had spent the day cleaning the cottage from top to bottom, burning everything they didn't need on this journey. No trace of them ever having been there remained.

"Safe journey," said the driver, throwing Imran the keys to the removals van. "I shall meet you in Somerset."

"Inshallah," said Imran.

He watched Mohammed Khawaja's car disappear into the distance. He followed in the removal van ten minutes later. Their ferry left at nine-fifteen. They were on schedule and on their way. Nothing would stop them now.

Tuesday 20th into Wednesday 21st November 2012

Just before eight-thirty in the evening, the two vehicles had joined the rest of their fellow travellers on the ferry at Rosslare. Three and a half hours later, they docked in Fishguard.

The Olympus agents would be waiting, whether they knew they were coming or not.

Rusty and Kelly were driving. Phoenix and Hayden rode shotgun; both men were armed, alert and ready for action. At nine-thirty, Phoenix received communication.

Giles reported a possible sighting of Imran Nawaz in the Rosslare ferry port. A man known to be an ISIS sympathiser was driving a saloon car with Belgian plates as he drove onto the ferry.

Tarek Qaadir had been active in the past twenty-four hours; he had delivered the so-called 'cigarette' boat to Salma Begum at Welcome Break near Swansea before catching the ferry to Ireland in his removals van. Unfortunately, Giles and his team had not captured that piece of intelligence.

After an uncomfortable crossing in high winds and

driving rain, the ferry docked safely in Fishguard. Cars and vans drove off in a steady stream. Tarek made his way to the exit. A security guard stopped him, checked his papers, and inspected the car and the boot.

A cursory check found nothing because there was nothing to find. The guard waved Tarek on his way. Without a backwards glance to see what might happen to Imran and the others, he drove off towards the M4. His next destination was in the English county of Somerset.

"There's the car with the Belgian plates," said Kelly. "Do I follow?"

"It's just the driver," said Phoenix into his earpiece headset microphone in the other van. "We need to find our four prime targets. Let him go for now. Inform Giles that he has left the port. He can track him on the motorway and discover where he's headed."

Imran Nawaz stopped the big van. He knew a check was inevitable. Imran got out of the cab and went to the back doors. He called out to the nearest two guards.

"Lads, you'll want to get a good look at this lot. I'm booked for a house move from Ireland to Tenby. I could do you a nice carpet if you're interested."

Imran Nawaz had changed his appearance on the ferry journey. Tarek Qaadir had supplied him with a bodysuit undergarment, which thickened his usual medium build with the loose Western clothing he had donned. It made it appear he was a heavy-set individual with a beer belly. Jeans slung low, well-worn working boots, and a bobble hat to hide his long unruly hair completed the transformation. He looked like the archetypal slobbish lorry driver that has been the cornerstone of the British transport cafe for generations.

As he held the door open, the guards took a look. A

quick shine of the torch at the floor-to-ceiling stack of tables, chairs, beds, and wardrobes was enough.

"No, you're OK." said a guard. "If you want to get on, close her up and be on your way. An hour's drive ahead, look you, so steady as you go."

Imran took his time as he drove out of the terminal and headed for Tenby.

The guards moved on to check one of the last ten vehicles rolling off the ferry.

"I don't envy that guy's job, do you?" said one.

"Especially on his own. I suppose in the morning, when he drops his load at his destination, there will be someone there to help him?" replied the other.

The final car they chose to check over contained four young women returning from a hen weekend for a mate from their university days. Good-looking girls, too, most of them. More than enough to stop the guards from wondering about the lone occupant of the removal van or thinking about how he could unload that huge van on his own.

"That's the last vehicle," grunted Rusty. "We should have followed that bloody Belgian car."

"Giles has eyes on him," said Kelly Dexter.

Phoenix tried to recall the cars and vans he had seen leaving the ferry terminal. They were an assortment of old and new, small and large. There had been that removals van, but nothing that sparked any alarm bells. The foot-passengers, too, had been scrutinized. No one answering the description of the four men they sought had materialised.

Back to square one. The crew could park nearby for the night and get ready to do the same thing tomorrow at lunchtime. Maybe Giles might send them the green light in the morning, a confirmed sighting of the men boarding at

Rosslare. They had to hope so. Missing them was not a choice.

While the Olympus agents slept, leaving any decisions until the morning Tarek drove, without speeding, on a deserted M4. He reached Bristol around four o'clock. Careful negotiation of the M5 brought him to Watchet Harbour in Somerset.

Not that long ago, Watchet was a small working harbour handling coasters. The Marina opened around ten years ago. Tidal ranges along this stretch of coast are massive, with a ten-metre range quite common. The Marina made use of this to allow boats always to stay afloat. Depths were maintained in the marina by a flap sill, with access available for a few hours on either side of the local high water.

Tarek Qaadir was not a seafarer, but he knew that Salma Begum had done her homework well. The crossing from the Welsh coast should get them here inside that margin of error. High tide was just after six in the morning. The weather was the only fly in the ointment.

This is England; isn't the weather always fickle? In common with harbours along this coast, entry was not possible with strong onshore winds. Tarek got out of the car, licked his finger, and stuck it in the air. Was the wind onshore or offshore? He had no idea. He looked at his watch; it was five-forty. He got back in the car and waited.

While Tarek Qaadir took a long way to the Somerset coast, back in West Wales, Imran Nawaz had parked the removals van next to Salma Begum's Passat. She got out of the car, stretched her stiff, tired limbs and greeted him warmly.

"No time to waste," Imran admonished. "We must get the others out of their hiding place."

They opened the doors and removed a few pieces of

furniture. It took longer for Imran and Salma, but the side gangway finally became accessible, and the three men were, very gratefully, released from their hidey-hole. Salma laughed as cramps and various aches and pains struck the three men when they tried to walk around the car park to loosen up their stiff limbs.

"Fresh air at last," said Jamshed. "You have no idea of the smell in there."

"You men should shower more often," laughed Salma.

Hassan and Mohammed kept quiet. They were less enamoured with having a woman involved in this mission. They were even less pleased when they learned what was happening next.

"We must get this trailer through the dunes and onto the beach," said Salma. "We will leave the trailer and the car. In the boot of my old Passat, you will find the materials to destroy them. A five-minute delay will be enough."

Imran organised the team, and after a good deal of pushing and shoving as the car tyres and trailer tyres found soft sand, they had made it. The boat was in the shallow water. Hassan and Mohammed took responsibility for the vehicles. They removed the number plates for use on the other side of the water.

The police would assume this was just a 'dump and burn' of an old banger — something they encountered weekly somewhere along the coast.

Salma started the engines and eased the boat further into Bristol Channel. They reached a reasonable distance from shore when the car's petrol tank exploded, and the flames tore through the vehicle and incinerated the wooden parts of the trailer.

Despite the wind and rain - and given that the waters of the Channel were decidedly choppy, the go-fast boat kept going at forty to fifty knots. The four terrorists sat in cramped quarters, and even Mohammed Khawaja had to admire the skills of their driver. Salma was in her element. Her hair flew in the wind; the spray spattered her face and clothes. It mattered nothing. She was determined to deliver them to the small harbour on the other side of the Channel, many miles up the coast towards the Severn Estuary.

Using the cigarette boat to spirit the four men away from the Welsh side of the Channel had been her idea. Handling the boat in the choppy waters was challenging, but she knew two more significant challenges lay ahead. First, they had to find their friends, and then she had to negotiate that tricky entry into Watchet Harbour. If only the wind and rain eased.

Imran moved from his shelter under the canopy. He stood by Salma.

"How do we find the boat?" he yelled. "The Channel is so big, and we are a cork bouncing around in a pond."

"I must radio them," Salma shouted back. "It's dangerous, but we will keep it brief."

As they got closer to the Somerset coast, they spotted lights ahead. Salma grabbed the handset.

"Royal Hunt to *Storm Chaser*; come in, *Storm Chaser*."

"*Storm Chaser* to Royal Hunt; we are ready for you, welcome."

Salma eased back the throttle and brought her craft to the far side of the yacht anchored just off the coast. To anyone watching on such a stormy night, they had sheltered in a calmer spot, weathering out the storm. They would carry on up the Severn Estuary to dock in Bristol or carry on further out to sea in the morning.

They lowered fenders from the side of the yacht, and Jamshed and Mohammed secured the cigarette boat.

Several men appeared at the rails of the vessel. Item after item was then lowered carefully and stowed in the hull of the go-fast boat by Imran and Hassan.

Minutes later, Salma moved carefully away again and tackled the final challenge. The crew of *Storm Chaser* cleared the decks and returned below to wait out the storm for another hour or two. The terrorist cell members now had possession of the explosives, weaponry, and other materials they needed tomorrow in Bristol.

Salma expertly brought the go-fast boat to the harbour entrance, waiting, watching, and listening for the perfect moment. It was seven in the morning; dawn was breaking; Tarek should be waiting for them. There it was!

Salma gunned the powerful engines; briefly, the boat surged forward. They cleared the seawall on her right by just one foot. They were past the worst. Inside the calm waters of the marina, everything was quiet. She looked for the mooring she had booked with her mother's credit card last month. Salma might not speak to her father, but the two women had kept in contact in secret.

As she brought her craft into the reserved space on the quayside, she spotted Tarek Qaadir. He helped Hassan get the boat secured.

"We must get on and transfer the equipment," he growled. "This weather delayed you. It is light now. Someone could see you."

The four men who had endured an uncomfortable five hours in the cramped quarters on the boat were in no mood for hanging around either. They wanted to be as far away from water as possible.

"I've experienced enough of the sea for a lifetime," said Mohammed angrily.

Hassan Ashiq looked at Jamshed Saswar; they smiled at one another.

Mohammed glared at them. "What's so funny?"

"Don't worry, brother. You won't go to sea again," said Imran putting a hand on his shoulder. "Tomorrow, we will be in paradise."

Mohammed passed the Passat number plates to Tarek.

"Make yourself useful and put these on the car, Tarek; those Belgian number plates will be spotted in no time tomorrow."

The transfer of equipment passed as quickly and quietly as possible. With the car boot lifted, they had a partial shield to hide what they were off-loading. The rest of the marina felt empty. It may have been full of little boats, but nobody was up and moving around this early in the morning.

Salma ensured everything was secure on the boat and said goodbye in her head. Tarek's role in the mission was now complete. He said his goodbyes to his colleagues and set off on foot to the town. He took the bus into Taunton, walked to the railway station, and travelled back to his home in Birmingham.

Imran Nawaz drove the car, his four passengers, and their equipment out of Watchet and took the road to West Quantoxhead in the Quantock Hills. They turned off the minor road onto a narrow country track a mile past the village. Once they were out of sight of the road, they stopped and rested. Everyone needed sleep. It was just before eight in the morning.

As the terrorists nodded off, one by one, in the car in Somerset, the Olympus agents started their hunt for their targets afresh in West Wales.

"We must check with Giles to see if they're travelling

this morning. They should be at the Rosslare terminal by now," said Phoenix.

Rusty made the call. After a five-minute one-way conversation, he ended the call.

"Okay, listen up," said Rusty, connecting with Kelly and Dexter in the other van as well, "First, Giles tracked the car with the Belgian plates beyond Bristol. He took the M5 west towards Taunton. They lost any CCTV contact with him around Bridgwater. His best guess is that he headed for the coast. We have people looking for him there. Over in Ireland, Fintan O'Sullivan, our man in Wexford, has unearthed a small holiday cottage near Kilrane. It's a short hop from there to Rosslare. He inspected the property and reported that it was 'too clean'. Someone went to the trouble of hiding that they had been there. A farmer who lives a mile up the road towards the ferry terminal told Fintan he thought he saw a furniture van on that road early last night. But he didn't see where it headed."

"That removals van we saw in Fishguard!" shouted Phoenix. "They were inside that!"

"We've missed them!" cried Kelly Dexter. "We need to get back to Bridgwater sharpish."

Colin thought over the events of the past days. What had they missed? Were there any clues about where their targets were headed? Was it Bristol, or could there be other targets they planned to hit west of England?

He re-ran the scenes in the Fishguard ferry terminal through his mind. The removals van: which way did it go when it left? He asked Rusty to get Giles to check for any sightings of the van on the motorway.

"The guy driving the car with the Belgian plates is near Bridgwater, possibly on the coast. Why go there? Where did they go if the removals van had our targets aboard and didn't follow by road to the same destination?"

Nobody spoke in either van for a minute or two until Giles broke the silence by returning Rusty's call. There had been no removal vans on the motorways early this morning.

"So they went to the coast near where we are now and then across to the other side," Phoenix thought out loud. "We could search near here, but they're bound to be long gone. We need Giles and the lads to find this damn car driver. They could have landed a dozen places, from Minehead to Sharpness. That's one helluva stretch of coastline to search."

"We need fresh orders from Larcombe," said Rusty. "We're no good to anyone here."

"Let's head home," said Colin, looking at his watch. "We can re-group at Larcombe and then relocate wherever they think fit. The clock is ticking. There are only twenty-four hours until the Royal party rides into Bristol."

Chapter Ten

It was half-past eleven when the two vans swung into the driveway that led to the old Georgian Manor. Somewhat deflated, the four agents left the vehicles by the stable block and walked to the main building.

Erebus, Athena, and the others needed to decide what they should do next. A Royal visit requires considerable protection. The police and the secret services were bound to be there in numbers. The nature of the attack concerned Phoenix. What type of raid would this be?

He was aware of their reliance on the team in the icehouse to uncover helpful information. These four terrorists, plus any others recruited for the task at hand, were formidable opponents. So far, they were always one or two jumps ahead of them. Colin Bailey wasn't used to that, and he hated it.

Erebus was in London, meeting with several money men who helped finance the Olympus Project. Athena whispered to Phoenix so the others couldn't overhear that Erebus had requested an urgent meeting.

"I think the time has come, Phoenix," she whispered. "I believe he has gone to tell them he is ready to retire."

Colin nodded. Now was not the time to think how Olympus might look after Erebus had sailed into the sunset.

"It is essential we find the driver of the car with the Belgian number plates," he said. "He was not one of the four targets, but he is an ISIS sympathiser. Is he part of the hit-squad? Who took them if they crossed by boat, and where did they land? The number of terrorists involved could be in double figures; are they heavily armed? Are we dealing with one suicide bomber or half a dozen? Could it be a rocket attack? We know less now than when we left for Fishguard."

Athena was the voice of calm.

"I understand your frustration, Phoenix. I've called Henry Case and Giles to attend as soon as possible. We'll look at the latest intelligence and devise our action plan."

Fifteen minutes later, Giles and Henry entered the room.

"What do you have for us, gentlemen?" asked Athena.

"The driver is Tarek Qaadir from Aston in the West Midlands," said Henry. "He's not considered a fighter, just a driver and general dogsbody. The car belongs to our friend Mohammed Khawaja in Brussels. He drove it to Cherbourg, crossed to Rosslare, and then holed up in Kilrane before crossing to Fishguard. Khawaja is dangerous; he's the explosives man on the team."

"Imran Nawaz must have travelled as a foot passenger, possibly alone, but they may have split into two groups of two," Giles continued. "The four of them came to Wales in the removals van. We don't know how they pulled that off yet because Qaadir drove Khawaja's car, not the van, as they left the ferry. You saw that for yourself, Phoenix."

"There's something about Nawaz that might shed light on the crossing from Wales," said Henry. "He was friendly with a Salma Begum. They met in 2010, and police monitoring Nawaz may have assumed that Begum might have a taming effect on him, but such couples often do the opposite, radicalising each other. Female terrorists have a long history of exploiting gender stereotypes to avoid detection. She's not an exception; she's an example of a trend. We often assume that women are forced or tricked into following the cause. Salma experienced strong feelings of alienation. Her last photo shows her wearing a veil and aiming a Kalashnikov at the camera. Counter-terrorism investigators brought her in for questioning early in 2011, but they didn't have enough to charge or monitor her. It was clear Salma Begum was active. She wanted to share in the violent nature of the jihadist ideology."

"They knew the possible threat this girl posed," said Rusty, "and the police had her in their hands in 2011. Why didn't they stop her or put her under surveillance?"

"They weren't aware of her Muslim fundamentalism," said Giles. "It would take more than heightened surveillance to stop someone like Salma Begum. The clincher that she is part of the attack cell is that she went powerboat racing in her late teens and early twenties with her father."

"That's how they got across the Bristol Channel," said Phoenix. "Why didn't we pick up on this Begum girl earlier?"

Henry raised his eyes to the ceiling.

"With hindsight, we might have flagged up the connection to Nawaz earlier. In our defence, hundreds of suspected terrorists are on our shores these days who might have joined forces with the four we originally sent you to eliminate. They outwitted us by getting past you at the ferry terminal. Without that deception, you could have trapped them in Fishguard, and it would have been Goodnight Vienna."

"There is one final point on the Wales business," added Giles. "The burnt-out remains of a car and trailer have been found by South Wales Police this morning on a beach a few miles east of Tenby. They abandoned the removal van in the beach car park. There was only furniture, etcetera inside, but there was evidence that people had stowed away in a hidden compartment behind the driver's cab. The police are hunting for a handful of illegal immigrants in the vicinity."

"Understood," said Phoenix. "Let's move on. How do we stop them from reaching Bristol for tomorrow's Royal visit? Or am I wrong to assume that's the target?"

"We're confident that the Royal visit is their primary target, Phoenix," said Henry Case.

"We don't have a complete schedule for the day's activities," said Athena. "That has been kept a closely guarded secret. The main points are the caravan factory, the Old Vic, and the M Shed."

"Don't worry too much about a schedule," said Phoenix. "It might not matter if they strike early. Let's get back to the boat. They crossed with Salma Begum driving, agreed?"

Nobody disagreed.

"So which harbour has a powerboat or similar moored in it today that didn't have one yesterday?" asked Rusty.

"Good thinking," said Phoenix.

Giles left to get back to the ice-house. The hunt was underway.

In Portishead, police service personnel ran through the

final preparations for the big day. The Chief Constable briefed the troops.

"We need bodies on the streets early. You have details of where you are to position yourselves. Several of you will be at the station when the Royal Train arrives. When they drive off to Ashton Vale to visit the caravan factory, you will relocate to King Street to watch the crowds gathering there. We are aware of a small but noisy, anti-royal protest group outside the Old Vic theatre when the Royal couple arrives at half-past eleven. The tour will take in the refurbished theatre, which recently reopened after being closed for eighteen months. The Queen will then see a special performance from the Christmas spectacular - Peter Pan. Just after noon, they move on to the M Shed. Thousands of people will line the streets. We have to ensure the event goes off with minimal disruption and congestion. No walkabout is on their schedule, but we can't rule it out. If she decides she wants to trot off, shaking a few hands and passing bunches of flowers to her security guard, that will happen. Those officers at Ashton Vale will have joined your colleagues on the roads around the Old Vic and the M Shed. As always, we rely on you to be vigilant."

DS Phil Hounsell risked a question.

"Sir, do we have any known threats to this visit, apart from the anti-royal protest? Will there be a significant security presence from the other agencies?"

"The protesters cleared their actions with us beforehand, DS Hounsell; we have police protest liaison officers that will walk with them; that should deter any problems from arising. As for the secret services, they don't tell me what they're up to, I'm afraid. But, as usual, the Royal Protection Squad bodyguards will be in evidence; over and above that, any action will depend on any perceived threat from whatever quarter."

"Thank you, Sir," said Phil out loud. Under his breath, he added, "Helpful as always."

DI Zara Wheeler looked at her duties for tomorrow on the other side of the room. First, she was at Ashton Vale for the caravan visit. Then she had to lurk in the side streets by Prince Street. Finally, Zara was to be with a team trying to spot someone who might throw something nasty at Her Majesty's limousine.

A minor supporting role was what she expected after her daring rescue of baby Grace. Her superiors had warned her against standing out from the crowd. They much preferred officers who behaved like those cardboard cut-outs you see in shopping malls that can't afford security guards: full of smiles and never putting a polished boot out of step.

The Chief Constable swept from the room; his acolytes followed at a respectful distance. Everyone who was left checked through their duties for the morning. If you've done one Royal visit, you've done the lot, seemed to be the laid-back mood of the room.

Further along the coast, the car's occupants with the false number plates from the VW Passat stirred from their sleep. It was now early afternoon, and they had tasks to perform.

Mohammed Khawaja took charge. The next task was his speciality.

"Here are our vests; I will prepare one for each of you. I shall place the explosives and detonator on the vest, which you will wrap around your torso. A wire connects the detonator and bomb with a small arming device and trigger. When the time comes, you will detonate the bomb with the trigger in your left-hand pocket. You will keep firing your weapons until the ammunition is gone. Then it is time."

Jamshed raised a hand.

"I am left-handed, brother,"

"Then I shall place your trigger in your right-hand pocket, Jamshed."

"Why have we got so many explosives and only handguns?" asked Hassan.

"It's true we only need a few kilogrammes for our vests," replied Mohammed, still working on completing his tasks, "but we have two distinct types of targets tomorrow. First, attacks with these vests kill four times as many people on average as with other methods. Second, a person wearing a bomb is far more dangerous and difficult to defend against than a timed device left to explode in a busy street. We can make last-minute changes based on our surroundings. Three of us can move to a more crowded place, possibly jump on a bus, or do whatever will cause the largest number of casualties."

"What is our other target?" asked Jamshed.

"When two of the most important people in Britain drive to the M Shed for the final stage of tomorrow's tour, this car will be packed with over fifty kilogrammes of explosives. The explosive will have metal fragments scattered through it. We will trigger it remotely as our first move to create panic. The damage to people and property will be devastating. The car will be parked near the expected route they will take. The carnage caused, if we are fortunate, will kill the Royal party. If not, the security surrounding the Queen will tighten, and they will try to speed her away to safety. Imran and Salma will get as close as they can to the ring of bodies that protect her. They, too, will fire their weapons until they are empty, and then they will detonate their vests."

"It sounds so easy when you tell it, brother," scoffed Jamshed, "but how will Imran and the woman draw close enough?"

"Salma's bomb will differ, my friend; we will conceal it in a false pregnancy stomach. She will be allowed nearer the front so that her baby isn't pinched or crushed in the jostling of the crowded streets. Imran will wear the fat suit he wore in the removals van. He will play the role of the devoted husband and keep pestering the people around him for safe passage for his heavily pregnant wife. Have faith; they will get close enough. The British love fair play; they will make sure older adults, pregnant women, the disabled, and little children get the best view. Tomorrow, they will be the ones in the most danger. The effect on the nation's morale will be huge. We martyrs without borders will become legendary."

Jamshed and Hassan appeared content. Mohammed continued to work steadily and carefully. Imran and Salma stood apart from the rest, hand in hand.

In the late afternoon, Rusty walked along the quayside in Watchet Marina. It hadn't taken long for the cigarette boat to be spotted. Kelly Dexter and Hayden Vincent were on board. They had searched it for clues but had reported nothing so far.

Phoenix stood by the van with a map in his hand. The car was no longer here. Where had they gone next? Were they going to drive straight to Bristol to lay in wait or hide between here and the city until tomorrow? Giles hoped to pick up the car on the M5, but his lads hadn't seen it so far. What other roads might they use?

There were so many questions. They must have

weapons and a form of IED. Had that been in the removal van?

Colin tried to put the pieces together, but his train of thought was interrupted. Giles was in his ear.

"We've just had a slice of luck, Phoenix. One of my lads suggested that if they contacted Tarek Qaadir from the boat, we could have it in the 'chatter' we record as a matter of course. It was tough, but with a few keywords in our filters, I believe we've got it. It was relayed at six forty this morning."

Giles played the message Salma Begum had made to the yacht and the reply she received.

"So, this *Storm Chaser* could have been the pickup point for the weaponry?" said Colin. "That makes sense. They couldn't have risked carrying it from Belgium or even Ireland. Royal Hunt confirms one hundred per cent that the target is Bristol tomorrow. Where is *Storm Chaser* now? Do we know?"

"En route to Padstow. We could discreetly tip off the local police that they may be carrying drugs, I suppose?" suggested Giles.

"Have a word with 'Head' Case and see if he thinks it's worth the effort. Their part in this may be over and done. They're small fry as far as we're concerned."

Colin cleared his head and thought of where they should be and when. They must assume that there were only five cell members: the four original targets plus Salma Begum. Tarek Qaadir was now out of the frame. Colin searched the local area for a spot they might use as their launch point for the attack.

Rusty, Kelly, and Hayden returned from the boat. They had found nothing that suggested the terrorists' final destination. However, Kelly had noticed the distinctive smell of plastic explosives. That was a given, as far as Phoenix was concerned.

"I'd travel to Bristol on the A road, avoiding the motorways," said Colin. "The A39 and A38 will take them as far as Long Ashton. The first visit is near there in the morning. The A370 and then Brunel Way can get them over the River Avon, and then Cumberland Road skirts the waterfront right to the doors of the M Shed. The new mayor is hosting an official reception before the Royal party shoots off to the suburbs. The trip to Kings Street and the theatre is a possible target, but it might be more difficult to access that part of the city. I favour the M Shed: that has the largest concentration of people, either inside the building or lining Prince Street."

Rusty looked at the map that Phoenix held.

"We need to get the four of us into Prince Street and spread out, moving systematically over the bridge to the M Shed; we will aim to identify our targets and cut cut the threat."

"That's the logical approach, Rusty," said Phoenix, "but consider what Kelly said. Plastic explosives could mean suicide vests. Five vests might only contain ten kilos, fifteen at the most. Yes, the smell lingers, but if it was pervasive, as she said, then we could expect there to be a far larger volume brought ashore. That suggests a car bomb, plus the vests."

"So, it's still Prince Street and the bridge over to the M Shed," said Hayden Vincent, "that's around six hundred metres to search between us. Do we have a photograph of Salma Begum? We have the four men's IDs memorised by now."

"I'll ask Giles to get us the latest photograph of her. Without a veil, of course," said Phoenix.

The four agents returned to their vans and headed home to Larcombe. Nothing was happening tonight. There was nothing to be gained from chasing around the Somerset coast between Watchet and Bristol, looking for a car with five passengers in the dark. A night of good sleep and an early drive into Bristol were what the doctor ordered.

In the countryside, the car with five passengers was quiet. Everything had been made ready. They would rise at dawn, pray, and then drive the car into position. Mohammed's preparations were complete. The disguises he had prepared for them to wear tomorrow would put the joyous spectators at their ease. They planned to mingle with the crowds, entertaining them with their colourful costumes and painted faces.

Only the minority who suffered from coulrophobia would shrink away in fear. The real fear would strike the vast majority when the car bomb exploded, and the guns began firing. When the shooting stopped, the clowns would disappear.

Thursday, November 22nd, 2012

An unusually wet day dawned with widespread flooding problems across the West Country. In addition, torrential rain and high winds threatened to cause structural damage to the length and breadth of the country. Nevertheless, the Royal visit was still going ahead; the show must go on.

At Larcombe Manor, the morning meeting began at eight instead of nine. This early start was so agents could move swiftly to counter the terrorist attacks, wherever they occurred and whatever form they took. Erebus was back at the helm, returning from his urgent meeting in London.

Erebus stood at the head of the table. He had read the mission reports so far; little new intelligence had arrived overnight, so he chose his words with care and told them his decision.

"These are, without a doubt, the most dangerous opponents we have faced since Olympus has been in business. I sent my best agents to Wales, and they outwitted us at every turn. I attach no blame. Today's operation will attract a heavy police presence; the RPS bodyguards are highly trained and prepared to give their life for their Queen. Henry Case understands that armed personnel from the security services will be in Bristol, but not in large numbers. I have seconded two more pairs of agents to join the existing team. They are known to you. Your task is this: - find that car and disable any bomb it may contain. That is your number one priority. The shock and awe of a massive explosion and multiple casualties can be immeasurable. Remove that threat, and the five terrorists will be containable even if heavily armed and wearing suicide vests. We must expect that containment will come at a cost. When I gave you your instructions, Phoenix, and Rusty, before you left for Fishguard, I said that the terror squad needed not to leave there. They won that round; we must win the contest. So that they cannot detonate their bombs, confine your shots to the head. They must die at once. No matter if it proves fatal in minutes, a body wound will allow them to get to that detonator. That must not happen. Do I make myself clear?"

"Crystal," replied Phoenix.

The meeting broke up, and everyone left the room.

"Phoenix," called Athena. She ran to him and took him in her arms.

"Come back safely, darling," she whispered. "I love you."

"Don't worry," said Phoenix. "We'll be fine."

As she reluctantly let him go and he followed the others, Phoenix wished he was more confident of things turning out 'fine'. This job had the signs of being a bloodbath.

Rusty had met up with a few familiar faces in the foyer before Phoenix finally left the meeting room. Jack Mould, the sniper who had been invaluable in the Weymouth beach mission, had arrived. Brad, the ex-SAS guy from Birmingham, had come down with his usual crew.

Phoenix was pleased to see the two explosives experts who had been with them at the Westfield Stratford City shopping centre earlier in the year.

"Hello, lads," said Rusty. "Trust you to pick a cushy number."

"Sounds as if you needed a helping hand," said Brad grabbing his friend's hand. "We're only too happy to get you out of a tight corner."

"There are tight corners, and then there's this," said Phoenix, welcoming Brad. He knew that these were great guys to have with them. Brad had turned up trumps in Milton Keynes, Oxford Circus, and the Olympics Park. With eight agents on the ground, they had a better chance of success. Planning and coordination were the keys.

"I suggest we get over to the ice-house and visit the armoury; we can ensure we have everything we need today and then drop in upstairs to see Henry and Giles. They can give us a heads-up on the latest intelligence. You never know; something may have landed on their desks in the last hour. We can study our plans in the operations room. Let's go."

Phoenix led his team out of the main building and across the manicured lawns to the ice-house. They travelled two floors in the lift for a quick visit with Bazza and Thommo. Extra ammunition, comms equipment for the newcomers, silencers, various bomb disposal paraphernalia and street maps of the centre of Bristol were collected.

"Bring it back safe and sound mind, boys and girls," joked Bazza Longdon.

Humour was in short supply this morning. The mission threatened to be tough; no one was under any illusions.

They took the lift to the control centre. Colin never ceased to be amazed at the volume and complexity of the technical wizardry available to the Olympus intelligence gatherers. They ran through their plan of action, collected several intercepted messages from Giles, and, happy with what they had put together; they left the ice-house.

They ran to the two vans still parked by the stable block and got on board. Kelly and Rusty drove. They exited Larcombe Manor driveway at nine thirteen and headed for Bristol.

DI Zara Wheeler was already in Ashton Vale. Her day had started early, too — a trip to Portishead in the driving rain before dawn, followed by another briefing and pep talk. Then transport to the caravan factory.

By nine o'clock, ninety minutes before the Royal party was due, she had rallied her troops and positioned them in the most strategic spots. She had walked the perimeter with her uniformed colleagues, looking for something where it shouldn't be. The crowds, such as they were, had started gathering. It was sodden underfoot, but the rain had moved on to batter someone else further up the country for now.

It looked set to be a typical November day.

Imran Nawaz and the others had woken up at five. They wanted to pray pre-dawn on this day of days; the fajr was to begin at five forty-five. The four men prayed together; Salam Begum kept her distance and prayed alone. The five terrorists knew that dhuhr was at noon today. If everything went to plan, they were going to be too busy.

They drove into Long Ashton and parked in the supermarket car park. It was nine-thirty. They purchased food and bottles of water. It would take them fifteen minutes to drive into the city and park the car in the chosen spot.

They then had to cross Pero's bridge, and a further five-minute walk brought them to an independent food outlet run by men who donated generously to the ISIS cause. They were to change clothes in the upstairs rooms and wait for when the crowds were at their height.

The longer they remained on the streets, the more chance the police or the authorities might become suspicious. So they took every precaution to make the mission a success.

Mohammed Khawaja took over the driving seat, with Salma sitting beside him. The other three men squeezed into the back as they set off into the city. The traffic was heavy as usual but moving fitfully. No one gave their car a second glance. Everyone was either going about their business or thinking of the forthcoming visit.

Mohammed eased the car into Prince Street and then entered Farr's Lane. Traffic cones had been placed in various positions to reduce the number of vehicles near the Old Vic and along the Royal limousine route. The crowd would be kept back by barricades, behind which they could cheer and wave their flags to their heart's content.

In the lane towards Narrow Quay, one lorry was parked

while it was being unloaded. Mohammed checked the restrictions for the Controlled Parking Outer Zone. A spot fifteen metres away on the opposite side of the truck gave him two hours. So that was where he was leaving the car. The digital readout on the car's dashboard read five minutes past ten.

"Did you lock the car?" asked Salma as they walked away with their bags containing their guns, vests, and clothing.

Someone stifled a laugh behind her.

"No, sister, I didn't, although it was not because we won't be coming back for it. If the police sweep the streets before the Royal car drives past the end of the lane, they will discover I have left a surprise for them. It will be their undoing, and we will have to attack earlier than planned. Even so, the damage will still be catastrophic."

When they reached Anchor Road, they soon found the shop they sought. It opened at eleven to catch the lunchtime passing trade. Two members of staff busied themselves inside preparing food. Imran and Salma arrived at the door first. Mohammed and the others hung back and looked in a shop window. They waited for the couple to enter and followed a minute later.

Their friends quickly brought them inside and led them upstairs to the living quarters. They ate the food and drank the tea their hosts brought them. They sat and waited until it was time to change and return to the bridge and their destiny. The clock on the wall read ten-thirty.

The Olympus agents had driven around Queen's Square earlier, and Kelly Dexter had headed for Prince's Wharf. Rusty had parked in the NCP car park on Prince Street at ten minutes past ten.

Rusty, Phoenix, Brad, and one of his explosives experts,

Travis Knight, made up the crew. They split up and patrolled the limousine's route once it left King Street and the Old Vic theatre.

Kelly was on Wapping Road. She found a place to park, and Hayden, Jack and the second explosives guy, Calvin Lyons, went their separate ways, carrying out the same task as the other crew.

Each agent was looking for the car Tarek Qaadir had driven from West Wales to Watchet. They knew now that they had switched the plates. The make and model identified it as a Renault Grand Scenic. It was around seven years old. The plates it now carried had come from a VW Passat registered to a Salma Begum from Kings Lynn, Norfolk.

At the caravan factory, the Royal party had begun their tour. The crowds waved and cheered, the management puffed out their chests, and the caravans gleamed. Zara left Ashton Vale with a handful of her colleagues from Portishead and drove into the city. She was confident that the team they had left behind could cope.

She parked on Wapping Road, and they walked towards Prince Street. Brief conversations with uniformed officers now on the ground and the primary observations of her colleagues gave no sign they were going to experience any problems. As every minute passed, the number of women and children gathering at the barricades grew. Zara looked at her watch. Ten forty.

Phoenix and his three companions made slow but steady progress along Prince Street. Kelly Dexter and her crew followed a similar pattern on the other side of the bridge near the M Shed. The Olympus agents were conscious of the need to keep a low profile. They were a clandestine organisation. Nevertheless, their presence was necessary today, based on their intelligence about Imran Nawaz and the terror squad.

Even so, they couldn't be sure that MI5 and MI6 hadn't stumbled over the same information, despite their usual bumbling inefficiency. The existence of Olympus, other than as a charity, had to be protected. Every step they took was calculated to uncover the car bomb, find the suicide bombers, and stay under the authorities' radar. It was a delicate balance.

Zara turned off Prince Street into Farr's Lane. A small white van had just pulled away from the business premises in front of her. She watched it as it left the lane. She passed three large green commercial waste bins and continued walking towards the only car now left parked in the alley. It looked like a Renault. One of those seven-seaters that were so popular. It didn't appear to be dropping deliveries off anywhere. She looked around for the driver.

She glanced at the windscreen as she reached the front of the car. That was odd; the vehicle appeared to be foreign. There was a blue zone parking disc on the windshield that might be Belgian, yet the number plates were in the usual UK format. Something didn't make sense.

Zara tried the front passenger door; she discovered it open and moved to the Renault's rear. The interior of the car appeared to be empty. She reached for the handle on the boot.

Someone lifted Zara off her feet. Strong arms encircled her, and a voice whispered in her ear.

"Don't touch that, sweetheart; I don't want you to get blown to bits, nor me for that matter."

Zara squirmed and struggled; she couldn't free her arms.

"Let go of me. I'm a police officer. Who the hell do you think you are?"

"Well, officer, the hi-viz jacket and being a nosey parker gave the game away, sweetheart. Who I am isn't important, but I may have just saved your life."

Zara found that the giant who held her had relaxed his hold a little. She turned around enough to look up into his face.

Rusty looked into her fiery eyes. If he let her go, she might kill him. The more he looked at her, though, he didn't want to let her go. Zara looked up at her captor. He had his hat pulled over his ears, and a scarf covered the lower half of his face. It was his eyes that she was unable to resist.

Zara prayed this man-mountain wouldn't set her feet on the floor, at least, not yet, as she needed to compose herself. She knew her knees were so weak she would crumple to the ground and look a complete fool.

"Are you sure there's a bomb?" she asked at last. Rusty nodded.

"Go back to Prince Street, get several traffic cones, and close off the lane. Without panicking the crowds waiting for the Queen, get your people to move the barricades back five to ten metres on either side of this turning," said Rusty. He gently lowered Zara to the floor. "This could be forty to fifty kilos worth of big bang, so we need to disable it as soon as possible."

Into his mouthpiece, he said, "Can you hear me, mate? We need your help, pronto."

"Who were you talking to?" asked Zara. "Are you Special Forces? Why didn't we get informed of the threat?"

"All in good time," said Rusty, smiling at Zara. Her heart melted. This man was who she had been waiting for; she didn't know his name, yet she knew that those lonely nights, crying into a wine glass, were history. She couldn't let her saviour leave without finding out his name.

Travis arrived at Rusty's shoulder. He was surprised to see the rough, tough ex-SAS guy talking to a policewoman; this wasn't the accepted 'under the radar' protocol they usually adopted. He nodded to the two of them and then set to work on the Renault.

Rusty led Zara to the end of the lane.

"Off you go then, miss," he said. "We'll handle things here."

Rusty studied her reaction; she seemed reluctant to leave. Rusty was tongue-tied himself. He was not at his best with women. Close relationships had been sparse with the life Rusty had chosen. He had been with the odd bar girl this policewoman might disapprove of, but since he had been at Larcombe Manor, there had been no one.

Zara walked over towards her colleagues.

In the end, he blurted out, "I'm Rusty."

Zara turned and called back, "I'm Zara Wheeler. Don't worry. It's the same as riding a bike. You never forget."

Rusty blushed from his neck to the top of his red-haired head; Zara realised what he had meant, and she blushed too. They smiled awkwardly at one another. Both implicitly understood things would never be the same for either of them again.

Chapter Eleven

Travis was inside the Renault Scenic when Rusty returned. He had checked the interior and the underside of the vehicle. He found no unwanted wires or attachments to cause problems.

"You can leave this one with me, Rusty," he called out. "Get on with finding the bad guys."

Rusty checked in with Phoenix and Brad. They were further along Prince Street on the opposite side of the road. They reported no signs of the faces they were searching for so far.

"Any news from the others?" asked Rusty.

"Same old story, mate," said Phoenix. "No sign of them."

"What time was the party leaving King Street for this official reception at the M Shed?" asked Brad.

"Noon. But you can never put a stopwatch on these occasions," said Phoenix. "It's not long after eleven now. So if that bomb is on a timer, we know they'll look to break cover a few minutes after it is due to explode to take advantage of the shock."

"If it's a remote detonation," said Brad, "they're close by already. They'll wait until the Royal party cruises along Prince Street. Keep looking. We don't expect them to detonate that bomb this early, do we? There's no point. The buildings and the crowds nearby might be history, but the supposed target would be too far away. They would be whisked off to London sharpish."

"I can hear this chat, you know," said Travis. "I can't rush this job. I'm checking the back seats for wires. If my luck holds, the boot handle will be the only booby-trap."

The minutes passed. With great care, Travis released the catches and brought the back seats forward, exposing the contents of the boot. Phoenix and the others heard a low whistle.

"Impressive," said Travis.

"Size or complexity?" asked Brad.

"We've got over fifty kilos of PE with the extra shrapnel that generally accompanies bombs of this sort. It would do serious damage. The good news is there's no sign of a timing device. Everything I see in front of me indicates they will detonate it by mobile phone. So I'm going to make one final check through everything and then start cutting wires."

"Sorry. I missed that last bit," said Brad. "I had my fingers in my ears."

"Game head on, you two," said Phoenix. "This is serious."

He looked at his watch. It was twenty-five past eleven.

"It looks fine," said Travis, "however, I have a problem."

"Go ahead," replied Phoenix.

"The bomb-maker added a trap to the boot handle. Even without the bomber's mobile call, this explodes when you open the door. From where I'm perched, I can't see whether the bombmaker is sophisticated enough to have rigged it, so if I cut the main contact wires, it explodes with the same mechanism as if I've opened the boot."

"I'm guessing the only way to see the full picture is..." said Rusty.

"Open the bloody boot; you've got it," said Brad.

"On the other hand, if I cut the boot wires first and interrupt his devious little scheme, has he got another surprise hidden away for me?" muttered Travis.

Phoenix pulled a coin from his pocket. Rusty tapped his head.

The coin hung in the air; Phoenix caught it. It was tails.

"Cut the boot wires first, definitely," he said.

"Here goes nothing," said Travis and cut the wires.

A long sigh of relief followed silence.

Travis cut the wires that then immobilised the mobile phone. He pushed the back seats into position until they clicked into place. He hot-wired the car and drove along the lane, turning around at the bottom.

"Where do I go from here, lads?" he asked.

"Turn right and go over the bridge and park up on Wapping Road. We'll take it back to Larcombe Manor and dispose of everything there later. Well done, Travis."

"How come you're so familiar with these car bombs then, Phoenix?" asked Travis. "You were so sure it was the boot first. That gave me the confidence to do it. I was bricking it big-time here. I couldn't be sure."

"I just follow the KISS principle, Travis."

Rusty and Brad just shook their heads and smiled. One down, five to go.

The search for the terrorists continued.

Imran Nawaz and the others prepared to move from the

rooms above the shop. They checked the clock on the wall for the hundredth time. It was eleven forty-five.

"Time to go," Imran said. They walked downstairs and waited to exit the shop. The elderly couple who stood by the counter turned their heads and stared. Three garish clown masks stared back at them. The couple also saw an overweight Muslim man and a heavily pregnant woman.

The terrorists left the shop one by one. The clowns went first and walked towards Pero's Bridge. Each carried a bunch of coloured balloons. Mohammed flicked open his mobile phone. Ten to twelve. He selected a number and made the call. There was no explosion. He rechecked the mobile phone. He dialled again. He tossed the phone into the river. They could still achieve their goal. His bomb must have malfunctioned. Mohammed would do it himself. He would open the boot. He left Hassan and Jamshed as they walked off to Prince's Wharf and into Farr's Lane from the quayside.

The car had gone. It was approaching five to twelve, and the Royal car would leave the Old Vic in minutes. He could mingle with the crowds and pass out balloons to the children. When the vehicle passed by him, he would detonate his vest. He would be victorious, his name legendary.

As Mohammed Khawaja stood gazing at the spot where his beloved bomb had been waiting to cause carnage, he looked up towards Prince Street. A man with a hat pulled over his ears, and a scarf around his face turned towards him. Mohammed pulled his gun from under his outer clothing. He didn't get the gun up into a position to fire.

Rusty's bullet entered Mohammed's brain through the left eye of his clown's mask. He slumped against the wall and slid to the pavement. The balloons rose slowly into the air and floated off towards the quayside.

"Phoenix," said Rusty into his comms mouthpiece, "I need a hand with this clown. Let's get him in a dumpster for now. We can pick him up later. Everyone listen. Clowns! We're looking for clowns with balloons."

Travis parked the Renault on Wapping Road. Jamshed and Hassan had crossed over to Wapping Wharf and approached the crowds gathered by the M Shed. Jamshed looked back to see if he could see Imran and Salma. They were due to be walking up Prince Street towards the oncoming Royal limousine. He could only see balloons floating in the sky. Why hadn't the car bomb exploded by now? It had to be ten to twelve by now.

Hassan didn't see the balloons. He was looking up Wapping Road. The car that had pulled into the side of the road looked familiar. Was it the Renault? Surely it couldn't be? Had the British authorities discovered it and moved it to a place of safety? Was the bomb still armed? He walked across the road. He released his balloons. Hassan was determined to detonate his vest once he reached the car. He must give the others the distraction they needed to complete the successful mission they craved.

Hassan drew his gun and held it by his side. The driver stepped out of the Renault. Hassan raised his weapon and fired.

The driver fell to the ground. Hassan closed the distance between him and the car; he fired at the man on the ground. It was unnecessary; Travis Knight was already dead.

Hassan moved his hand towards the side of his costume to detonate his bomb. Jack 'Jelly' Mould lay on top of a building, on Canon's Way, on the other side of the river. He was a mere three hundred metres away as the bullet flew. He sent two shots unerringly into the back of Hassan

Ashiq's head. Jack Mould packed away his gear and contacted Kelly Dexter to tell her they had lost an agent. He moved towards Pero's Bridge to rejoin his crew.

Kelly instructed Hayden Vincent to clean up as best he could for now.

"Put Travis in the front of the Renault and the suicide bomber in the back. We'll sort it out once we find the other clowns."

Jamshed Saswar heard the sounds of a car backfiring. Everything was confused by the din of the crowds surrounding him. He looked up and saw balloons high in the sky. What was happening? Children tugged at his costume, asking him for a balloon. He thrust the lot into the hands of a young boy and ran towards the M Shed.

Jamshed fumbled for his gun with his left hand. Bristol police officers on duty outside the M Shed museum spotted him. Someone shouted a warning. Two young officers ran towards him. They tackled him, and he hit the ground slowly. He was winded.

Brad's second explosives expert knew that staying in covert mode would not hack it in this situation. So as Jamshed Saswar struggled with his assailants, Calvin Lyons ran to help. He stamped a booted foot on Jamshed's right wrist.

"Cheers, mate, but we've got this," said one of the policemen.

"He's got a detonator in his right-hand pocket for the suicide vest he's wearing under that costume," said Calvin. "He carried his balloons in that hand. My guess is he's left-handed. That gun you've just wrestled from him was in his left hand, yes?"

The two policemen nodded and, chalk-faced, looked up at Calvin Smith.

"Shit," they said in harmony. "What are you, RPS?"

"Near enough," said Calvin, who disabled the detonator and watched the colour return to their faces. He walked behind them as Jamshed was securely handcuffed and taken away to a waiting police van.

The police officers handed their prisoners to their colleagues and returned to get a statement from the man who rushed to help. He was gone, nowhere to be seen. Calvin Lyons had slipped away into the crowds and found Kelly and Hayden. They had moved back across the bridge into Prince Street. There were no more clowns on this side of the bridge. What happened to the rest of the squad?

Phoenix and Kelly counted the cost of the mission so far.

"We've accounted for Mohammed Khawaja," Phoenix reported.

"Hassan Ashiq is dead; Jamshed Saswar has been taken into custody by the police," added Kelly. "I'm sorry, Brad, but Travis Knight didn't make it. Ashiq shot him just after he had parked the Renault."

"Thanks, Kelly," said Brad. "He saved hundreds of dead and wounded when he dismantled the car bomb. He can be proud. We need to find the other two and finish the job. We owe him that."

The remaining seven Olympus agents spread out on both sides of the street, searching the crowds for balloons and people in clown costumes. The police had spread the news of Jamshed's arrest at the M Shed to their colleagues and the royal bodyguards with the Royal party.

The limousine had left the Old Vic and headed along Prince Street towards the scheduled official reception. An immediate decision was necessary. Was this man operating alone? Was he part of a cell? Although the authorities always planned an exit strategy for this, they prayed it never became necessary.

The Royal car glided through the cheering, flag-waving crowds of happy, smiling faces. Any threat of danger to the occupants seemed impossible. The driver received a brief message. He turned sharp left into Queen Square and headed for Cabot Circus; he had been joined by an escort of police cars that accompanied him at speed via the M32 and onto the M4.

The Royal couple was tucked up in the Palace by half-past two, shaken but not stirred. They had horse racing from Kempton and Market Rasen to enjoy on television. Missing lunch with the great and the good was disappointing. One had to hope there would be other days.

DI Zara Wheeler and her colleagues awaited instructions. The crowds had to learn the reason for the Queen's sharp exit without causing panic. The situation needed a cool head and a steady hand. While the authorities searched for the right person for the job, the two remaining terrorists, Imran Nawaz and Salma Begum, moved closer to the limousine.

They panicked when it disappeared without warning into a turning twenty metres in front of them.

"Why did they turn off the route they were supposed to follow?" asked Salma.

"I've no idea Salma; something has gone wrong. Look, that's the lane where we parked the car. Stop here as if you are resting. I will look to see what happened to the car. These traffic cones weren't here earlier."

His 'pregnant wife' paused as if to rest. Her 'overweight husband' in his fat suit glanced towards the bay where they had parked the Renault. There was nothing there. Imran knew that their carefully laid plans were unravelling. Had the others been taken too?

"Salma," he said, "our car has gone; our primary target has driven off to safety. Nevertheless, we must hope our brothers still await the sign to begin their attack. We must give them that sign. Our sacrifice must not be in vain."

"What do you propose, Imran?" she asked, gripping his arm.

Imran looked at her. He spotted people moving on the other side of the street just over her shoulder. The spectators stood and waited patiently to discover why the limousine had changed direction; these people searched the crowds methodically. They had to be from the British secret service.

Imran turned and dragged Salma back into Farr's Lane.

"Back to the bridge; we will leave our mark on this city."

Phoenix spotted the sudden movement on the other side of Prince Street.

"Gotcha!" he shouted, "the suspects are in Farr's Lane running towards the quay. Cut them off before they reach the bridge. I urge extreme caution; they will explode their vests in any crowded spot they find. The others were armed; we must expect that both were carrying weapons. Whatever happens, we must prevent a 'human shield' or hostage situation. If we get a headshot at BOTH targets, we take it straight away. These side streets are going to be getting more crowded by the minute. People will soon realise there's nothing left to see and disperse."

Kelly and her crew had got nearer the quayside.

"There are no clowns here, Phoenix; are you sure it was them?"

"You're looking for a large husband and a heavily pregnant wife. Look closely at their faces. That's Imran Nawaz and Salma Begum. When I saw the removal van driver at the ferry terminal in Fishguard, I dismissed him as being just that, a fat trucker. I've seen that trucker leaving Prince Street and ducking into Farr's Lane."

"We've split up, Phoenix," said Jack Mould. "Calvin and I are on the other side of the footbridge. Kelly and Hayden are near the Farr's Lane exit."

"Excellent," said Phoenix. "They're trapped in Farr's Lane. Brad and Rusty will follow me in there."

"Understood," said Brad.

"Rusty, are you receiving me?"

"Loud and clear, Phoenix; I'll see if I can catch that copper I chatted to earlier. If the police have megaphones available, we can stop the numbers near that end of the lane growing and empty the footbridge."

"It's time for damage limitations, Rusty," said Phoenix. "These two will empty their weapons before detonating their vests if they have time and plenty of targets. We need to leave them with no options. Isolate them so they kill themselves and the absolute minimum number of members of the public. Just make sure she uses her head when she gives any message."

Rusty searched the street for Zara Wheeler. He saw several police officers walking along the road, watching the crowds. There she was, and he ran over to her.

"Zara, can you warn these spectators to avoid the quayside and Pero's Bridge for the next ten minutes at least? Tell them it's temporarily closed because of congestion."

Zara blushed and pushed her glasses up her nose. Her colleagues must wonder who this guy was, running up and issuing orders. She turned to a uniformed sergeant.

"Did you hear that? Get that message out at once."

The sergeant ran back to the nearest vehicle and grabbed a loud hailer.

As Phoenix and Brad made their way up Farr's Lane, they heard the message repeated twice. Rusty ran up behind them.

"Fat guy and a woman; up there, on the bridge," he shouted. "They're on the bridge now."

Imran and Salma had managed to evade Kelly Dexter and Hayden Vincent in the clamour of people. Jack and Calvin were on the far side, preventing people from walking onto the bridge and encouraging others still on the footbridge to run towards them. They had their weapons in plain sight.

When Phoenix, Brad, and Rusty joined Kelly and Hayden on the quayside, Imran Nawaz and Salma Begum were the only people on the walkway. They stood on the central section of the so-called Horned Bridge.

They clung together. Imran looked into Salma's eyes. Her love for him shone back.

Phoenix told everyone to hit the deck and cover their ears.

"It is time," Imran said.

"Fi amanillah," replied Salma.

They pressed their detonators simultaneously.

Chapter Twelve

The blast was tremendous; the bridge's central span suffered severe damage. Its horns were now a twisted and tangled lump of metal. Phoenix raised his head. His ears were still ringing, or were they alarms in the buildings surrounding him?

There were several casualties on either side of the bridge. The vests contained metal fragments travelling at sixteen hundred feet per second. So, of course, there would be casualties. The blessing was that things would have been ten times worse if they hadn't reduced the numbers in the vicinity dramatically.

Phoenix decided they had to withdraw, to leave the official authorities to manage the aftermath. There was nothing left for them here. Their mission was complete.

"Time to go," he said. "Kelly, you pick up Jack and Calvin. Guys, you must take a ten-minute hike along Anchor Road and Hotwell Road. I'll contact Larcombe to arrange a clean-up crew for the bodies in both the dumpster in the lane and the car on Wapping Road. We can't be dealing with that now."

The Olympus agents slipped away. Rusty drove Phoenix and Brad back to Larcombe Manor. Kelly Dexter arrived around thirty minutes later with her crew intact. Calvin Lyons came straight over to the stable block to find Brad.

They hugged one another; there were no words. Travis had been a good friend.

Rusty set off towards the ice-house.

"Where are you off to, mate?" asked Phoenix.

"I want to check the latest news on casualties," replied Rusty.

"She got to you, that young copper, didn't she?" said Phoenix. "When you collared her in the street, I nearly had kittens. That was Zara Wheeler, the DI who came here checking out the Charity Commissioners beef. She is one dangerous cookie."

Rusty's face reddened.

"No, I was just concerned that those two beggars didn't kill anyone except themselves."

"Wait for us then; we need to return as much of the kit we took from stores we brought back with us. We have to take the lift below before getting cleaned up and having a bite to eat. No doubt Erebus wants a word too. But you're right. We should check if Giles knows what damage those two caused on their way to paradise."

The trip below from the ice-house left them with a more sombre demeanour when they returned to the surface. The ordinarily cheerful Bazza and Thommo were gutted that Travis Knight had died. The agents checked in their kit and moved up to visit Giles and Henry Case in the control centre.

"First," said Henry, "let me say how sorry we were to

learn of Travis's loss. But, overall, the positives outweigh the negatives. Four of the terrorists are dead; the local police have arrested one. The car bomb that Travis put out of action would have destroyed half the nearby buildings. The loss of life could have been at least a hundred with three times as many seriously injured."

"What fall-out did we suffer from the IEDs on the bridge?" Rusty was concerned, and it showed.

"Numbers are still unconfirmed," said Giles, "but we believe it to be six dead, around forty injured, seven of those seriously. The vast majority came from commercial properties along the quayside. There wasn't time to give any warning to evacuate. Your message asking people to keep away from Pero's Bridge saved dozens, Rusty."

"Erebus is keen to talk with you before you get stuck into something else, Phoenix," said Henry Case. "He's called a full meeting for us at six tonight. He wants to see you before that."

Colin nodded. He had a good idea of what that concerned. He hoped to see Athena before he talked with Erebus. Days such as today made you realise just how lucky you are if you have someone to come home to after the job they had just suffered.

Athena waited for Phoenix in the foyer.

"Darling, you're safe; thank God," she said.

"It wasn't a picnic," replied Colin. "I'm glad I saw you before I met the old man."

"I'll be there too; it's just the three of us," Athena said.

Erebus came downstairs from his apartments, and they followed him into the lounge. He invited them to sit in the chairs on either side of the elegant fireplace. He brought them each a drink and stood in front of the fire with a large gin and tonic.

"I don't suppose that this will come as a great shock. I told our friends in London that I wish to retire at the end of the year. My health is still reasonable for a seventy-two-year-old man, but I find that this old house contains too many memories since Elizabeth passed. I shall fly out to Ibiza as soon as the handover is complete. That is where Elizabeth and I honeymooned, as you are aware, so naturally, I will see out my days there. I have employed an ex-Royal Navy man, Gavin, to sail my yacht to a mooring in the Santa Eulalia del Rio marina. I hope to revisit places Elizabeth and I fell in love with all those years ago and sail around the islands. The affairs of the Olympus Project here at Larcombe Manor are in your capable hands."

Athena rose from her chair and kissed the old gentleman on his cheek.

"Thank you, my dear; I shall miss the cut and thrust of our job, but the time has come for younger hands to hold the reins. Phoenix, I know that today was difficult. Losing team members is part of the job, I'm afraid. Every time someone doesn't make it back, I wonder whether I should have sent them or whether I could have done something to prevent their death. Command responsibilities are often heavy; I hope you are ready to accept them?"

Phoenix nodded.

"Yes, I'm ready; we're a team, Athena and me. Together we will ensure that Olympus maintains the high level of integrity you installed in it when you began this enterprise."

"I'm sure you will, dear boy," said the old gentleman. "We will tell the others at six this evening. Our priority will be to debrief today's direct action and get the latest updates from Giles, but then it's on to my piece of news. After they have left us, perhaps the two of you will join me for dinner in my apartment. As soon as our friends in London learn that you have accepted the challenge, you both need to be at your first meeting. I want to go into the details of that when we dine tonight. It isn't fair to throw you in at the deep end."

They discussed how the mission had gone, and when they finished their drinks, Erebus returned upstairs.

Phoenix went back to his quarters and showered. He slept for an hour before being woken by his watch alarm at five-thirty. He changed into fresh clothes, and when Rusty knocked on his door, he joined his friend to walk over to the main building.

Erebus had arranged for the alteration of the layout of the meeting room. The traditional seating pattern, since Colin had arrived, was no more. Instead, two new chairs stood at the head of the table on either side of the one Erebus had always occupied. The Three Amigos were seated on the window side of the room while Rusty, Giles, and Henry Case sat opposite them. The remaining minor attendees could sit where they chose further up the large table.

Before everyone had arrived, it was clear what the announcement was going to be. Thanatos, Alastor, and Minos knew, too, that the layout suggested that their status in the organisation wasn't under threat. Erebus had always favoured Athena as his successor. Phoenix was relatively new, but his reputation was without blemish. He got things done. As for the three men who sat opposite them, they were vital team members. The Three Amigos realised that together, their eight-strong team was a match for anyone.

Erebus came into the room at six o'clock on the dot. Athena and Phoenix took their places beside him.

"Today's direct action in Bristol was a qualified success. The Royal party escaped unharmed. This terrorist cell was hell-bent on striking the heart of our community. They planned hundreds of deaths of ordinary citizens celebrating the Diamond Jubilee of our monarch. They hoped to kill her and her husband too. The five terrorists wore suicide vests designed to wreak terrible havoc wherever they chose to detonate them. Phoenix and his crews prevented the worst-case scenario. Bristol suffered several deaths, injuries, and damage to structures and properties. We lost a valued comrade, but this is what we do. We protect this country against its enemies."

Erebus paused, and then he continued,

"The time has come for me to stand aside for younger blood. Athena will be my successor. Phoenix will be her right-hand man. The six men you see at the top of the table are now the senior management team. They will carry on the work Olympus has been undertaking. However, there will be a change of focus; we will become more proactive. We will increase our cyber-intelligence wing as this will undoubtedly be where our greatest threats will originate in the next five years. I leave you in capable hands, but mark my words, dangerous times lie ahead, and you will need to be extra strong and vigilant. This nation doesn't appreciate it yet, but Olympus is the only organisation capable of standing up to the forces of evil flooding onto our shores."

With that final speech, Erebus stood aside, and Athena became the head of Olympus at Larcombe Manor. Erebus kept his promise. After the meeting broke up, he took them to the lounge again. He told them a few details of the upper echelons of the organisation.

"Remember when you first arrived here, Phoenix, literally wet behind the ears?"

The three smiled at the memory.

"I had placed an advert in The Times personal column

in 2006 seeking help, looking for anyone eager to prevent Britain from going to hell in a handcart. I found a handful of like-minded people with the intelligence, the will, and the necessary access to extra funds to help bring my ideas to fruition. Our friends have chosen to stay as silent partners, and soon you will meet them when you attend your first meeting. You must take their true identities to your graves. Do you understand?"

Athena and Phoenix nodded in agreement. They glanced at one another from one side of the fireplace to the other. Just who were these people?

"When you attend the meetings, they will be addressed by their given names. Here at Larcombe, you know me as Erebus. In London, you will meet Zeus, the king of the Gods. By that grand title, you will gather he is the real head of the Olympus Project. Hera, Poseidon, Demeter, Apollo, and more will attend. You will recognise several of these people; they are well-known faces with massive funds available. We could not function without them. You must never refer to them by their real name."

"A few of your late nights in London over the past months - were because these people are still somewhat unsure of me," said Phoenix. "Is that correct?"

"Somewhat," Erebus agreed, "but the facts speak for themselves. A rough diamond can expose a jewel of unparalleled beauty."

Athena smiled, "Good luck with that."

"You're not seeing me from my best side," said Phoenix.

"I convinced them that the two of you were the 'real deal, as I believe they say in modern parlance."

They dined and then talked late into the night. Athena and Phoenix longed to steal away for a night together, but they both recognised that the time was short. The old gentleman was soon leaving. But, before he sailed into the sunset, they needed to learn as much as possible.

Colin Bailey slept in late the following day. When he finally got up, showered and dressed, he popped next door to see what Rusty was doing. He wasn't there.

"Anyone seen Rusty?" he asked at any of the rooms along the corridor where agents were in residence. Nobody had seen him today. Colin decided it was time to hit the gym and then go for a long swim to take the stresses and strains of the past week out of his system. He had lunch with Athena in the canteen, and they spent the rest of Friday afternoon in bed. Later that evening, Athena decided whether to return to her apartment or stay the night; they heard someone next door.

"Rusty, is that you, mate?" called Colin.

Athena thumped him and ran to the bathroom to get dressed.

"Sorry, never gave it a thought," said Colin.

Rusty tapped on the door and poked his head into the room.

"Okay, to come inside, Phoenix?"

"No worries; where did you disappear today?"

"I went over to Portishead to see Zara."

Athena flushed the loo and came back into the room. She casually sat on the end of the bed.

"Sorry. Didn't realise you had company," said Rusty. "I'd better go."

"Don't worry," said Athena. "We both need to hear this..."

"Look, mate," Colin broke in. "You don't know everything I did before I appeared here at Larcombe. You may have heard a few whispers and worked things out for yourself, but Zara Wheeler and I have a history."

"Whatever happened between you two is none of my business," said Rusty.

"Not that, you idiot," said Colin. "Much of what we do here is unlawful, no matter how righteous it might be. Well, before I arrived at Larcombe, I did unlawful things. A copper called Hounsell was the only one who guessed I was responsible for the deaths of several evil people. So he chased me high and low. He was after me the last couple of months; he had Zara Wheeler in tow. She was the brains of the outfit. I would have been banged up for life if I hadn't gone in the water in Bath. I was fortunate to live to tell the tale. Back in September, while we were up in Cropredy dealing with our rogue clean-up crew, Zara came here asking awkward questions concerning Garry Burns."

Rusty looked perplexed.

"She had the photo we gave her of the guy Boko Haram probably killed. Because I pitched up here just after he went MIA, they used his picture as a guide when they carried out my facial reconstruction. We had vaguely similar facial features, even if he was physically bigger than me. The ICO people who raised their concerns over this place thought it was the bloke that collapsed in a heap in front of them. But you can bet your last Rolo that Zara wasn't convinced. Why were you so keen to see her?"

Rusty took a deep breath.

"I grabbed her when she was going to open the boot on the Renault. She looked up at me and…. You'll think I've lost it, mate. Things like that don't happen to me."

"What are you saying? Love at first sight. Crikey, Rusty, I knew you weren't gay, but I can't remember you ever mentioning a woman."

"When did I ever have the time, mate? I joined up at sixteen to get away from my old man. Soldiering is all I've ever known. Killing people for a living isn't the most attractive occupation for a wife to mention on a coffee morning. Looking for someone to settle down with was always there in the back of my mind. I never took the plunge because I didn't reckon it was fair to a woman, especially in our game, where we could end up the same as Travis Knight one day."

"So, what's changed?"

"You and Athena have shown me it's possible. What you two have has been great. I looked into those fiery eyes glaring up at me and the spirit she showed trying to get away from me. I knew she was the one. Zara is my Athena. I'm even surer after I met her today."

"What did you do?" asked Athena, who could keep silent no longer. "Wander into the police station and ask for her at the front desk? Do you have any idea how risky that could be? Not just for you, but us here at Larcombe and beyond these gates."

"Give me credit, Athena," said Rusty. "I drove over early doors and hung around near the headquarters, trying to decide what to do next. Then, I walked up the road to get a coffee and a newspaper. I thought I'd look less of a stalker if I carried something. As I stood in the queue at the counter, I looked out of the shop window, and there she was, parked on the pavement. She drops in to get a granola bar and a can of fizzy lemon most mornings. It was fate. She had to get off to work, but we met at lunchtime and chatted for an hour in a pub in town."

"What the hell does she think you were doing in Bristol?" asked Colin.

"She thought I was Special Forces or RPS, and I didn't tell her otherwise. I know that she's pissed off with her job. She's had a massive falling out with this Hounsell bloke, and her bosses gently shunted her into a siding. Her career was flying, but she rescued a child in the floods in Somerset in July. She ignored health and safety protocol and put herself and two other officers at risk, so now her career's stalled. That's why she was on crowd control yesterday."

"We never heard that in the summer. I suppose other things occupied our minds," said Athena.

"How are you planning to play this, Rusty?" asked Colin. "Will you keep seeing her in Portishead? Does she live there?"

"She lives in Bath," said Rusty sheepishly. "She's got her own house now."

"It gets better and better, doesn't it!" said Colin sarcastically.

"I want us to be together. Today just sealed it; Zara feels the same way, mate, I'm positive."

Colin lay back on his bed with his hands behind his head. He thought for a minute or two.

"This might be the most stupid thing I've said since I got here, Rusty, but keep working the angle that she's pissed off with her job; and that there's no future in staying with the police service. We'll give it six months. Then, if you're still together and you can persuade her to quit, we'll bring her to Larcombe and introduce her to the real Olympus Project."

"Leave it to me, Phoenix; I'll get her here somehow. I don't want to leave this place."

Epilogue

New Year's Eve, 2012

Erebus held a grand dinner for the senior Olympus members at Larcombe Manor. Christmas had been a boisterous time, with lots of parties. They consumed food and drink in large quantities.

Tonight was a much more sombre affair. It was time for goodbyes. In the early afternoon of the first day of 2013, Erebus was leaving his family home for the last time. Gavin had left two weeks ago to sail the old gentleman's yacht, *Elizabeth*, to the Mediterranean.

William Horatio Hunt OBE was flying out to the island of Ibiza to begin his retirement.

Athena and Phoenix remained with their former leader after the rest of the guests had left.

"I have no regrets," said William. "I have served my country for over half a century. I wish you both every success in the future."

He embraced Athena, whose tears dampened the shoulder of his dinner jacket. He shook Phoenix warmly by the hand.

"Bringing you into the fold was the best day's work I ever did, dear boy."

He asked them to leave him. He wanted to have one last walk around the place before he retired to his apartments.

Erebus never told them he had arranged to slip away after midnight. He was spending the night in a hotel in London before being driven to the airport. William didn't want a fuss.

Zara Wheeler had spent the festive season at home with her parents near Durham. A few days before New Year, she'd made a phone call and then returned to her house in Bath. Rusty had been waiting outside with a large bunch of red roses and a bottle of wine. So far, they hadn't left the house.

Rusty hadn't spoiled the mood by mentioning 'work' yet; that could wait for a while longer. Instead, the past nights had given him every incentive to persuade his new love to throw her lot in with Olympus and convince her to join a winning team.

On the other side of the city, the Hounsell family had enjoyed a typical family Christmas. Mary Trueman had to be visited, of course, in the care home. So they had made a trip up to the Midlands to call in on Phil's parents, where Phil and Erica fell asleep on the sofa while Shaun and Tracey were spoiled rotten.

On New Year's Eve, Erica curled up in her comfy chair

with a glass of mulled wine, watching a film she'd seen several times. Phil was working. He sat in a car, waiting for it to kick off outside one of the city bars. As the country welcomed in 2013, Phil ticked off the days to retirement.

Next in The Phoenix series

vinci-books.com/lap-of-the-gods

Chaos rises on the streets. Shadows gather from within.

The Olympus Project, an undercover organisation intent on fighting injustice, faces its most lethal foe yet—a ruthless Bulgarian gang wreaking havoc across South West England. Phoenix, the force's deadliest operative, races to stop indiscriminate attacks, but conflict within Olympus' leadership turns the mission into a battle on two fronts.

Turn the page for a free preview…

In the Lap of the Gods: Chapter One

Saturday, June 29th, 2013

"This is modern policing, is it?" thought DS Phil Hounsell as he watched two police officers walking through the crowds with giant sunflowers attached to their helmets. Day Three of Glastonbury 2013, and he was visiting the police command centre at Worthy Farm.

The police had been present on the Festival site since 1989; these days, the Festival became a large town in its own right for the few days in June when it occupied this quiet part of Somerset.

As a senior detective in the Avon and Somerset service, Phil was assigned many duties in these austere times. Just his luck; this year, his name came out of the hat for a Worthy weekend.

He would rather endure a few hours' root canal work or a shopping trip with Erica and the children than this duty. Anything other than being at Festival HQ. Despite the well-documented history of mud in the previous years, the weather gods smiled on Worthy Farm this year.

A brief shower last evening did nothing to change the conditions underfoot. Nor had it dampened the spirits of the great crowd of revellers, hell-bent on enjoying what had become one of the highlights of an English summer.

Phil perused the reports from the opening days and glanced too at the events of Saturday so far. Everything was 'par for the course'. The expected number of searches at the entrances to uncover items that might be 'used illegally or offensively'. Somewhere in the command centre or back at Portishead, there would be a collection of laser pens, fireworks, questionable knives and sharp instruments. With the penchant of festival-goers for a chemically enhanced glow accompanying the music, you could also guarantee to stumble across a stash of confiscated drugs.

The CCTV coverage was extensive; throughout the weekend, officers monitored those images for public safety, crowd management, and crime prevention. Phil tore his eyes away from the mind-numbing reports and switched back to the screens.

He spotted the two giant sunflowers again. The local lads from the neighbourhood patrol were photographing a couple of scantily clad females. They looked young; the girls did too.

"Nice work if you can get it." thought Phil.

This 'touchy-feely' policing was fine and dandy but jibed with Phil's 'old school' approach. Phil wanted criminals off the streets and banged up, if possible, for a long time. He had frequently expressed those views, and his superiors knew where he stood. But, unfortunately, those superiors also understood precisely where he was going - nowhere.

He felt himself slipping gently into the long grass, perhaps thinking he wouldn't notice. Phil glanced at the young girls as they wandered on from their brief encounter with the Flowerpot Men and felt every one of his forty-seven years.

"Only three more summers," he thought, "and I can get the hell out of this charade. I prefer to wear jeans and a t-shirt to do something useful."

Phil knew they had plain-clothes officers on the ground, plus the uniforms the CCTV images now showed. Their main targets were thieves and drug dealers. So far, it had been quiet. Fingers crossed, it stayed that way. Phil sighed; he was bored to tears. The stuffy atmosphere in the room was causing his eyelids to droop. He needed to get up and stretch his legs before he nodded off to sleep.

He searched for a chaperone. No way would you persuade him to go out there alone. Walking alone around a site populated by well over one hundred thousand people was his idea of hell. A door opened, and a constable poked his head inside.

"I'm on the ice cream run; what can I get you, Sir?"

Phil jumped out of his chair and headed for the door.

"I'll come with you; this sunshine might not last much longer. We are in England, after all."

As they emerged into the sunlit site, close by the farmhouse, Phil checked out his companion, the same age as himself and yet still a constable. That seemed curious.

"Been in long?" he asked.

"Since eight o'clock this morning, Sir."

"No, sorry; I meant been on the job long."

"Eight years, Sir, and a paramedic before that. I joined the RAF straight from school but didn't enjoy it much, so I got out and tried various jobs until I found something I enjoyed. I worked as a traffic warden, a zookeeper, and a security guard out at Cribb's Causeway."

All relatively uniform, thought Phil. He had his answer. If his mother had let him have a dressing-up box as a nipper, he would have got it out of his system by the time he reached sixteen. He might have made something of his life. The further they walked, the bigger the crowd became. It proved difficult to stay together.

"Over here, Sir," called his companion as they neared an ice-cream stall, "what do you prefer?"

Phil made his way back through a sea of people and elected for a choc-ice; not that he particularly liked them, but with its wrapper, he hoped it gave him half a chance of polishing it off without getting his suit plastered.

"Cheers," said Phil as his guide handed over the ice cream, "what's your name, by the way?"

"Wayne, Sir."

"OK, Wayne, how many orders have we to carry back to HQ?"

"Eleven."

"Terrific," Phil could foresee problems.

Wayne had made this trip before; he had a system. Phil spotted the man-bag strapped across Wayne's chest but didn't pass a comment. Phil had met several gay officers during his career and always resisted saying things that might get misconstrued. Wayne fished out plastic vending cup holders from his bag. Each triangle was designed to hold six cups. The resourceful Wayne had modified the openings to accept a cornet and even a lollipop.

"Hey, Presto," said Phil, impressed at the ingenuity.

"E-bay," said Wayne, not getting the reference.

Phil finished his choc-ice before they reached the command

centre. He held the door open for Wayne, and ten grateful people inside soon got chilled relief from the warm conditions. Wayne started to devour his Magnum. He eyed Phil.

"Do you want to carry on having a walk around, Sir?" he said, with a shiny chin.

Phil looked at the constable. He sensed his desperation to get back outside, mingle with the crowds and listen to the music. Well, it was marginally better than being stuck in this place.

"After you, Wayne; you know your way."

As they walked back to the site, Wayne gave Phil a running commentary on what had happened yesterday and what lay in store for the fans today.

"Glastonbury isn't just the music; it's the people too. I arrived early yesterday, and things were grim — the usual long queues for the showers and the toilets. But, by lunchtime, as last night's hangovers had disappeared and today's cider started taking hold, the mood lifted, and you saw a few smiles. Then the music starts, and you see smiles all the way, no matter what the weather's doing."

"How many times have you been here, Wayne?" asked Phil.

"This is my twelfth Festival. I've done three as a copper, three as a paramedic and six as a punter."

"I'm impressed," said Phil, "I'm a virgin. You'll never catch me in a tent; I don't queue for showers or toilets, and I'm not a great music fan. Of course, I enjoy a few songs I hear now and then, but I couldn't tell you who sang them for the life of me."

"You could always go 'glamping' over the far side if you didn't want to rough it with the great unwashed," said Wayne with a laugh.

Phil eased past a swaying teenager who looked as if his

day could only get worse and thought of his wife. Erica would probably enjoy the Festival experience, but it wasn't something he wanted to bring up at the breakfast table. He shuddered as the contents of the teenager's stomach hit the grass behind him.

"No fear. Give me a warm bed, with a shower and a loo five yards away, thanks," said Phil.

Wayne ploughed on, regardless. He adopted his tour guide persona, for which a uniform was available, and pointed out various attractions. Based on the crowds, they negotiated as they passed; they lived up to their name. Wayne interspersed this information with brief reviews of the performances he witnessed. Occasionally, Wayne shouted these observations over people's heads as the two policemen zigzagged their way through the vast site.

"Over there, you've got Arcadia, the giant spider. After midnight, it belches fireballs into the night sky, and they hold a rave. See that marquee? It's where you can queue up to complain that Glasto isn't what it used to be. The place is quiet, though. So who will hang around here when you can have a good time? Dizzee Rascal smashed it yesterday; he did a crazy set. The Arctic Monkeys sounded great, too—lots of lights, smoke and lasers. Bill Wyman played somewhere too, but you can't be in two places at once, can you?"

"Bill Wyman? Wasn't he with the Stones? Now that's a band I have heard before. What happened to them, I wonder?" shouted Phil.

Wayne gave him a sympathetic look.

"You don't have much of a clue about music, do you, Sir? The Stones are the main attraction tonight on the Pyramid Stage. They're still belting it out after fifty years on the road. That's the Pyramid over there. Can you see the big screen? That big voice and a bigger smile belong to Laura Mvula; she's superb."

Phil Hounsell glanced over towards the stage. He couldn't see or hear much at this distance, but she sounded okay. If only there hadn't been so many people around them. He was no longer watching where he was going. The inevitable happened. His shoulder collided with a man moving fast in the opposite direction with his female companion.

"Sorry," said Phil, turning to apologise for his clumsiness.

The man was arm in arm with his attractive partner; they hardly broke stride. The man grunted at Phil but didn't turn around again, and in seconds, the crowds swallowed them.

Phil massaged his shoulder.

"You can't beat meeting the public face-to-face, can you, Sir?" said a grinning Wayne.

"My fault for not watching where I was going," muttered Phil as his shoulder regained feeling.

"A smart couple, I thought. I guess those two come from the same neck of the woods as Mick Jagger and his entourage, enjoying the benefits of a more glamorous outdoor living style. I doubt they put up their tents as I have had to over the years. How the other half lives, eh?"

Phil didn't reply.

"Everything okay, Sir?" asked Wayne. The two men were now side-by-side and back in step.

"The woman is definitely out of the top drawer. But there's something about the bloke. Just seeing how he walked and made his way through the crowd. It was a familiar gait. No doubt I'll remember in time."

"I never recognised them; if they've been on the telly,

I've missed them," said Wayne, slowing as they neared one of the many food stalls.

Phil could smell heaven. He put thoughts of Erica's caustic comments relating to his growing waistline and why his shoulder hurt out of his head.

"A great idea, Wayne; it's rude not to check that these people are providing food to an acceptable standard. We're truly serving the public for the next ten minutes."

As Phil and Wayne chose what was very unhealthy but tasty food from a limited menu, the two festival-goers they had been discussing strode further and further away. For now, they were unaware of their identity.

Annabelle Grace Fox was indeed a lady, as the police officers surmised. She liked her creature comforts. Her companion that sunny afternoon was Colin Bailey. His features were subtly altered by cosmetic surgery on two occasions in the past decade; no way Phil Hounsell would have recognised him even if he had caught his eye as they bumped into one another.

What distinguishes an excellent detective from the run-of-the-mill plodders is the millions of details they have stored away in those tiny grey cells. Despite his loss of enthusiasm for the job he used to love, Phil Hounsell still behaved like a dog with a squeaky Christmas toy. He would search among those grey cells until he remembered who walked that way; and where their paths had crossed. Then, in time, the name would come to him.

Phil and Wayne spent the rest of the afternoon and evening moving across the site, gradually threading their way closer to the main stage. More by Wayne's design than any wish on Phil Hounsell's part to have his ears battered by the sound system. Wayne loved his music.

The crowd noise grew louder and louder as the main

attraction of the day was due to begin. The Stones were to make their long-awaited appearance.

As they took the stage, the Phoenix raised itself and belched fire for the Stones.

That was not a metaphor, nor a reference to the vigilante killer in the same corner of the site with Athena. Instead, it was the sculpture of a vast bird perched on top of the symbolic Pyramid stage. With its enormous moving wings, the Phoenix announced the Festival's return after a two-year absence.

Meanwhile, the human Phoenix and his partner Athena stood in the crowd as the Rolling Stones opened with 'Jumping Jack Flash'. The standout songs for Colin Bailey were 'Paint It Black', 'Gimme Shelter', and the encore 'You Can't Always Get What You Want'. Athena danced with Phoenix for most of the set. Then, suddenly, she saw her and her partner on the big screen as the cameras panned around the crowds between numbers.

Phoenix turned away and shielded his face by moving Athena in front of him.

Phil Hounsell watched the show and listened. He saw the crowd scenes on the screen. Phil prayed the director of those camera shots wouldn't pick on him. Phil didn't need the hassle of his superiors thinking he was out on a 'jolly', enjoying himself when he was supposed to be doing a proper job.

As the set ended and the Festival wound down until the final day, he reflected on what he had seen; a one hundred thousand crowd, the Stones and lots of fireworks.

Phil turned to Wayne. "No doubt it will be three times as many in ten years that swear they came here. Good fireworks, though."

"Did you clock that bloke that pulled his girlfriend in

front of him when the cameras picked him out, Sir?" said Wayne. "That seemed odd."

"What did he look like?" asked Phil, who had to admit the incident never registered.

"I reckon it was that couple from this afternoon," Wayne said.

"I need to remember who he reminded me of," said Phil. "I knew he had something to hide. We'll keep an eye out tomorrow, and if possible, I want to have a word."

On Sunday, the day started slowly again, and the atmosphere and the excitement built and built. Phil was back on duty, and once he checked that everything was shipshape in the control centre, he went to find Wayne.

"Okay, Wayne, anything you can tell me?"

"A baby got delivered during the Stone's set last night; mother and baby are doing well. It was a case of 'Gimme Gas and Air' rather than 'Gimme Shelter'. I understand. Prince Harry also visited the ground last evening, enjoying life as usual. He was mostly on rum & coke."

"Coke from a bottle, I trust?"

"So I heard, Sir," said Wayne with a smile. "Brucie's on this afternoon, so that should be a riot."

Oddly enough, Phil reckoned it might be; you can't buy experience, can you? The day rocked and rolled along without the two policemen catching sight of their person of interest. As night fell and the final act took to the stage, The Phoenix belched fire again to welcome Mumford & Sons. Phil resigned himself to watching them round things off for another year. If they kept to the timetable, it would end; just before midnight.

Phoenix and Athena were still on the site and enjoying a quiet day together. Athena wanted to revisit the Pyramid stage, but Phoenix preferred his clothes cut from a heavier cloth. He endured the afternoon's offerings. Somehow, he persuaded Athena to go off-piste for a while and take in the Smashing Pumpkins, the Heavy from their home city, and they even caught a French band with a highly original name, Phoenix.

They were too lightweight for Colin Bailey. Athena enjoyed them; Colin sulked throughout their set, wishing this Eavis bloke could have booked Judas Priest or Iron Maiden for the main stage. Great memories of nights in the Crown from his youth and on tour with Maiden's Hair in 2010 came rushing back.

While Phil Hounsell and Wayne suffered a bout of indie folk-rock sickness, Athena and Phoenix made plans to pack their things, empty the yurt and drive back to Larcombe Manor. Just after midnight, Phil gave up the ghost and said farewell to Wayne. He drove towards Bath but never closed the gap between him and Athena in her high-end Range Rover.

As Phil put the key in the door just after one in the morning, he made a note to don his thinking cap later for that elusive face.

Erica and the kids were fast asleep. Oh well, with luck, that was his last weekend on Glastonbury duty. So the only thing to do tonight was to get a few hours' sleep before that alarm shattered the silence at seven o'clock.

Monday, July 1st, 2013

Getting out of bed on a Monday morning can be challenging.

On one side of the old Roman city of Bath, Phil Hounsell padded to the bathroom, trying not to disturb his wife, Erica. He glanced towards the two bedrooms where Shaun and Tracey still lay fast asleep. Phil knew from experience that as soon as they heard him get in the shower, they would scramble downstairs to snatch a few minutes watching television before they began the countdown to the school run.

Erica usually awoke by half-past seven; either she heard her husband creeping around, despite his best efforts, or the kids had started arguing over which channel to watch. Once in a blue moon, she didn't stir until the alarm on her mobile phone shattered the relative quiet with a few bars of 'Sweet Child of Mine'.

The routine and order Erica established when she reached the kitchen got them through this rigmarole every weekday morning. As Phil stepped out of the shower and gathered his wits and shaving kit, things downstairs grew calmer by the minute. Erica had awoken. Phil looked in the mirror, lathered his face and started shaving. His mind drifted back over the weekend at Glastonbury and to the day ahead at Portishead.

Phil attempted to recall that French phrase that said the more things change, the more they stay the same, but it wouldn't come to him. He finished up in the bathroom and wandered back to the bedroom to get dressed, ready for work. By the time he reached the kitchen, the first coffee cup and his bowl of cornflakes should be waiting. The tried and trusted routine all over again.

Erica would be wide awake, bright-eyed and bushy-tailed, all set to pack him off to work so she could go to the bathroom herself. Shaun and Tracey were always eager to tell their Dad everything that had happened over the weekend and what they expected of him over the coming days. There were those summer fetes, end-of-year plays and other occasions he was probably due to miss, no doubt, because of the job.

Phil entered the kitchen, and three faces turned to greet him.

"Ha-ha. Cut yourself again, Dad," sniggered Shaun.

"Don't worry, darling," said Erica, "there's another clean shirt ready in the wardrobe."

Phil sipped his coffee and sighed. Then, as he wolfed down his breakfast and carried his mug back upstairs to repair his face and change his shirt, it came to him; 'plus ca change, plus la meme chose.'

Yeah, that was right, he thought as he drained his mug. He picked up the car keys, went downstairs, kissed Erica goodbye and waved at the kids, who had already flopped on the sofa watching the box. He barely noticed the glorious summer's day outside the house as he got into his car and headed for Portishead.

Elsewhere in Bath, Zara Wheeler was also experiencing those same Monday morning blues. Ever since that chance meeting with Rusty on the streets of Bristol during the terrorist attack on the Royal visit last November, her weekends, her whole life, had been transformed.

Gone was the cosy but loveless time spent with Toby Drysdale, her long-time colleague from her days at Manvers Street police station. Gone were the hours spent alone at home with her cats and a bottle of Chardonnay, pining over her boss Phil Hounsell. Rusty had changed that.

Zara was an intelligent young woman. She appreciated that Rusty had secrets. In those first few weeks of their relationship, it had been wonderful discovering things about one another in the bedroom. Zara had no complaints in that department. Rusty was a robust, athletic and capable lover; they spent much of their time together in bed.

Although she wanted to learn so many other things about her partner, Zara understood that Rusty needed to be sure he could trust her before revealing anything he did when they were apart. It was clear he was in the SAS or a special ops unit that targeted terror threats on the UK mainland. That much was clear from his presence in Bristol, where he suddenly appeared to stop her from checking the boot of a suspicious car. Rusty's prompt action saved her life.

The details of which branch of the secret services he was attached to were unimportant; she just wanted to know he would be coming home to her safe and well for years to come.

One Sunday evening in late January, they had curled up on the sofa with a glass of wine.

"It's easy enough to work out why they call you Rusty," said Zara, "but what did your parents name you? Are they still alive?"

"My mother died when I was twenty-five. She had cervical cancer. She and my dad split up five or six years earlier. So I've no idea whether he's dead or alive."

"Really?" she asked, "Aren't you in touch with him?"

Rusty snorted.

"I joined as soon as possible to escape from the bullying bastard. My father treated my mother as a servant, not a wife. He was a regular soldier and demanded everything in his life be regular, too; mealtimes, sex, you get the picture. If not, she got knocked around. I felt guilty leaving her with him, but I need to to get away. If I'd stayed, I'd have killed him. So when she wrote to say she'd escaped and found peace in a women's refuge, I was happy for her. Unfortunately, she never lived long enough to enjoy her freedom. She always used the name she christened me in her letters,

David. That was his name too, which is why I never use it. David Scott. That was me until my first few weeks as a boy soldier. After that, the red hair branded me as Rusty, and that was good enough for me."

Zara had cradled Rusty's head on her shoulder and kissed his closely cropped hair. More small details emerged over the following weeks as he told Zara where he had been in his early time in the army. He mentioned operations he had been involved in and made her laugh at a few of the lighter moments he and his young colleagues shared when they were on leave in far-flung places worldwide.

Eventually, she learned he had applied for the SAS, where his real soldiering began. Of course, he couldn't tell her where he had served or what he had experienced. But he could say he was already an old hand in the first intake of the Special Reconnaissance Regiment in 2005.

"This red hair is often associated with people with a short fuse and a fiery temper Zara. The discipline drummed into me from day one in the army keeps it under control most of the time. But, now and then, someone winds me up so tight I explode — every corner of British society suffered at the hands of the idiots that preach liberalism and appeasement. Even in a proud, action-based organisation like the SAS, some officers should never have had the honour. These officers are weak and spineless. Instead of getting in amongst the bad guys and sorting them out permanently as soon as they arrive on the scene, every step has to be weighed, risk-assessed and rubber-stamped by faceless mandarins before anything is allowed to happen. We were on a mission deep in bandit country, and I headed a team of seven. A sandstorm struck without warning, and two of my lads separated from the group. A young colonel sat thousands of miles away and ordered us to pull out. He was still wet behind the ears and had never seen any real action. He didn't want to risk us being captured by hanging around searching for them. He said they were capable of finding their way home. We never left anyone behind on one of those missions, Zara. When we got back to base and debriefed the confusion, we learned that their bodies were found by the Americans, who had their special forces on the ground there. My two lads survived for a few days in the searing heat but died when their water ran out. I stormed out of the room after I got the news and tracked down the superior officer responsible. He ended up in the hospital with a broken jaw, and they dismissed me from the service. That was back in 2009."

Zara listened in silence to what had been the longest speech she had heard from Rusty.

"I don't blame you for lashing out," she had said. "I joined the police force to make a difference, but we've both suffered from the same disease strangling the fight against terrorism and crime. My career has been 'on hold' since I rescued little Grace from the floodwaters last year. I can't face being side-lined into crowd control and pointless PR exercises until I collect my pension."

Rusty had shut down after that for a while. Zara bided her time before she tried to get him to open up about what he had been doing for the past three years. Then, over the Spring Bank Holiday weekend, they travelled north to her parent's home and spent hours walking in the countryside near her hometown of Durham.

"Can you tell me what you do now, Rusty?" she asked as they stood on a hillside looking across a wooded valley. The sun was gathering strength and warmth so that gradually everything around them woke up after a cold and lengthy winter prolonged by the coldest spring in fifty years.

Rusty had gathered his coat about him and thrust his hands deeper into his pockets. He had known that this day would come. Rusty drip-fed snippets of information to Zara over the months, and time was running out. He had promised Phoenix that he would resolve the situation within six months. Rusty had to decide whether now was the right moment. He resolved to plough ahead.

"I work for someone in the private sector. The people approached me a few months after the SAS showed me the door. This outfit operates how our security services should, but you need to understand that what I tell you goes no further. It will change your life forever. You know how I feel about you. I want us to share the rest of our lives. Bringing you into the fold alongside my colleagues and superiors is the only way for that to happen. Will you trust me?"

Zara stood on tiptoe and kissed him.

"If it means we're together, then I'll go anywhere, Rusty. I need you to promise that you and whoever you work for aren't involved in any criminal activity."

Rusty smiled.

"A typical copper to the last," he said "start with the difficult question. I can guarantee that villains and terrorists are the opposite of my employers. Criminals work outside the law. We work in a somewhat grey area. Maybe that goes on in an area above the law. But we prefer to consider that the law has become so lax of late that we are merely operating at its rightful level."

Zara and Rusty had continued their afternoon walk and spoke nothing more on the matter for a few days. Then, finally, the couple returned to Bath and were at her home, preparing to return to work the following day. Rusty was in the shower. The door opened, and a naked Zara joined him.

"To what do I owe this pleasant surprise?" he asked.

"I've made my decision," said Zara, wrapping her arms around him. "I'll hand in my resignation, which will set me free from these mundane non-jobs they keep assigning me. Then, in four weeks, I'm all yours."

Rusty grinned.

"I think you can already tell that waiting four weeks won't be an option for that young lady."

Minutes later, they were under the duvet, and any thoughts of resignation forms were forgotten until the morning. After an early breakfast, Zara drove into the Police HQ at Portishead and started the ball rolling. She chatted to Toby Drysdale to let him know her decision. She had been nervous about Phil Hounsell finding out; she wasn't sure of his reaction. Toby had plenty of questions, and Zara knew this would be a familiar pattern over the coming weeks.

"Why on earth are you leaving, Zara? Where will you go? Has someone been head-hunting you already?" Toby asked, concerned about his friend leaving.

Zara had thought long and hard about answering these questions; she had to be firm in her decision to leave yet guarded about where she was working next. She needed to be vague on that front but not so ambiguous that it might draw attention to the possible hidden nature of her future job. A delicate balance, but Zara was confident she could cope.

"I have to leave, Toby," she had replied "ever since we did the right thing and pulled baby Grace from that car, They've shunted me into a corner. My ambitions for further promotions and a dream of becoming a Chief Constable one day ended. There's no way they'll consider me for any significant advancement in the future. I'm not sure where

I'll go eventually; I'll take time to review my options. I reckon I deserve a short holiday."

Zara had asked Toby not to spread her news around the building. She knew the cat would be out of the bag soon enough, but every day of the twenty-eight, it remained a secret was a bonus. Zara had downloaded a copy of Form 232 and provided the required written notice of her intention to leave the organisation. So far, she hadn't handed it to her Department Head.

Thank goodness that wasn't Phil Hounsell these days. Since that night in Bristol and the subsequent fall-out, they spent less time increasingly in contact at work.

After filling in the form, she then took a few days wondering about Toby's second question. Where *would* she go? What would they ask of her? Rusty must be based somewhere near Bath or Bristol, that much she realised. Otherwise, he wouldn't always be able to find his way to her house or Portishead without prior warning.

The same as her, he wasn't doing a nine-to-five job. Now and then, he told her he'd be 'off the grid' for a few days. He never said where. Zara never asked.

In a month, they were due to be living and working together. As Zara had driven home after work that Friday, she had waited for Rusty to drop by so that she could ask him. That evening, the ground fell from under her feet, and she wondered what she was getting involved in.

The pair had shared a meal and a bottle of wine, and then as they relaxed listening to music, she plucked up the courage to pose a few questions.

"Can I ask for a few details, Rusty?" she began.

"What do you need to know, sweetheart?" Rusty had replied.

"Where will I be working? Will I be able to continue to

live here, or do I need to move? What salary can I expect to receive? What type of work will they expect me to carry out?

"Woah, steady Zara; let's take these one at a time, shall we? Firstly, you already know the place where we'll be working. We'll live together, but if you want to keep this place, rent it out or sell it, that's up to you. Based on what I know of the salary structure in the organisation, I reckon you will receive something around twenty per cent above the figure you earn now. As for the work, I recommended you for attachment to the intelligence section. The team there needs strengthening; being a woman will help. We're thin on the ground in that area at Olympus. As well as gathering intelligence, we'll increasingly need a sharp mind like yours to develop strategies to fight cybercrime and cyberterrorism. Do you think that could keep you gainfully occupied while I'm off hunting down the villains you identify for me?"

A dim light went on in the corner of Zara's brain as Rusty was speaking. Then, when he had finished, she jumped up from the sofa.

"It's Larcombe Manor, isn't it?" she squealed. "I bloody knew that place was suspicious. That shower gave me the run around when I was there last September chasing up that ICO enquiry. So they did have something to hide with that bloke Garry Burns."

Rusty held his breath; had that been one step too far, too soon?

In the Lap of the Gods: Chapter Two

Colin Bailey and his partner Annabelle Fox slept late at Larcombe Manor that same Monday morning after the Glastonbury glamping weekend. But, despite the relative luxury of their festival accommodation, nothing compared to the sumptuous surroundings of home.

Since Erebus vacated his suite of apartments and sailed away to a well-earned retirement in Ibiza, Athena and Phoenix had remodelled his rooms to suit their taste. But, in deference to the older man's history with the Georgian house and the memory of his beloved wife Elizabeth and daughter Helen, Athena kept a selection of photographs and ornaments on a table next to one of the large windows that overlooked the rolling lawns leading to the woods on the perimeter of the estate.

Phoenix had been sad to leave his old quarters in the stable block even though compensations were full-time with his partner. He missed those hours alone with the thoughts he always valued so highly as a young man; the extra leadership responsibilities within the Olympus organisation were time-consuming. He yearned to get back to direct action. He longed to have a chance for a little 'street cleaning' — the good old days.

There was no going back, though. As soon as Phoenix had been dragged away from his hidey-hole in the New Year, Athena arranged to extend Rusty's quarters next door in readiness for the planned new arrival. If Zara Wheeler decided to join the organisation, it was only right they should be together. Athena knew too that keeping Phoenix in the Manor House, a comfortable distance from the stable block and the operations room beneath the ice-house, where Zara would be working, was her absolute priority.

It wasn't merely a selfish wish; she was head of the Olympus Project at Larcombe Manor. She shared a post with Phoenix, and she was eager to have her partner at her side when they reported to the organisation's upper echelons in London. The nuts and bolts of the operation Phoenix always got involved in must be left to more junior staff. Athena understood, too, that Garry Burns and Colin Bailey looked alarmingly alike. Phoenix and Zara Wheeler had a shared history and needed to be kept apart for as long as possible. Perhaps in the fullness of time, her assimilation into the Olympus family would be such that they could reveal his true identity.

As Annabelle Fox and Colin Bailey slept undisturbed by the Monday morning blues that troubled many others on the other side of Bath, DS Phil Hounsell drove to Portishead with bits of tissue on his chin. All the fun of the Festival was behind him, and another meaningless working week beckoned. As his car idled in the building traffic, he dreamt of lazy retirement days with nothing more taxing than deciding which shorts to wear or which golden beach to visit and sunbathe.

Meanwhile, Zara Wheeler sat in her car a few hundred yards behind him, praying that now that the Divisional Commander had signed off on her resignation, the remaining items on her exit checklist would be dealt with quickly.

Zara still promised herself that short holiday. The shock of discovering that Larcombe Manor was her new home continued to make her brain hurt. Her decision to leave the police service, though, remained rock solid.

God, how she hated that word. Service my eye. What was wrong with a police *force* that knew when to apply a firm hand where needed? But, as the days ticked remorselessly on towards her final Friday at Portishead, Zara was only too happy to quit that tiresome pussy-footing around behind her. She wanted to see real progress in fighting crime and ridding the country of all the evil that strangled it. Working alongside Rusty might well give her that opportunity.

Zara had eventually calmed down after her initial outburst that Sunday evening when Rusty dropped the bombshell about the Olympus Project. He filled in most of the blanks to appease her and get her to take the time to think before giving him her final decision.

Rusty explained how a wealthy group of similar-minded patriots joined forces around 2008 because the nation they loved was going to the dogs. These men and women came up with the idea of masking the Project's true nature with a charitable organisation treating veterans with PTSD. Larcombe was their HQ in the UK, and it housed many more on its grounds that the Charity Commissioners or visiting local police personnel never got to see.

Rusty had kept quite a few details back. She understood that. If her final decision was to reject a move to Larcombe, she needed to pursue a different career path. However, rusty assured her that no matter how the coin fell, their relationship would be unaffected; it would carry on as it had done for the past six months, with them getting together whenever their busy schedules permitted.

The only difference was that Zara now knew the secret behind the Olympus Project. That fact was the most significant cause of the questions banging around in her brain and leaving her sleepless nights. Would Rusty keep her close because he loved her, or did he need to guard against her passing that red-hot information to her soon-to-be former colleagues? She briefly wondered if she was in any danger.

Zara had dismissed that thought from her mind without question. She loved Rusty unconditionally and knew that feeling was mutual. Rusty would make it work somehow; of that, Zara had no doubt. The holiday she promised herself gave her enough time to sort those Olympus issues out in her head. But, for now, she needed to deal with the last few tasks on that exit checklist and, if possible, avoid Phil Hounsell before making her escape from the job she had come to detest.

Zara spotted Phil's car in the car park. He had arrived on the site already. She parked far enough away to be comfortable that they didn't cross paths later in the day when heading home. Then she made her way inside the building to her office. There were exit interviews on the cards this week with superiors to endure. Also, she needed to finalise her details with the finance department and then arrange to return the paraphernalia she'd acquired over the years. Her phone, laptop, ID access badges, parking permits, uniform, warrant card, pocketbook and other odds and ends must be handed over.

Zara knew full well where to lay her hands on ninety-nine per cent of it already, but a couple of items might need tracking down. She had few belongings to gather and put in a cardboard box. Anything relating to the cases Zara currently worked on, which these days were few, could be transferred to whoever took them on after her departure. She peered around her office over the top of her glasses. Zara reckoned it would be easier to walk away from all this than she'd thought.

Of course, she would miss a few people at Portishead. Toby Drysdale, for one, had been friends for ages, lovers for a brief period. She gazed across at Angela Chambers had once sat and realised how much she still missed her murdered colleague. She searched through her desk, wondering if a memento remained somewhere of Angela that she might take back home, wherever that might be so that she could keep her memory alive. But, unfortunately, there didn't appear to be anything.

Her hand rested on a folder at the bottom of a drawer. Zara knew at once what it contained. That photograph of Garry Burns. She opened the file and inspected the picture for the umpteenth time. Should she pass this on to someone? There was no point; nothing more had surfaced via the ICO after Portishead reported back with the results of the interviews she carried out at Larcombe last September.

The ICO had covered their backsides by raising a concern; the police found little unusual. Water under the bridge. As Zara took one last look at Garry Burns, she wondered whether he left to go travelling. Perhaps he was out there somewhere putting the world to rights for Olympus. She hesitated as she prepared to shred the photograph and copy of the paperwork gathered that day.

Had she begun to cross the line between sticking to the letter of the law and aligning herself with Rusty? In that grey area operating outside and above the law along with his colleagues?

Zara pressed the button.

DS Phil Hounsell caught up on news of yet another ram raid as he sat in his office on the other side of the building. Last year there were several similar robberies. A gang from somewhere in the country; they had never learned whether they came from the capital, or the Midlands. They had travelled along the M5 as it crossed his patch and paid fleeting but profitable visits to a collection of small towns bordering the motorway.

They spent many working hours at the crime scenes. Those had included jewellers and other stores that stocked high-end clothing. The target might be a relatively isolated ATM in the smaller towns that they crudely smashed from its housing and spirited away to be opened and emptied elsewhere. The amounts of money varied, but the sum now ran into the millions of pounds accumulatively. There was increasing pressure from his superiors to get this gang out of commission. Phil read the details of the recent attack in Taunton, where dozens of designer handbags worth tens of thousands disappeared from one of the town centre's premier stores.

Residents described hearing a massive bang as raiders hit the flagship branch on North Street, crashing a car through the reinforced windows of the store.

One local woman from a nearby flat said, 'I heard a huge crash like a giant door slamming. It was a very unusual noise, and when I checked what happened later, I saw police and tape all hanging around the shop.'

A neighbouring camera store owner who lived in rooms above his business said, 'I heard a terrible scraping of metal and then the crash. I knew straight away that it was a ramraid. Thieves have raided the business several times.'

The raid took place around half past four in the morning. The raiders used a stolen Audi to smash through the glass and steal bags that retailed up to two thousand pounds. Typical of this gang's *modus operandi*, they abandoned the Audi where it lay jammed in the shop storefront and used another stolen car to cover the trip to the motorway. Officers found a burnt-out Vauxhall Zafira on the road leading to Junction 25 of the M5.

Traffic on the arterial routes at that time of day is light but considering that the gang could have transferred to any vehicle, maybe a high-performance BMW or even a people carrier, it didn't help much. Unless they drew attention to themselves by driving like lunatics at high speed, Phil could tell this mob was too clever by half to commit that schoolboy error.

There appeared to be a lot more reading matter on the subject. Phil had already read enough. The score in the game currently: – Ram Raiders 1 Police Leads Nil.

Events that week carried on in much the same vein. Zara went through all the hoops required to secure a speedy and relatively amicable release from the job that had become her private hell. Phil Hounsell continued to search for ways to break down the stubborn defence that the ramraid gang and the villains behind the other cases on his desk constructed. The Police score remained resolutely at nil. Both officers welcomed the weekend with open arms; Zara couldn't wait for Monday to come around again so she could start her last week. But, on the other hand, Phil dreaded the prospect of more setbacks and stern faces from his superiors.

Monday, July 8th, 2013

Phil Hounsell avoided the shaving mishaps at the start of this new week, but it had hardly started before his mood darkened. Mid-morning on Tuesday hadn't arrived yet, and disenchantment had set in already. Phil flicked through the dozen or so items in his in-tray. There were a few reports to skip-read and sign; he would end up rubber-stamping holiday requests, even though he knew it promised to leave his team more stretched than usual. Notification of confirmation of Form 232? What's this? One lucky beggar must have decided enough was enough and handed in their papers. No doubt, off to pastures new for a lot less stress and a good deal more money?

Before he read it, he got up and walked over to get himself a coffee. He checked to see how soft the biscuits had become in his top drawer and decided they might still be safe to eat. Phil took a bite out of his hobnob and read.

"Bloody hell," he shouted, almost choking on his biscuit. He started coughing and gulped steaming hot coffee. That didn't help matters. "Zara Wheeler? Where the hell is she off to, I wonder?"

Phil raced through the form, searching for details, but they were few and far between. Her actual leaving date was almost upon them as it seemed she planned to take a week's holiday as part of her notice. The Divisional Commander and the ACC were interviewing her this week. Although they regretted that such an excellent young officer had decided to end her career, they agreed not to be bloody-minded and make her work every last minute.

Phil sat back in his chair and reread the information while finishing his coffee. He was confident that her leaving the service related to her superiors' response regarding the rescue of that little mite during the floods; it wasn't her being pissed off with his reaction after they slept together during the Kelly family trial in Bristol. But either way, he wasn't sure how he felt about seeing her go.

Ever since he'd clapped eyes on her in that incident room in Durham three years ago, they had been working closely together. What happened in Bristol had been inevitable; he could have handled things better. He shouldn't have insisted they stay overnight in the first place and resisted her advances when they returned to the hotel. There had been so many opportunities to do the right thing before and after the event. Instead, Phil failed to act upon them. Deep down, he knew that was because he wanted her just as much as she had wanted him that night. Once they got it out of their system, they avoided one another as far as possible, both in Bath and here at Portishead.

So much so that she had decided to leave. Zara had completed her forms and was almost through the leaving process without him even hearing a whisper. So much for the grapevine. Phil Hounsell pushed his chair away from his desk and walked towards his office door. He was determined to have a final chat with Zara Wheeler before the end of the week. He couldn't let her slink out of his life for good without at least saying goodbye.

Zara eyed the small cardboard box on her desk. So far, it only contained her Queen's Gallantry Medal, a few certificates for long-forgotten training course achievements and a calendar that Tracey Hounsell made for her at school. It was in 2012 when she and the Hounsell family were on better terms. Nevertheless, it possessed that innocent charm that kids convey to each item they bring home from school after completing a craft project, and Zara couldn't bear to throw it away just yet.

Her first meeting of the week with the Divisional Commander was thirty minutes away; her door swung open, and a flustered DI Phil Hounsell loomed in the doorway.

"So you're off on Friday then, Zara?" he said. "You didn't think to keep me in the loop, though? What brought on this urge to leave? Where are you going?"

Zara didn't reply straight away. She wasn't sure how many questions he might have thought of on his way across the building to confront her. He may as well get them off his chest; then, she would decide which ones she chose to answer.

The silence stretched out between them. Then, finally, it appeared there were no more questions.

"I am off on holiday from Friday; I won't be returning to Portishead. My career has nosedived because of one error of judgement, and there isn't any point in me staying. I detest traffic duties and jobs nobody else wants; to be lumbered with that burden for the rest of my service is a demoralising prospect. I need a new challenge."

Zara saw Phil's reaction to her mention of an error of judgement; he couldn't disguise the discomfort her choice of phrase had caused.

"Don't flatter yourself," she said "my day out with Toby and Dave down at Shepton Mallet led to my downfall. I'd do it all over again. Saving Grace from drowning is the one good thing to come out of my career since I came south three years ago. Not that it's any business of yours, but I'm in a stable relationship and my partner and I will work together in the private security sector. I'm sure you understand the word 'private' means I can't divulge where I'll be working or with whom."

Phil slumped into the chair near the door.

"What the hell happened to us, Zara? What became of Cat and Mouse? We worked well, and I always hoped we'd stay together until my retirement."

Zara allowed herself a weak smile.

"Bristol happened; the Kelly family trial fiasco happened. Angela Chambers died; the baby Grace rescue took place. The criminals got stronger and stronger while we, the police, got weaker and weaker. What chance do a Cat and a Mouse have against the Lion or the Elephant? I can't stop to chat. I'm afraid. I need to prepare for my interview with the Divisional Commander. Goodbye, Phil. It was good working with you most of the time."

Zara Wheeler swept past Phil Hounsell and left the room. She headed for the Ladies, where she spent ten minutes taking deep breaths and getting her nerves under control. There were no tears. She realised how much stronger a woman she had become than that frightened little ingenue Phil first met up with at Durham.

DS Phil Hounsell sat alone in Zara's office; he had been stunned by her evident loathing for how the whole ethos of police work was heading. Phil sympathised with her on that score; he had been a vocal opponent of the softly, softly approach for years. Yet back in the summer of 2010, Zara insisted that they must work with the system rather than turn a blind eye to a vigilante killer such as Colin Bailey. Phil had wondered whether Bailey was a 'necessary evil' in the society successive liberal governments had created. How cynical and life-hardened Zara had become since then.

He was shocked, too, to learn that Zara was now in a relationship. Her colleagues had never said a word here at

HQ; he knew how difficult it was to keep anything quiet on that score in a relatively close-knit community such as Portishead police headquarters.

Most of all, he was gutted that their situation had become non-existent. How much worse could things get around here? Well, he would find out in a few minutes.

Phil strolled back to his office. He spotted new files in his in-tray and an urgent email from his boss. Something must have hit the fan at a high rate of knots. The all-important meeting his boss had summoned him to would give him more than enough to think about in the coming weeks. Indeed, it would stretch the entire Avon & Somerset police to the limit, and the repercussions would send tremors across the country.

In the Lap of the Gods: Chapter Three

Wednesday, July 10th, 2013

At the Olympus Project HQ at Larcombe Manor, morning meetings differed little from when Erebus was in charge. Athena and Phoenix were now at the head of the table, with Annabelle Grace Fox firmly in control.

The three senior Larcombe residents, Alastor, Minos and Thanatos, occupied the seats on the window side of the long table. They generally arrived earlier than the other attendees. As they lived in quarters within the old manor house, it gave them a head start, but it was more than that; Athena knew these three well. They enjoyed being in the appropriate position when Giles Burke and Henry Case turned up from the ice house loaded with data gathered over the past twenty-four hours. They aimed to continue to confirm their superior standing in the organisation, justified or otherwise. Phoenix watched this charade each morning with an amused expression on his face.

Athena understood what Phoenix was up to; she knew

what game The Three Stooges played. However, it was the five attendees of the meeting themselves who were nonplussed. When Phoenix wasn't scowling or deadpan, it unnerved them; it didn't seem natural.

"Good morning, gentlemen," said Athena. "Can I have your reports, please?"

Minos, the former High Court judge, opened the morning's business.

"The European Court of Human Rights has ruled that whole-life tariffs breach a prisoner's human rights. Eventually, such sentences have to be reviewed because the judges have declared that not having any possibility of parole was inhuman or degrading. But, of course, our government has criticised the ruling; the verdict stands, but they have six months to consider their response."

"Surely this wasn't what the authors of the human rights conventions envisaged?" asked Phoenix. "This is another asinine intrusion by Strasbourg on our ability to make the punishment fit the crime."

"On top of sticking their noses in over the deportation of Abu Qatada and giving prisoners the vote, it does cause you to wonder who's running the country," said Alastor.

"I think we have the answer to that," muttered Henry Case, "and they don't live over on this side of the Channel."

"If my sums are correct, the best part of fifty people might profit from this ruling," Giles commented.

"That is our understanding at this point, Giles," said Minos. "One can only imagine the public outcry when the names of those who might see the light of day outside a prison cell become general knowledge. Sutcliffe, Bamber, Brady and even Rosemary West might get parole hearings."

"Anything else on the legal front, Minos?" asked Athena.

"Not today," he replied and sat back in his chair.

Thanatos spoke next.

"I'm sure we were horrified by the events of yesterday morning in Clevedon. What we might imagine being a 'big city' crime carried out in a small seaside town less than forty miles from our doorstep is shocking. What data have we gathered so far on who may have been responsible?" He directed that question towards Henry Case and Giles Burke.

"Very little that one might call 'concrete' information, I'm afraid," said Giles.

Henry Case continued. "We are re-doubling our efforts to secure the relevant CCTV footage. All our attention in the ice-house focuses on this matter for now. Giles has access, for instance, to the number plate recognition programs used by our police services. We tracked no discernible suspicious mobile phone activity in the Clevedon district yesterday. The gang kept communication to an absolute minimum."

"This was well planned and professionally executed," said Giles. "If we have an Eastern European criminal organisation operating within the UK, they will have surfaced earlier. Somewhere in our data banks, we shall find the tiny threads of detail that will lead us to their door."

Phoenix glanced at the two intelligence officers. He hadn't thought about it previously. It might appear odd to an outsider that Olympus relied on a Burke and a 'Head Case' to run their intelligence section, but these blokes were good. He was confident they would find clues the police didn't. He longed for the day he led a group of agents to take these killers out. But, unfortunately, that day couldn't come soon enough; he'd spent far too long sitting around on his hands, waiting to get into action.

As he half-listened to Alastor, inquiring whether anyone knew what had happened to the ram-raid gang active in the same area over the past year, his mind switched to Zara Wheeler. Phoenix knew she was as sharp as a tack. Her brain added to the mix over in the ice-house would be very interesting indeed.

How would the boys take to having a female in their midst, he wondered? There was always something to consider when you held a position of responsibility. He craved the good old days when all he needed to think of was how to get rid of the next person on his little list.

Phoenix concentrated once more on Henry Case's response to Alastor's question.

"Regular forays took place somewhere in the Home Counties by a group of thieves, who used crude methods to obtain cash and goods over a lengthy period. We didn't pay them too much attention as they didn't commit crimes we consider to be within the Olympus remit. There's nothing to suggest this latest attack has any connection, whatever. This new outfit might even emanate from a different part of the country for all we know at this stage."

Phoenix now became fully engaged. He thought for a few seconds.

"Except for one similarity, Henry; the top of the range motors they used to get from A to B as quickly as possible. I appreciate that there are loads of Beemers on the roads these days, but coincidences bother me. So, Giles, can you look at the CCTV and ANPR data for the times this ram-raid gang carried out their raids and satisfy my curiosity?"

"Certainly, Phoenix," said Giles.

Athena decided the intelligence section needed to be back at work sooner rather than later. She suggested they return to the ice-house to follow up on suggestions the morning session yielded.

When the five senior staff were alone, she discussed the

first meeting in London with the top people in the organisation. That was on Friday, July 19th. It would be her first meeting as Larcombe's head. Plus, the first opportunity for Phoenix to be present.

"Do you know what's on the agenda?" asked Thanatos.

"It will mostly be a meet and greet," said Athena. "Erebus never received a written agenda; nothing is ever committed to paper. He received a phone call roughly two weeks beforehand inviting him to attend. He got another message twenty-four hours before his trip to London, relaying only a few keywords. Secrecy is paramount. I have learned the time and place, the dress code and that I may be accompanied by my plus one on this occasion."

Phoenix raised an eyebrow.

Athena smiled. "Sorry if you're miffed at being described as my plus one, Phoenix, but everyone here knows of our situation. Also, Erebus informed our superiors we were a couple and now shared the responsibility for Olympus matters here."

"No, Athena, it's not that when you mentioned a dress code. I hoped to wear the Rory Gallagher t-shirt and blue jeans you bought me for our Glastonbury weekend."

"Ah, you might need to keep those for another occasion. But, then, you will be suited and booted, and I shall wear one of my best dresses."

Phoenix groaned.

"Let's move on," said Athena. "Rusty is missing from this morning's meeting. We've sent him on a fact-finding mission this week and next. There are two reasons for this. First, his partner leaves her present job on Friday. She is taking a week's vacation; she will decide whether to throw her lot in with Olympus here at Larcombe during that break. If she does, she and Rusty will live in their quarters in the stable block, and she can start work in the ice-house. Second, her focus will be to develop our cyber-intelligence strengths together with Giles Burke. This mission is partly to take his mind off that situation and to give us a closer insight into the exploitation by landlords of migrants in areas such as Slough and Ealing."

"How much do we know about this woman?" asked Minos.

"How much does she know of Olympus, more to the point?" bridled Thanatos.

"Rusty trusts her," said Phoenix, "that's good enough for me. I prefer concentrating on what Rusty investigates in the big, bad world."

Athena allowed a few moments to pass before she continued.

"It is estimated that they have three thousand people living illegally in the borough of Slough alone. Our thermal imaging cameras have flown over that borough and several neighbouring council boroughs in the South East to confirm that the incidence of suspected illegal dwellings is fast becoming a significant problem. Outbuildings often don't need planning permission as long as they meet size restrictions and are *not* for sleeping accommodation. Snap inspections are forbidden. Councils must give twenty-four hours' notice before inspections, meaning landlords have ample time to remove evidence. If caught, the fines are only a fraction of the monies they can make from the rents they are charging. Any law-abiding residents who get fed up with such over-development in their area and seek to move away soon discover that their house value has been adversely affected because of the problem. The odds are that the only prospective buyer of their property will be a landlord eager to convert their home into another multi-occupancy money-making machine."

"If this is rife in the South East, then that suggests many individuals are involved. So how can direct action by Olympus be deployed to make a difference?" asked Alastor.

"The government position appears optimistic, even in the face of a hopeless situation. Local authorities want more controls placed on landlords. The response from the government is that the councils have enough enforcement powers to cope with matters. We believe that as councils face further stringent cutbacks, minimal constructive action will occur as things stand. Rusty will report back with what he discovers at the end of next week, and we will decide whether Olympus can remove a handful of the main players."

"Happy days," said Phoenix quietly.

After a few minor issues concerning the movement of agents around the country to carry out investigative sorties, Athena brought the meeting to a close.

Grab your copy...
vinci-books.com/lap-of-the-gods

About the Author

Ted Tayler is the international best-selling indie author of the Freeman Files and Phoenix series. Ted lives in the English West country, where his stories are based. He was born in 1945 and has been married to Lynne since 1971. They have three children and four grandchildren.

His thought-provoking mysteries appeal to readers of Sally Rigby, Joy Ellis, Pauline Rowson, and Faith Martin. His action-packed thrillers are a must for fans of Mark Dawson and J C Ryan.

Gus Freeman's cold case investigations are carried out with reasoned deduction rather than bursts of frantic action. In each of the 24 books, unsolved murders are accompanied by romance, humour, and country life. The core message in the 12 Phoenix novels is that criminals should pay for their crimes. Unfortunately, the current system fails to deliver the correct punishment, so Phoenix helps redress the balance.

Acknowledgments

The love and support of my family; without them, this would have been impossible.

Acknowledgment

The love and support of my family written this book would have been impossible

www.ingramcontent.com/pod-product-compliance
Ingram Content Group UK Ltd.
Pitfield, Milton Keynes, MK11 3LW, UK
UKHW040119190326
469155UK00004B/1233